KAIJU RIFT

IAN WOODHEAD

SEVERED PRESS
HOBART TASMANIA

KAIJU RIFT

Copyright © 2018 Ian Woodhead
Copyright © 2018 by Severed Press

WWW.SEVEREDPRESS.COM

ISBN: 978-1-925711-66-0

CHAPTER ONE

The sudden dull thump shocked him awake and the man's instincts took control, forcing him out of the makeshift cot and into the corner next to him. Another dull thump shook the rotting door off the frame. Sliding slowly down the crumbling stone wall, it splashed into a shallow pool of grey mud.

Sergeant Harry Scrimshaw kept his gaze fixed on the only opening in this building, not daring to blink in case he missed the tell-tale signs of enemy activity beyond the remains of this ancient ruined church. Would the enemy investigate anything as tedious as a piece of falling timber? It seemed unlikely. However, he needed to be sure.

This whole mission depended on him not taking any risks, to stay alive and to follow out his orders no matter the cost. Their area commander had made it perfectly clear what the consequences of failure would mean.

He recalled that feeling of anticipation which settled in his guts when he caught sight of their platoon commander escorting some big cheese down into their cosy burrow. It took Harry a couple of moments to recognise the old man. His last meal, a delightful concoction of meat paste and warm beer, threatened to come back up as General Flanders, the man solely responsible for the defence of the Northern Front, headed straight for him.

Harry listened as General Flanders explained the details of what they expected him to achieve. He had nodded at the appropriate moments and did his best to maintain a sombre expression while so needing to shout out in triumph as the old man explained what their boffins had discovered. General Flanders, the only man ever to stop a Goliath, then wished him and his squad good luck and shook his hand.

The shelling was for his benefit. They assured him that it would provide the much-needed distraction to allow his squad to penetrate the enemy's inner sanctum. Harry swallowed down a hard bubble of frustration and grief. As a result of the bastards initiating the bombing several hours ago as agreed, Harry might still have a squad.

Harry had followed his instructions to the letter. They all had. His fingers tightened around his adopted gun. Like most of the surviving soldiers, they used weapons stolen from the enemy; they called them fleshmeltas, as that's basically what they did.

He got ready to move out. The fury which threatened to burn him up so needed boxing. Harry had to purge himself of all extreme emotion before setting out on the last leg of this mission. If he failed, then his entire species would not last another six months.

He left the illusive safety of his corner, scuttled across the debris-covered stone floor, and crouched next to the door opening. Judging from the distant booms, the bombs were landing a good few miles from his position. Harry guessed that the Royal Ordnance Corps were trying to destroy the meat factories on the other side of the city. He wished them good luck with that one. Aside from the Goliath stockade, those endless lows of brick sheds had to be the city's most heavily protected section. Harry hoped the idiots at HQ hadn't targeted that hellish place. The familiars were likely to respond with deadly force if anything happened to any of their precious buildings.

Two more bombs detonated, but they sounded a lot closer now. Harry peered around the edge of the doorframe and prepared himself. He wouldn't have much time to do this; bombs of that magnitude were incredibly valuable, which, he guessed served to illustrate just how important this mission was.

A defiler patrol floated close to his position, a moment before he readied himself to dart across the next stretch of open wasteland. Harry scrunched his body into a ball and hurriedly rolled into the nearest mud puddle, hoping it would help to disguise his heat signature.

On this occasion, it appeared that those pair of familiars had other tasks on their mind than searching for more flesh to add to the meat factories. He dared to lift his head a couple of inches to watch them continue their journey.

It was a defiler that took Private Johnson, the first fatality of this fateful mission; David Johnson, a young recruit from the distant shores of the Southern African States. So eager to prove that he was just as good as the others in the squad despite having no real battlefield experience.

Well-trained men were almost as rare as human-made ordinance these days.

Harry watched the two defilers float past the remains of another ruined building before he emerged from where he spent the night. He ran over to a crater and dropped into it. The defilers hadn't paused; they hadn't detected him. As soon as they moved out of sight, Harry would move again.

Of all the familiars belonging to the local Goliath, the defilers were the easiest to kill. Not really much of a shock, as the creatures were basically a big bag of helium with a dozen pencil-thin tendrils trailing out from under them.

A well-placed shot from a standard Lee-Enfield into that bag and the blasted creature simply exploded. Harry couldn't remember the last time he saw any ammunition for their rifles. The powers that be decided a long time ago that diverting valuable resources to manufacture more bullets was a total waste when the scavenged weapons of their enemy were good, if not better, than their own ailing rifles.

The top brass, safe in their bunkers on another bloody continent, would soon change their tune if they were the ones who had to use these bloody abominations during a fight. For a start, the fleshmeltas were useless against the defilers. The energy streams just bounced off their reflective surface. You could shoot off their tendrils until the cows came home, but what was the point of that when the dirty things could regrow another set in a matter of seconds?

The two defilers disappeared behind a collection of blackened tree trunks. He waited for another few more seconds before he left the crater and ran over to the next building, all the time watching where he put his feet. Harry did not intend to allow any burrowers to catch him.

Another four defilers floated over the ruined city, a few hundred yards to his left. He was too far from them for their sensors to detect his movements. At least, that's what Harry hoped. The unexpected barrage must be attracting them. With luck, this would mean he would be able to enter their inner sanctum without any familiars noticing him.

Harry silently made his way through the building and out the other side. There it was! Just beyond a row of houses which displayed remarkably little battle damage was his final destination. The domed-shaped structure rose out of the ground like some giant toadstool. It was the first time he had been this close to the enemy's centre of operations. It took effort not to shiver in a combination of fear and disgust. The surface resembled the hide of their Goliath, similar to a grey lizard's skin, only covered with a thin covering of the wet-looking slime that coated every familiar.

This was it; he had done it. The way looked clear too, thanks to the bombings. By the looks of it, all the familiars will have rushed over to the meat factories to try to defend the position. Even with the apparent lack of enemies, Harry was too experienced to go charging down the middle of that cobbled road. They wouldn't leave their main base undefended.

He settled down to watch both the road and the black, windowless holes in the row of houses. Harry shivered again, as he knew time really was running out. The time between the bombs exploding was getting longer, meaning they were quickly running out. He needed to get inside that complex before they returned.

Patience rewarded him when three of the cobbles close to the first house began to move. The stones bubbled upwards. An opening appeared in the tops and three jets of dark green gas erupted from the openings. The stones then reverted to their original shape.

"Astonishing," he whispered. Harry had never seen traps so complex. The ones they usually found were all pretty crude affairs, hiding under pools of mud or in long grass. It didn't stop them from being deadly. Harry thought back to a few hours after they lost Johnson to those defilers. They were now three; himself, Corporal Benson, and Corporal Harris. Harry had fought with both men in countless campaigns going back over a decade. Neither of them was reckless, and they understood how their enemy worked. They were perfect for this mission.

Watching that trap expel its waste before reverting into its camouflaged state made him understand how his two experienced men both fell victim to those horrible devices. Now that he knew what to look for, Harry spotted another two more traps disguised as stones. The shade was just a little too dark and their sizes were more uniform than they should be. Harry turned his attention to the houses and their overgrown gardens. It would have been easier to approach the dome by going through those gardens, as the tall plants offered plenty of cover. Now that Harry knew of the existence of those more complex traps, he dared not go anywhere near that undergrowth. Harry wouldn't have a hope of spotting any traps.

If Harry had known about the bloody things beforehand, perhaps his squad mates wouldn't have died such a pointless death. Harry let out a quiet moan of anger. He would avenge them. Harry swore that their deaths wouldn't be for nothing.

Something moved in one of those windows! He threw himself to the ground, brought the weapon up, and looked through the gun sight. Harry held back that usual feeling of panic and revulsion as the fleshmelta's wet flesh grew around his eye socket. The few hundred yards of space between him and that window vanished. The magnified view showed Harry the interior of that room in great detail. He could even make out the grain on the back of the peeling wallpaper. Yet again, it upset and angered him at just how many his diminished species had to rely on their enemy's technology to survive. Harry remembered listening to the old ones, the survivors of the Great War and the coming of the Goliaths, when he was a young boy. They used to tell stories of the fantastic achievements their race had made in the last two thousand years. Harry listened, enthralled at stories of their huge cities full of people, of buildings as tall as mountains, and of trams, and cars, and carts fighting for space on the crowded roads. It all sounded so magical to Harry. They also dreamt of a possible future where those hateful Goliaths never arrived and stomped their wonderful cities into dust, at what the human species could have achieved.

Harry panned the weapon a couple of degrees to the right. A table came into view, along with a transparent cup containing glowing green fluid. He spotted a weapon next to the cup. It looked similar to his stolen weapon but much smaller. A side-arm perhaps? Why not? Harry had always assumed that the Goliath's foot-soldiers would use more than just their fleshmeltas.

The old ones used to talk about weaponry a lot too. That wasn't much of a surprise considering they all fought in the last war. They used to ask themselves if we, the human species, could have invented anything as sophisticated as the weapons used by the familiars if we hadn't been invaded. Most agreed that, given time, anything was possible. Harry distinctly remembered one old chap announcing that it wasn't beyond the realm of science fiction to imagine that one day, humans could go into space, even visit the moon.

He moved the gun a little more to the right then stopped when a single foot-soldier came into view. Was that where these dirty things originated from? Was he looking at something from the moon? Harry had no idea, nor did he really care. All he wished for, right now, was to kill that vile-looking beast and get away with it.

Harry relaxed his finger, took a deep breath in order to still his murderous thoughts, and moved the gun past the foot-soldier so he could see the inner doorway. There was more movement coming from beyond that room, but it was beyond even this weapon's ability to make out more than a few vague shadows. It was enough though to convince Harry that it wasn't alone up there.

The gun sight made an audible pop when he removed it from his face. Harry knew that he would never get used to the feeling of nausea he felt every time the thing touched his skin. He stood up while rubbing the area over his left eye. The side-arm on that table showed him exactly which direction to go and it wasn't the road, not if he intended to keep breathing. Every window equated to a gun port. Harry wouldn't get ten yards before a dozen fleshmeltas turned his body into a puddle of steaming meat.

His only remaining option suited Harry just fine. It was fitting that the only way left for him would make the last leg of his mission up close and personal. He clipped the weapon onto his back and caressed the eight-inch serrated knife strapped to his leg.

"Lads, it's time for payback," he snarled.

Harry skidded down the embankment, ran across the narrow strip of weeds, and pressed his back against the side of the house. He looked around the corner. The closest point of entry was just a short distance from his position. Thankfully, none of the houses on this row possessed doors or glass in their windows, meaning gaining entry wouldn't pose much of a challenge.

He did not believe the familiars would expect a frontal assault either. The dirty bastards revelled in their arrogance and feeling of superiority over the lesser creatures they preyed upon. Harry took out the knife then ran along the side of the house and slipped into the cool dark interior.

It took him a couple of moments for his eyes to adjust to the difference in light. He used those few seconds to press his body into one of the corners and drop closer to the floor. The bare wooden boards were spongy due to rot. He would have to watch for that. Harry blinked a couple of times while waiting for the indistinct shapes to solidify.

One of those shapes slid across the floor. Without hesitation, he leapt up and swung the knife in a low arc, catching the creature in the mid-section. Harry pulled the blade out and slammed it into the top of its head, grinning in delight at the sound of the crystal inner-housing, which held what served as a brain, shattering.

Breathing heavily, Harry wiped the gunk off his precious knife and got back on his feet. He looked down in disgust at his first kill and let loose a thick ball of saliva. "Vile, dirty, murderous fiend," he growled.

It did feel good to kill a foot-soldier. Harry hoped to kill a lot more before his mission ended. Each one despatched helped the war effort far more than bombing those meat factories. Foot-soldiers were a finite resource. Unlike the other familiars, these things actually came from the Goliath, meaning that he had just killed some tiny piece of the monster that watched over their city.

He stepped over the dead thing and hurried across the room, eager to find and kill another one. His blade had tasted their flesh, and he knew it was eager to taste more.

The doorway was almost within reach when a skeletal, slimy arm slid out from behind a wardrobe and grabbed Harry's wrist. He slammed his jaw shut to stop his shocked cry from giving him away. He pulled his arm back, transferred the knife to his other hand then stuck the blade into the side of its neck.

Harry jumped back as the foot-soldier collapsed onto the floor. He froze and slowed down his breathing while straining his ears, desperate to pick up any giveaway sound which might indicate the presence of any more of those things close by.

There was something, a noise which hadn't been there before. Harry tightened his grip on the knife handle and darted his head from side to side, growing more uneasy at his failure to locate the source of the sound. It was nothing he had ever heard before. The noise reminded him a little of somebody trying to breathe with blood-filled lungs. Finally, Harry looked down at the corpse. It wasn't coming from that; the foot-soldier was as dead as a rock.

The foot-soldier's fleshmelta then caught his attention. "I do not believe this," he said while watching, perplexed as the semi-organic weapon spat out black fluid from the ventral ports under the forestock. It was trying to call out to the others and give his position away. "No you don't." Harry lifted his boot and stomped down on the front of the stock where its nervous system was located. The noise stopped immediately and the soft green glow running down the length of the weapon went black.

It surprised him a little to feel a soft vibration down the length of his spine. Harry unclipped his own fleshmelta, lifted the leathery flap which covered the weapon's own health indicator, and discovered the green light oscillating. It took him a moment for the realisation to sink in. As weird as it sounded, his weapon must be mourning the death of one of its comrades. Right at that moment, he so wanted to give this traitorous piece of stolen weaponry the same treatment. Harry didn't care if the thing was broken-in and neutered. What use had the bastard thing been to him during this mission?

"Calm down, Harry," he muttered. Taking out his frustrations on some stupid gun would not bring his friends back to life, nor would losing his temper help him in any way complete this mission. More than likely, losing his focus would kill him and if that happened, his species would die with him. At least, it would according to what General Flanders disclosed. Harry clipped the weapon back where it belonged, pulled the knife out of the creature's neck then hurried over to the next doorway.

He crouched down, making himself into a smaller target. There were another four foot-soldiers in the next room, and by watching their twitches and listening to the sound of the grunts and squeaks, emitting from the flattened wet pipe they used as a mouth, something had seriously spooked them. The foot-soldiers must be reacting to his presence, what else could it be? Perhaps one of the creatures that he had just put down had signalled in, or maybe Harry had not been as furtive as he believed? The reason no longer mattered. The things were alerted to his presence, meaning stealth was no longer an issue. Still, although secretly pleased, Harry still needed to find out exactly what they were doing in that dome before officially announcing his presence.

Harry rushed into the next room. He slashed the nearest foot-soldier across its secondary abdomen, and snatched its fleshmelta out of the beast's limb fingers. He so wanted to turn them all into wet stains. The overpowering desire to follow his orders stopped him from doing something he might regret. He turned the weapon around and smashed the stock into the other creature's multifaceted, insectile head.

Just one remained. Harry spun around and faced the thing. He growled low in his throat, all the while keeping his gaze fixed on the fleshmelta side-arm gripped in its right hand. Harry spun the snatched weapon around so the business-end pointed at its lower chest.

It let out a couple of high-pitched squeals before dropping the pistol. It was about to make a run for it. Harry dropped the fleshmelta, brought his arm back, and threw the blade. The knife completed two graceful loops before the blade slammed into the back of the creature's head. It fell to its knees before keeling over.

He ran over, eager to retrieve my knife, only to pull the handle out of the green mush and find the blade lodged deep in a thick rope of knotty sinew running up the thing's back. Dammit, he'd had that knife for almost a decade. His options were reduced to the one. Harry unclipped the weapon, swore softly at the corpse then ran as fast as he dared alongside the edge of the wall.

Just as Harry expected, most of the interior walls had gone, demolished and removed at some earlier date. The familiars had extended the base into here. All Harry had to do was to continue running along this wall to reach the inner sanctum. At least, that's what he hoped.

It took him another minute or so to reach the last corner. He almost smacked his face into the rotting plaster due to his attention focused solely on the four exits he picked out in the dim light. Not one of them displayed any movement. For one glorious moment, Harry actually believed that perhaps he had been wrong about them sensing an intruder, that one of their prey animals walked amongst their number. His triumph vanished when the movement he had been dreading now materialised under the four exits and three more that Harry had failed to notice.

With his back against the wall, Harry shouldered the fleshmelta and uttered his last prayer, knowing that he would get off four shots, perhaps five, before one of them returned the favour. Foot-soldiers might be easy to defeat up close, but they were all crack shots with their weapon of choice.

"I go with dignity." Harry squeezed the trigger and the meat of one of the vile beasts slid off its crystal skeleton. "I go with honour." He fired twice more, each shot finding their targets. Harry saw three of them had now dropped into firing position. His life, such as it was, had come to an end.

"I go with…" The last word remained unspoken when the wall he had been resting on fell away. Harry stumbled backwards. He spun around to stop from crashing onto the floor. Harry cried out in shock when his eyes found what he first believed to be his celestial exit from this world.

His befuddled mind sought order from the chaotic vision before him. He wasn't dead, the things hadn't melted him. He was still alive, and that swirling mass of blue and red light hovering about a foot from the floor was his sole reason for entering this hornet's nest. Harry also knew that the temporary reprieve he had just gained from stumbling had just run out. He only had one chance left.

***

Harry Scrimshaw raced into that light and left this world forever.

The sergeant had no way of knowing, but he hadn't been the first individual to cross through the enemy-built trans-portal. Several others had already gone ahead to prepare the ground for the next invasion. This dying world offered nothing but scraps. It was time to move on, to find another world. The thousands of immobile Goliaths standing in the midst of their exhausted feeding grounds were impatient to move on.

CHAPTER TWO

The last number seventy-three bus for the night had dropped off its last three passengers on the opposite side of the road next to the betting office. The bus rumbled towards the turning circle, leaving the departed passengers wobbling inside the dilapidated bus shelter.

Callum McGuire felt that familiar hard knot grow in his guts when three inebriated gentlemen noticed him. He stood perfectly still, feeling like a rabbit caught in the glow of a pair of headlights while they staggered across the now empty road heading straight for him. They giggled, laughed, and pointed, acting like a set of naughty school kids.

He guessed they were all at the borderline legal drinking age, which, in his opinion, made them the worst kind of person to bump into on a street utterly devoid of anybody else. Callum wasn't usually bothered by the appearance of kids their age. Or any kids really. Oh sure, the little terrors called him names on occasion, threw stuff at him, and generally tried to make him feel like some low-grade animal, but they never got physical, not even the older ones. He could handle himself and the locals knew that. Word got around.

Normally, the local teenage pissheads generally left him alone. After all, Callum had been a common sight in the town of Brandale for over two decades now. He might have mellowed in recent times, but he was sure that his younger violent exploits were still discussed.

That sneering expression plastered across their faces suggested that these jokers now approaching him didn't fit into that category. He released a low moan and attempted to unknot his twisted guts. So much for word getting around. Then again, what else did he expect? This part of town wasn't a part of Callum's patch.

He reluctantly dropped the pizza box back into the trade bin, then moved back until the cuff of his filthy parka brushed against the corner of the wall. Callum might be a relative stranger to this part of town, but that hadn't stopped him from memorising his escape route. Until now, Callum kinda expected his ancient bad boy reputation would protect him from having to face shit like this. Brandale wasn't a huge place, with only a dozen or so pubs and plenty of old fishwives who transmitted gossip with a religious furore.

They were all taller than him, with the tallest having at least a foot on Callum. He presumed him to be the boy who made the decisions, judging from the fawning postures the other two exhibited.

The brown-eyed thug, complete with an unimpressive collection of stray bum hairs under his nose, grinned, displaying a set of teeth which so needed work from a dentist's tools. The kid gave him the laser eyes treatment, while lifting a hand from the pocket on his baggy, grey sport's pants. Callum's guts knotted up once more when the fluorescent light from the takeaway shop window reflected off the silver handle, gripped in the kid's thin fingers.

A soft snick noise accompanied brown-eye's quiet chuckle and there it was, the lad had just officially revealed his intent. The other two stopped moving, but brown-eyes didn't. He was almost at arm's length when one of the other boys suddenly broke the tension.

"Go on, Sky. Stick the dirty bastard!"

Perhaps if Callum had been younger, like two decades younger, he would have taken them on, knife or no knife. In fact, back when he was in his prime, he ate scrawny brats like these three for breakfast, but time hadn't been kind to him, and Callum felt every one of his fifty-four years twice over.

Callum spun around, almost tripping over his own feet, and pelted down the high street before turning into an alley behind the Horse and Crown. His hope that perhaps a chase would be too much trouble evaporated when he heard their running footsteps hitting the wet pavement. Perhaps if that thug hadn't spurted out that kid's name, then they would have gone their separate ways. What sort of parent burdens their child with a name like Sky? No bloody wonder the bastard turned out like he did. Callum almost felt sorry for him until his ears caught their shouted insults, coupled with what they were going to do to Callum's face when they caught him.

Like he needed this sort of hassle after the day he'd just struggled through. All Callum had wanted to do was to find something to eat before settling down behind the old brick wall at the back of the park. Had that been too much to ask for?

The bastards were gaining on him. They obviously sensed this as the insults turned into triumphant laughter. There was no way he'd able to keep this up. Callum stopped dead, turned around, already prepared to ensure he would inflict as much damage to Sky with the hope that if he did hospitalise him, that knife wouldn't end up sliding into Callum's flesh. He wasn't bothered about the other two; they were just puppets. Cut the strings and they turned into rag dolls.

Had he already known moments before he turned around that his pursuers had also stopped? With his ears full of the noise made by his ragged breathing, Callum watched with interest as Sky and the quiet minion held onto the locked metal gates which led into the pub's loading bay, while the shit-stirred boy looked back towards the main road. They leaned over and proceeded to paint the alley floor. It looked as though the drinks they'd no doubt chucked down their necks weren't too disposed with all that running.

"I hope you both choke," he muttered, before turning back and continuing his retreat, this time at a slower pace. Callum stopped again, looking over his shoulder to check on their progress. They were still following him, but it looked that their need to catch him had lessened somewhat.

Callum severely doubted that any of them would be able to see him now. The shadows from the huge trees overhanging the wall which separated the alley and the town park obscured everything. Just to be sure, Callum stopped once more and glanced over his shoulder. As predicted, the three kids had slowed before finally stopping.

He nodded in grim satisfaction when the three turned as one then sloped back along the alley. "Yeah, and don't come back again," he whispered. "You have no idea how close you lot came to ending up in hospital." His words of relieved bravado went unheard, just how he liked it.

Callum climbed onto the top of the thick stone wall and dropped onto the other side, landing in a thick patch of nettles. "Great," he muttered. "Thanks for that." Callum jumped out of the nettles and sat in the damp grass, already knowing that some of those leaves had found the small tear just above his knee. He wrapped his arms around his shaking legs.

What a totally crappy way to end this already memorable day. The nettle sting would soon go, but the hurt caused by those kids would last so much longer. Not only had those cockwombles scared the shit out of him, they had also denied him of a substantial meal.

Callum hadn't had time to open that pizza box, but he just knew that the damn thing wasn't empty; in fact, he was willing to bet some proper folding money that there were at least three slices left, maybe even four.

He tipped his head back and gazed at the now upside-down, imposing-looking wall and wondered about the possibility that those three could still be hanging around. The chances were sure to be remote. After their little barf party, they'd make their way home, surely.

"Don't be too sure on that one," he whispered, "and don't call me Shirley."

He rested his left hand over his guts and already knew that he would be going back. That decision was as sure as mustard. Callum had no choice, not if he wanted to eat. There were only two hot food places in Callum's patch. The fish and chip shop wasn't open tonight, and Babylon Delight now had padlocks on their bins.

The old part of town opposite the New Harmony housing estate was the only patch left in town that hadn't been extensively mined. Well, it had. Old Joe Decker had claimed that patch as his own way back before Callum experienced his troubles. Back when he actually believed he would have a normal life.

Before this week had ended, word got around that Decker had gone. Just vanished into thin air, leaving nothing but a bed made from cardboard boxes behind the bank and his collection of carrier bags full of old sweet wrappers.

Thing is, also from what he had heard, Decker hadn't gone alone. As mad as it sounded, all the rats had vanished as well. The fact that this made no sense didn't enter into Callum's mind. As far as he was concerned, the absence of his main competitor meant the bins outside the takeaways, cafes, and grocery shops were now fully laden with practically unspoilt food. A veritable king's ransom.

All the cats and dogs had vanished as well. This scrap of info came from all the postcard-shaped notices he'd seen in the shop windows as he performed his daily trudge across his patch, looking for anything of value left on the paths or in gardens.

All this only happened a couple of nights ago. He found out about the news about Decker quite by accident. Thanks to the weather changing from a bright summer's day into a storm come six and coupled with the owner of his usual rain shelter suddenly deciding to bolt and padlock his shed, Callum had no other choice but to run down to the flyover in order to get out of the torrential downpour. A few of Brandale's other street-men obviously had the same idea. Four of the boys had already got a fire going in an old oil drum by the time he arrived. Once the heat from the fire began to start drying his sodden clothes, talk had already skimmed over the usual gossip and had settled upon old Joe Decker's patch and his disappearance.

Two of Brandale's originals both swore blind that they knew someone who knew someone who told them that the council had been using a new rat poison and Decker must have inadvertently eaten some as well. The remaining Brandale original slowly nodded before explaining to Callum that Decker used to have this habit of catching rats and using their pelts to line his underwear.

Callum missed the next line of dialogue from the two who claimed to know everything, but he was sure that they'd said that some guy from the waste treatment works had buried his corpse, along with all the dead animals in the land-fill site over on Beacon Road.

Gavin Styles, who was the youngest member of their cosy get together, disagreed, and despite the others telling him to shut his stupid gob, still managed to spurt out that aliens had abducted Joe before two of the others smacked him around the back of the head. They all knew that Gavin had a few problems in the upstairs department, but unlike the others huddled around that fire, the kid wasn't technically homeless. They generally only allowed the kid to hang around because, on occasion, Gavin appeared amongst them with cans of beer shoved into the deep pockets of his tatty Army jacket. Their patience with him recently was teetering on the edge due to Gavin telling them, last week, that aliens had stolen his jacket.

Two nights is a long time to wait, and Callum had known that if he hadn't made a move tonight, then some other guy would make the move and claim Joe's old patch. Down under the flyover, they had a laugh, told stories, and generally cursed the world. It was neutral territory. Down there, it was them against the rest of society.

All that bonding bollocks and camaraderie went straight out of the window when it came to expanding your patch. It was serious business. Joe's patch had three pubs as well as a couple of fast food shops. In Callum's eyes, as well as the others, claiming those extra shops could mean a difference to whether they lasted through the next winter.

Callum took his weight off the damp grass and wandered back over to the wall which separated his patch and Joe's patch. By rights, that patch ought to belong to him anyway; none of the other guys were anywhere close by. Well, Gavin did have an older brother who lived on the estate, but that didn't really count.

The pubs were shut now and the only takeaway still open was Khan's Kebab Shack, and that was right in the centre of town, a good mile from here. His three recent adversaries had no reason to hang around and plenty of reason to stagger home, and wash the dried vomit off their chins before climbing into a nice, warm bed.

He planted his hands on the side of the wall, surprised to find that they weren't shaking. His insides were still coiled up like a dozen wet, possibly slimy springs. He turned his hands around and stared at the pale white scars which criss-crossed his palms. In the pale moonlight, they looked like hand-shaped road maps. "I don't want to go down any of those streets and roads again." He quickly turned them back over and climbed up onto the top of the wall. "Please don't make me travel to that place again," he murmured. Callum dropped into the alley. "Please make it that they went home."

The journey back to that trade bin proved uneventful. It felt like a bit of a disappointment when none of those three kids jumped out on him. Callum lifted the plastic bin lid and rested it on the brick wall. Already, his mouth began to fill with saliva at the prospect of tucking into whatever the previous owners of that pizza had left in that box.

"Spicy chicken please," he whispered while leaning inside to retrieve the box. "Even pepperoni or donner will do me." Callum snagged the box and pulled it out of the bin. He sat down and rested the prize on his knees. "Anything but ham and pineapple."

Before opening the box, Callum double-checked the surrounding area, just to be sure that he was alone. He turned his head to the left and something just under the trade bin caught his eyes.

"That's unexpected." He reached out and folded his fingers around Sky's knife. Callum dragged it out from under the bin and held the object in front of him. The kid must have dropped it as he hurried home to clean his face. Callum grinned. What a shame. The poor boy will be distraught when he found out. He turned it over. This was no cheap knock-off either. Somebody had paid good money for this. He might be able to get a few quid for the knife. There were a couple of shops on the other side of Brandale who didn't ask questions. Oh sure, Callum wouldn't get a good price, but that didn't matter. If he got enough for a pint and a pie, he'd be happy.

Callum opened the pizza box and sighed heavily. So much for his luck turning around. It was sodding ham and pineapple. Still, it wasn't all bad news. Now that he had the knife, at least he didn't have to pick out all the disgusting bits of pineapple with his fingers. He pushed the small ridged button on the handle forwards and the blade thrust out of the front of the handle.

Three drops of blood fell off the blade and spattered over the pizza. "Oh Jesus!" he gasped, throwing the box off him. Callum jumped up and backed himself against the wall, his swirling thoughts trying to make sense of the scene in front of him. The knife, still with the blade open, lay by his feet. He wanted to kick it back under the bin; out of sight meant out of mind. Skulking back to his park, after picking up that over-turned pizza, now felt like the best decision he could ever make. So he'd have to pick bits of gravel and hair off the cheese before eating it, but that didn't really bother him. Callum had eaten much worse.

What stopped him from doing just that was the presence of that knife. Callum groaned aloud while bending over and picking up the weapon. He kept telling himself that he still needed this, that he had to clean off his fingerprints before selling it to the greasy Turk who ran the second-hand shop over on Bethel Road. Callum kept this line in his mind while carefully pushing the blade back into the handle without cleaning it.

He'd tell the boys that tale, no doubt about that. He'd have to embellish the story, perhaps add a bit of dressing and some relish before he boasted about how he fought off three huge men who, he guessed, were big enough to be rugby players. The blood on the blade? Well, that's what happens when you mess with Callum, simple as. The fishwives, when word got out, would love that one. His reputation would be back to where it belonged and, as a bonus, nobody would deny him old Joe Decker's patch. A win all around.

The truth of the matter didn't even come close to having a voice.

Had there been a bit of a scuffle before they went home? Some argument, possibly involving him? He sure hoped not. Callum didn't want any of those kids to be hurt, not even Sky. Before moving away from the trade bin, he gently lifted the pizza pieces over using his shoe and tried not to bite through his bottom lip when he saw that they'd all land in a puddle of muddy water.

A time taken to lament his loss was cut short when his ears picked up a scraping sound coming from around the other side of the bin. His desire to help whichever boy had received a potentially fatal stab wound threw out any thoughts that he might be in danger. Callum ran around the front of the large plastic receptacle, expecting to encounter one of the boys, hopefully the quiet minion, lying against the wall, with his hand over a gut wound and with hope in his eyes at the unexpected sight of Callum.

His suspicion that he wasn't alone proved to be correct, but something deep inside that tortured gut of his suggested that the man-shaped lump wriggling across the concrete floor like some huge, brown, fat caterpillar should be avoided. It was just a sack. Of course it was. What else could it be? Once the question was right there, out in the open, waving a little flag, Callum's narcissistic mind conjured up a whole host of demented possibilities.

"Bugger off, all of you," he said to his giggling mind, while backing away from the caterpillar-shaped monster. The blade snicked out from the handle. Did he just do that?

"Don't worry about it, lad. We'll soon get you out of that sack." It wasn't a sack. This thing really was some kind of mutated, giant, shit-brown-coloured, fat caterpillar. Now that he was almost on top of it, he could now see a network of pulsating veins underneath that thin, shiny skin.

"Did that Sky do this to you?" Every cell in his system urged him to stand up, turn then run as fast as he could to get away from this abomination before it was too late.

The time to actually listen to his inner voices had long since passed. Several tiny craters bulged through the skin. Callum blinked rapidly while whatever compulsion that had thrust a border between his body and Callum's common sense dissipated, but he didn't even have time to catch his breath before each of those craters vomited a pencil-thin tendril. They exploded towards him and wrapped tight around both his wrists before they started to shrink back, bringing him closer and closer to the fat abomination.

A thick seam of pale white flesh ran to the top of its body, zipping open by the time those tendrils had almost pulled Callum's two hands within touching distance of that slimy, mucus-like coating. From the abomination's cavity, a human-like head pushed out through the red mess. Callum was close to losing his mind, but that didn't stop him from recognising the remains of old Joe.

"This can't be real," he moaned. "It just can't be!" The eyelids slid back at the same time as its mouth opened. Callum pulled his horrified gaze away from those bulging red eyes as that jaw unhinged and opened wider and wider. Inch-long needle teeth filled that terrible cavern, and he just knew that those tendrils were pulling his hands towards that mouth.

"The knife, use the knife!"

That wasn't one of his own voices.

It didn't matter where the voice came from. Its sudden arrival broke the spell. Callum thrust the blade into that thing's left eye then jerked his hands up. To his utter shock, Callum stumbled backwards, with the snapped-off tendrils still attached to his wrists.

Somebody caught him, stopping Callum from falling into the middle of the road. He fell to the ground, breathing heavily, while finding it almost impossible to process what had just happened to him. The strange man, his rescuer, rose what looked like a mud-soaked Nerf gun and reduced the lump of gross into a puddle of stink.

"Are you injured?"

It took him a moment to realise that the mud was talking to him. He shook his head.

The man walked past Callum, crouched beside the puddle, and fished a piece of that filthy pizza out of the muddy water.

"I think I will need your assistance," he said, wiping the water off the cold food and stuffing the full piece into his mouth.

Callum wrestled with the notion that he had just gone insane while vaguely wondering why he had four rat tails wrapped around his skin.

CHAPTER THREE

Captain Thomas Copperfield moved a little closer to the upstairs window. He nodded to himself when his sharp eyes detected the reappearance of that elusive shadow. Copperfield had spotted his unwelcome intruder a couple of minutes ago, scrambling over the back fence. It was the sheer cheek of the situation which got his goat. The contractors had only finished erecting the last section of his new fence just two hours ago. It took some effort to stop his face from contorting into his trademark scowl.

Jenny kept saying that it made him look ugly. Copperfield pressed his nose against the cool glass. He found it a little spooky how that phrase became the one she used more than any other. His mother (God rest her soul) had a similar saying. She used to say that his face would stay that way if he didn't learn to smile.

Exactly what had the impudence to test his patience? He had previously put his money on a cat, but now Copperfield wasn't too sure. Cats didn't move in that manner. The animal hopped one second then raced along the ground at an incredible speed before stopping suddenly and changing direction. A squirrel perhaps?

"The species is irrelevant, Bullethead. The kink is that the shitter got in." The sound of his gruff voice in his ears made him more furious than ever.

The scowl found its favourite position. Fuck his mum, fuck Jenny, and fuck any other female who dared to tell him what to do with his face. He even released a low growl just for good measure.

It didn't matter what species had dared to invade his private domain. It was going to pay with its life. It was that simple. No shitter defied Captain Thomas Copperfield. He'd have to cross the grounds and enter through the side door in order to retrieve the key for the tool shed. Not a problem; that would only take a minute or so. He had a few old traps right at the back of the shed, near the vice. They'd come in handy. Obviously, this job would require the crossbow.

The shotgun would be better suited for the task of extermination, but the captain wasn't too keen on having some wooden-top coming up from the police station in the centre of Brandale and ringing the gate bell at one in the morning.

Shit, the bloody thing had vanished again. That shitter was a nippy bastard. From the direction it was travelling in, Copperfield guessed that it was heading towards the main house. That suited him just fine. The motion detectors will shed plenty of high-intensity light on his target. It didn't stand a chance.

He shifted his gaze towards the main house then tilted his head until their bedroom window came into view. God, that place looked so foreboding. That place, that room, now reflected everything he hated about that wife of his. Looking at that black hole felt like gazing into the blackness of her cold soul.

She'd probably be asleep by now, the rancid cow. Not that the lack of light made this obvious. She seemed to enjoy sitting in the darkness. Not that her state of consciousness made much difference these days, considering she doped herself up on whatever pills she'd managed to find throughout the house. His scowl increased. How she hadn't died from that cocktail of shitting stuff the rancid cow stuffed down her gob was the ultimate miracle of science. Instead of using the crossbow on the intruder, his life would be far less complicated if he put a bolt through her neck instead.

Copperfield heard movement behind him, followed by the reflection of a widening strip of yellow light in the window, utterly destroying any chance he had of spotting his intruder. "Shut that bloody door," he said.

"Sorry. It's just…. Well, it's just that I thought you said you would only be a minute."

He waited for her to obey his command before replying. "Jenny, why don't you go back to bed? I won't be long."

"But I'm cold."

His prey was still out there, somewhere in his extensive gardens, and while he was listening to her annoying whine, that little bastard could have already found its way into his vegetable garden, ruining his entire crop of cauliflowers, carrots, and cabbages. The shitter just had to die. It was that simple.

He turned around and while his gaze drank in his latest acquisition's superb shape, his mind had already mapped out the route to his crossbow, bolts, and the drinks cabinet. He would need a stiff one to help calm down the anger before going on his hunt. Stiff one? That almost cracked the scowl. He'd had one of those for the past hour.

Jenny sure enjoyed the attention he'd been giving her tonight. Strange; after sex, Copperfield's mood wasn't usually this volatile. Then again, considering the fun and game his day had been, it still shocked him that he hadn't murdered anyone. Still, the day wasn't over yet, there was still time.

He sighed to himself. Just what was she doing now? His daughter's best friend tried to adopt the pose of some sultry glamour model but just ended up looking like some back-street prostitute. The similarity didn't exactly fill him with a prudish sense of disgust. On the contrary, the sight of some nubile, if a little dense, twenty-two-year-old woman ready and willing to perform all sorts of depraved actions upon him did turn him on. At least, it would if she hadn't already done that to his own fifty-six-year-old body.

Copperfield would need her care and attention but not just now, not until he'd dispensed with his current situation. "Go back to bed, Jenny, and keep it warm for me." Before she could start with that oh-so-annoying post-teenage pout, he strode over to the woman, cupped her left breast, and roughly kissed her full lips. Her slender hand pushed up his inner thigh. It took a lot of self-control not to allow Jenny to drop to her knees. "Enough," he growled, pulling her octopus-like limbs off his hot body. "Go on. Do as you're told. I won't be long."

Jenny slinked back into the bedroom and as a final burst of defiance, the stroppy bitch slammed the door. The thought of him rushing in there and showing her just what happened to naughty little girls did help to remove his scowl. It also brought some life to his sleeping sausage. "No, control yourself, Bullethead. She'll taste sweeter if you allow the juices to simmer."

He counted the steps back to the window, all the while half-expecting her to open that door again with tears in her eyes and her tongue sliding across her lips. Copperfield knew that if Jenny did pull that trick, there'd be no looking back. The cat or squirrel would be able to have a barbecue in the garden, and he wouldn't care. The door stayed shut and remained in that position even as his back touched the glass. "Fine, be like that," he said, turning towards the door which led out of his office complex.

She could wait. It would be more fun to wake her up once this operation had run its course. That way, he'd have the advantage, at least until she came to her senses. Copperfield grinned to himself at that delicious future event. In fact, now that the grin had rooted to his face, the captain decided to leave it there. No more thinking about the rancid cow, alone in that cold bed, and he wasn't even going to go down the road which led to him kicking the two local contractors to death when he got his hands on those three work-shy layabouts.

Looking back, that probably had more to do with him trying to save a few thousand pounds on employing idiots from the Harmony Estate than anything else. Not one of them had any internal discipline or self-control.

Copperfield threw a shirt on and pulled on a pair of jogging pants before unlocking the door and stepping out into the warm night air. He made his way across the stone path, briefly stopping next to an ornamental well. As per tradition, the captain kissed the tips of his fingers then gently rubbed the roof.

As he continued to way towards the main house, he, as per the norm, mused on how his later life had gone from being the fairly average forces retired officer into what could only be described as a low-budget soap opera. The drama only existed in his mind which was where it would too. The outside world, as well as most of the players he operated, were utterly oblivious to the full picture.

Jenny knew everything, but she just didn't have the mental capacity to slot all the pieces into their correct place. As long as he continued to satisfy the brain-dead nympho with his downstairs equipment and continue to pay her credit cards, she caused him no trouble. She might be thicker than a whale sandwich, but Jenny knew which side her bread was buttered.

His wife had her pills, the doctor who looked after her as well as administering his own form of 'help' whenever she was surfing the Martian winds, and she had her doll collection to talk to whenever she found herself back on planet Earth.

The captain's only daughter was no problem either as she had decided to travel the world during her gap year. As much as he missed his little princess, her being as far away from the house as possible suited him just fine and her travelling across Saudi Arabia right now made him feel so happy.

Something at the left of his position flashed past a brick wall. He spun around, sure that whatever it had been was significantly larger than a domestic cat. He leaned forward, squinted his eyes, and focused on the top of that wall. Was it his imagination or was there something hiding behind it? If there was something there, then he'd need something more powerful than his small crossbow to take it down. The wall reached to his waist.

Despite being not having any weapon, he hurried across the grass, eager to see exactly what it could be. In his mind, Copperfield imagined it to be a medium-sized dog or perhaps even a goat. It wasn't as mad as it sounded. Up here, away from the town, there were still a couple of farm-holdings that hadn't sold their property to the estate agents. What did worry him slightly was how a goat or a dog had managed to get through the fence. It sure as hell hadn't chewed through.

He reached the wall and leaned over. Copperfield almost felt disappointed to discover nothing there. It had to be his imagination playing up. Those idiots from the estate might have been utterly lazy, but even they weren't so incompetent to leave out a section of fence. Which reminded him, while he was in the house, he needed to double-check the kitchen to make sure nothing was missing. He allowed them the use of the kettle and the microwave during their stay this afternoon. Granted, they hadn't made much of a mess. He'd give them that, but still, if anything was missing, even a spoon, then those thieving bastards would know about it. Nobody stole from Captain Thomas Copperfield, not if they enjoyed breathing.

Thomas did see the irony of his last mental threat, considering he had stolen Jenny from the arms of one of those stupid arseholes he'd employed to fix up his security fence. Granted, the event happened almost three years ago, and he was sure that Jamie Dawson had forgotten all about the incident by now. Still, it had happened, right here, in this garden too.

His daughter had brought her new friend over to the house to meet her mum and dad. Copperfield looked over to the wishing well while remembering how Jenny's hand travelled up his thigh. For the first time in his life, Thomas actually felt real fear. The thought of his wife or Maggie suddenly coming back down the garden path and catching the young girl's fingers unzipping his zip was even more terrifying than the heart-stopping moment of walking into that Iraqi ambush back in '91.

He didn't stop her though, not a chance. Hell, it had been months since his wife had shown any interest in sex and even then, the whole dull event had lasted just under four minutes, and that included the time to hold the struggling bitch down while he pulled down her panties. He remembered looking down at those doe eyes while she pulled out his equipment and shoved as much as she could into her warm, moist mouth. After a few more seconds of Jenny playing with him, he couldn't care less about getting caught.

It had been her who had cut the playing short, moments before the captain was about to explode. She had wiped her mouth then asked for his telephone number. He recalled the look of his wife's face when she and Maggie came back down that path laden with plates full of sandwiches and glasses of cold beer. She had known that something had happened. Copperfield had known her long enough to recognise the signs.

Not that he had been too bothered. Copperfield took his wife for the last time later that night. She didn't want it, but that hadn't been a shock; it hadn't stopped him from fucking her anyway. He just couldn't help himself, not after what that girl had done to him earlier on. Copperfield might have even cried out Jenny's name moments before he exploded into his wife.

He turned back around and reluctantly continued his way towards the main house. After all, those historic thoughts of sex had done wonders for his sleeping sausage and future thoughts of climbing back into that bed then climbing back into Jenny almost made him forget his mission altogether. Copperfield reminded himself about allowing juices to simmer and increased his speed.

Something had intruded upon his territory. That took priority over the enjoyment of his little play doll, it was that simple. Besides, it had been simply ages since the captain took down a live target.

He reached the side door, stopped, and frowned. His notions of sex with Jenny, what to do with his wife's doctor, and punishment for the estate layabouts ran to the back of his mind when Copperfield found kind some kind of jelly-like substance coating the bottom of the door and the top step. He placed the tip of his dark blue slipper into the stuff then lifted his foot. "What the hell is this?"

If Maggie was home, and she'd been ten years younger, Copperfield would have blamed her for playing with green slime again. As a kid, she loved all that gross stuff. Her mum bought her what they called alien eggs: a clear plastic egg-shaped canister, full of that vile slime and with some stupid, plastic alien baby in the middle. It was pointless tat, but Maggie loved them.

Copperfield slowly lowered himself and tentatively pushed his forefinger into the mess. It sure did feel like the same stuff. He got back onto his feet, wiped his finger against his jogging pants then pushed the door open. Copperfield couldn't explain it, so he filed it for later study. The cat problem came first. He'd decided it was a cat which had climbed the fence, simply because he hated the little shitters. Once he had grabbed the crossbow, Copperfield would perform a quick check in here, just in case the cat had got inside.

He entered the kitchen first. Nothing looked out of place since Copperfield had last been in here, nor was anything missing. That pleased him; it wasn't going to stop him from having a few words with those men. Copperfield reached the door which led into his study. He pulled out a set of keys, selected the one that opened the study door, and left the kitchen.

Something at the back of his head, a glimmer of an idea, managed to clamber past all the other notions currently fighting for attention. It raised a little flag and waved. Copperfield stopped dead. He spun around and peered back inside the kitchen. The fruit bowl, the bloody thing, was empty.

That had to be it. Sometime during today, while he'd been otherwise busy down in the summerhouse, that wife of his must have regained enough sense and come in here to raid that bowl.

The stuff on the step wasn't anything more elaborate than chewed-up banana. Her window was directly above the side door. Why she'd spit that stuff out of her window was anybody's guess, but it wasn't the weirdest thing she'd performed recently.

He unlocked the study, opened the door, and stepped into his second private domain. Nobody but him came into his study. The crossbow, as well as his other weapons, was hung on the far wall opposite his desk. Possession of most of his collection would put him inside for a considerable amount of time, if the authorities ever got wind of just how much ordnance he took with him when he left the forces.

Copperfield should have had these weapons locked away and out of sight, but what was the point of having these beautiful examples of fine engineering if you couldn't look at them? He walked over to the wall and ran his fingers along the barrel of his Sterling MK4 submachine gun. Such an incredible machine. This, as well as the others bolted to the wall, were taken from stores, picked up from the battlefield, or removed from vehicles during his twenty-year stay in the forces. He wasn't the only one who had taken a few trophies. Copperfield knew of at least two other COs who'd taken more equipment than him but unlike him, they had gone on to sell their ill-gotten gains to other people with rather dodgy backgrounds.

There used to be a Lanchester MK1 submachine gun above the Sterling, but he took that down a few months ago, with the intention of attempting to restore it to full working order. Despite it being a copy of a German MP28 and a Navy weapon to boot, it was still one of his most prized possessions.

He could spend hours in here. If he didn't have pressing matters attend, he probably would too. With reluctance, Copperfield left his collection before lifting the crossbow from the wall. He pushed several bolts into his pocket then walked over to his desk. If his video surveillance had been set up correctly, he wouldn't need to leave the study until his cameras had located the intruder. Unfortunately, the only camera properly connected was in his wife's bedroom. Good news for Copperfield; at least he'd known that the fault lay in him and his poor wiring skills and bad news for the doctor who he'd seen three times now diddling his wife whilst she'd been in orbit. He was on the captain's list. Once his territory really was secure, Copperfield fully intended to show the doctor exactly what happened to people who abused his trust.

He left the study, ensuring the door was locked before proceeding to the next room.

"Dammit, I should have reviewed the tape," he muttered. Copperfield hurried along the corridor, ran up the stairs, and checked into Maggie's old room. The place looked just as it should. He closed that door then bypassed all the other rooms before heading towards the second-floor staircase.

That tape wouldn't be reviewed. In fact, once all this was over, Copperfield intended to wipe the bloody thing. He simply didn't want to be proved wrong regarding the chewed-up bananas. Right now, his theory fitted the evidence perfectly and as far as he was concerned, that suited him down to the ground.

The bedroom door was wide open. "What the hell?" He pulled the line back and fitted a bolt. The closer he got to that open door, the more uneasy he became. Something was very wrong with this picture. The wife never left the door open, ever.

Copperfield rested his finger against the trigger guard and moved to the edge, away from the creaking floorboards which, if stood upon, might announce his presence. He passed the framed family portrait showing the three of them back when Maggie had left school and passed the group photo of his platoon, taken a few days before they were shipped out to Iraq. The only soldier not present in the shot was Callum McGuire, and that's because he was behind the lens.

He noticed his face in the light green door's reflection. Above the scowl and the iron-grey moustache, he saw fear in his eyes, something he never expected to see. What the hell was wrong with him? After the shit he'd faced over the years, the discovery of an open door shouldn't even enter his top ten. That soon altered when Copperfield realised that the only reason why he saw his reflection was due to the same gelatinous substance he saw outside also coated the door.

Copperfield covered the remaining distance in less than a second and got ready to shoot the first thing that moved. All that did move, apart from the nodding bird ornament on her side of the dressing table, were the bed covers. It looked like two dogs fighting under there.

"Anna!" he screamed. "What's going on?"

"Leave me be," replied a muffled voice from under the covers. "Go back to your whore, Thomas. Stay out of my bedroom."

It wasn't until he actually stepped across the threshold that the captain saw how wrong this whole situation was. There were things poking out from the side of her quilt. What the fuck was this? They looked like plant shoots or cooked spaghetti. Hell, they even bore a passing resemblance to rat tails.

"Oh God, Anna. Please. Tell me what's going on?"

The top of the quilt folded back to reveal her head. She sat up and the cover slipped down further. He stared, mouth agape, at the woman's grey, shiny body.

"Get out of here!" she yelled. The woman leaned forward. "Go on, go crawl up Jenny's arse, you vile, misogynist bastard." When Thomas didn't move, she reached across the bed and grabbed a phone lying next to the nodding bird. "This is your last warning. In a few more seconds, Jenny's father is going to know exactly where she's been going every night for the past few years!"

Thomas backed away. He no longer cared about what weirdness was happening in here. The woman wasn't in any trouble, apart from being bat-shit insane. He took one last look at that bed before shutting the door. It looked totally normal. No bits of spaghetti hanging over the side and no animals fighting under the cover.

Could he have imagined everything? He slammed the door. It was more likely that the bitch had decided to play mind games with him. The captain stormed along the hallway and down the stairs, taking them two at a time. So she knew about Jenny, did she? In that case, he'd see about trying to get her committed so Jenny could move up into the main house.

Copperfield moved through the empty house, his mind boiling over at the sheer ignominy of her behaviour. She even tried to blackmail him! That had to be the icing on the cake. Like he gave a shit about what Jenny's dad would do. Copperfield would tear the runt's head off his shoulders if he even thought about looking at him in a funny way. He reached the outer door.

"You're soon going to find that two can play at that game," he murmured. Copperfield still had the tapes showing the doctor having sex with his sleeping wife. That disgrace to the profession was going to help him to put the rancid bitch away or risk that numerous copies of those tapes ending up in the wrong hands.

Right now, all that nonsense could wait until the morning. So could the cat problem as well. It would probably go back to where it lived at some time during the night, most likely when it has crapped in Copperfield's cauliflower patch. It didn't matter, as tomorrow was another day, the first of many new days when his life was about to become so much less complicated. Once he had spoken to that dirty doctor, Copperfield would take a ride into that horrible Harmony Estate and find the incompetent fools who installed his fence. They were going to double-check and triple-check the security before any money exchanged hands. Once he was satisfied, he then intended to contact a reputable dealer to electrify the top. That ought to sort out that feline and any other which took it upon themselves to use his property as a toilet.

Copperfield pushed open the summerhouse door, leaned the crossbow against the wall, and padded over to the bedroom door. Before he opened it, he removed his clothes. The juices had simmered long enough. It was

Developmental Stimulation

While sleep is fundamental to newborn brain development, so too is age-appropriate stimulation. Neuroscientists are actively conducting research into the physiological and developmental effects of parental voice, music, light, and human touch, all of which are important for newborn brain development.[48] Human touch is the cornerstone of human interaction. Light touch, breastfeeding, and skin-to-skin care, all supportive human interactions, are significantly associated with stronger brain responses in the newborn.[21] What, exactly, is meant by positive or "supportive" stimulation? Positive, supportive stimulation is simply an age-appropriate social interaction, whether it be soothing, gentle strokes, an affirming smile, or a soft, gentle voice.[49] Skin-to-skin contact has been shown to promote both physiologic stability and mother-infant bonding.[50] Once again, positive, supportive stimulation is more likely to occur in the context of a healthy routine, which includes regular cycles of nutritional intake and sleep.

Developmental Reflexes and Milestones

Newborn development is a complex process, evolving rapidly in the first year. In the first 9 to 12 months, cognitive and motor function, primitive reflexes, posture, and tone are highly interconnected. Over time and with age-appropriate stimulation, higher cognitive and language function develops, fine and gross motor skills are honed, and adaptive reflexes emerge. Developmental assessments are simplified by parental report of age-equivalent milestones. In other words, milestones reflect a child's developmental status when compared with infants of the same age within the population. Minor deviations in milestones are common, so the experienced pediatrician brings an important perspective to these conversations. For example, failure to achieve one or two milestones might warrant close follow-up but need not prompt an extensive diagnostic evaluation. As long as milestones are followed regularly and achieved within a reasonable period of time, there is no need to be overly concerned. Reassurance is 90 percent of a pediatrician's job!

Primitive reflexes. Infants are born with primitive reflexes—innate responses to an external sensory stimulus. Some primitive reflexes are so important that they can be viewed as "survival instincts." The rooting reflex, for example, is a reflexive search for the mother's nipple when the cheek is stroked. The sucking reflex, which is paired physiologically with the rooting reflex, causes the newborn to suck when the nipple (or the examiner's finger) touches the roof (hard palate) of the mouth. The sucking reflex begins to emerge between 33- and 34 weeks' gestation but may not mature until 35 to 36 weeks' gestation. Full-term newborns are generally born with fully developed sucking and swallowing reflexes. The palmar grasp is a newborn's response to an object that strokes the palm of the hand. The moro reflex is a sudden, reflexive extension of the arms, hands, and neck when the newborn's arms/hands are gently but suddenly relaxed from the vertical plane. Sometimes referred to as the *startle reflex*, the moro reflex is active when the newborn is startled. These and other primitive reflexes are intact in the healthy newborn but gradually diminish over the course of the first six months of life. With time, as the newborn learns to roll over, sit up, crawl, and stand, primitive reflexes disappear.

Developmental milestones. Newborns are generally able to regard the mother's face, make eye contact, and turn to the breast or bottle when the cheek is stroked. Indeed, the most important developmental skills in the newborn period are innate, involuntary reflexes like the coordination of sucking, swallowing, and breathing. A healthy two-month-old is generally able to coo and smile, turn to sound, and lift his/her head when placed face down on a flat surface. Likewise, a four-month-old smiles spontaneously, enjoys social play, babbles, mimics simple noises, consoles with affection, now time to show her exactly what he was capable of. He pushed open the door, walked over to the bed, pulled back the covers, and climbed in beside her.

It took him precisely two seconds to realise the sense of wrongness had not finished with him when Copperfield touched Jenny's back and found himself stroking thick fur. He managed to release a single scream before several thin tendrils burst out of that back and wrapped themselves around the man's throat.

CHAPTER FOUR

The weird stranger poked Callum in the side, seconds after his eyelids dropped into sleeping mode. He jerked back and bumped the back of his head on the wall which separated the two patches.

"I'm awake, I'm awake."

Harry sighed. His new friend did a lot of sighing. The man then lightly booted Callum's ankle before nodding over at the other end of the alley. He wanted Callum to follow him, that was obvious, but right now, all he wanted to do was to climb over this wall, hurry over to his favourite spot in the park, and get some sleep. As far as he was concerned, today was finished. He had it up to here with the weirdness and so didn't need anymore, thank you very much. Callum crossed his arms and shook his head decisively. What the hell. Two could play at the non-communication game.

It was as plain as an unused tissue that this joker, dressed in mud and armed with a deadly Nerf gun, was obviously part of this weirdness that had invaded Callum's life. Despite him bombarding the guy with a bazillion questions, he'd answered precisely none of them. In fact, he had the bare-faced cheek to spit out a few of his own.

The weird stranger crouched beside Callum, placed the weapon on Callum's lap then stood up. "From where I come from, that is the second most valuable commodity a soldier could possess. With that weapon, the hunters became the hunted. Learning to break their conditioning was the turning point. Our species extinction no longer looked inevitable."

Callum so wanted to play touchy with the Nerf gun but found he couldn't pull his gaze away from the stranger's scary eyes. This man next to him had been to hell. The stranger blinked, breaking the spell. He looked down at the strange weapon. That man hadn't just been to hell, he had a frigging season ticket. "Tell me, where exactly are you from?" he whispered.

He jerked at the man's quiet reply. Surely, he must have misheard. "Say again?"

"I was born in Brandale, in the year 1978."

"Right, okay." Callum plucked up enough courage to place his fingers under the weapon and lift it a couple of inches above his knees. The surface felt a little unpleasant, a bit like wet clay, or dead flesh. He shuddered and dropped it back on his lap. Callum decided that he didn't want to touch it anymore. "Okay, so you're a local lad and recently you've been where? No, let me guess. You were kidnapped by aliens and were made to fight in some war on a far-off planet?" Callum licked his lips. "Sorry, I guess my sarcasm meter just melted. Please. Tell me what the fuck is going on?"

"From what little I've seen, friend, your world has become a paradise. It's rich and peaceful and so colourful." He plucked a leaf from an overhanging branch. "There's beauty everywhere." The stranger switched his gaze to Callum. "Here, you have thrived, aided by fantastic inventions pulled out of the heads of your own boffins." He picked up the gun. "And yet, I still believe the Goliaths and their familiars will still be able to turn this paradise into a vast killing zone with little effort."

"Gee, thanks for the detail there, Mr. Mud Soldier. Apart from pissing on my pretend happiness, you've told me absolutely bugger all."

"It would be best to show you," he replied, "as I feel cynicism runs thick in your veins." He bent over and dragged Callum onto his feet. "Stay behind me and keep quiet. The three who confronted you are close and, I believe, are observing."

As soon as the weird stranger mouthed out that the three kids were close by, a dozen ambiguous emotions rushed through his already battered system. Callum took the knife out of his pocket. It wasn't quite as impressive as the stranger's gun, but it did give him some reassurance. Not that it helped the original owner. Still, if he hadn't used this on that head in a bag, he might not have been here to witness all this wonderful roller-coaster ride of fun and joy.

The weird stranger stopped moving. He leaned to the side and tilted his head backwards, then grabbed Callum and pointed up into the tree. He craned his head back, not totally sure of what he was supposed to be looking at. Callum didn't ask the question as Mud Soldier told him to stay quiet, his scary eyes drilling twin holes into the back of his skull.

He was about to give scary-eyes the universal shrug when he did notice something odd. Callum let out a tiny moan when a pair of eyes blinked at him, followed by something up there hissing. A drop of slime fell from the leaves and splatted onto the floor between them. A thin plume of acrid smoke rose from where the slime hit.

"That is not good," said the stranger. He pushed Callum back, dropped to his knee, aimed the weapon up, and fired off a single shot.

An animal-like scream almost shattered Callum's eardrums. He jumped even further back when whatever had been blinking at him plummeted out of the tree and hit the floor with a wet thud. Bits of the creature's body flew out, landing in the surrounding foliage.

"Move it! Come on, man, we need to get out of here!"

Callum saw fear in those stranger's eyes and for the second time tonight, he wished the bottle he kept in his inside pocket was full of the hard stuff. The stranger ran over to him and pushed him backwards.

"This is your world, find us a safe place!"

Callum leaned to the side and looked over the stranger's shoulder and immediately wished he hadn't. The slimy mess on the floor wore Adidas trainers and the remains of a bright green T-shirt. He was looking at the kid who'd stirred the pot, the one who so needed to see his taller mate cut up Callum. As frightening as that was, it paled in comparison to the sight of all those lumps of meat which had flown off the main body upon impact. They were all crawling, rolling, and undulating towards the pair of them.

He didn't need telling twice. Callum spun around and raced back to the wall. He scrambled over the top and dropped down into his safe zone. Yet, thanks to what he'd just witnessed, those words had lost all their meaning. How could he be safe anymore, not after what he'd just seen? He cast a fearful gaze above him. Oh Christ, there were still two more of those things out there.

Callum hopped from foot to foot, waiting for the man to get over that wall. As soon as he was over, Callum raced across the grass, desperately needing to get out from under the trees. He headed for the playground. It wasn't usually an area of the park he frequented due to hysterical mothers during the daylight hours and gangs of youths sprawling across the equipment at night. This was an emergency, so all rules fell by the wayside.

Once he reached the slide, Callum stopped and leaned his head against one of the steel supports while vaguely wondering who had just blow-torched his lungs. Christ on a bike, how unfit was he nowadays? Callum waited until the other footsteps had crunched on gravel before standing straight. "So, that's your example of showing me? Thank you. I feel so fucking enriched now." He turned around. "I sure hope that's the end of it as I don't think I can take any more of this, not without a drink."

He instinctively tapped his inside coat pocket, just to see if his bottle really was still empty. Did his new best mate carry any folding stuff? He might have to ask that question before long. Before some mouse-sized slug ate its way through his foot! Oh Jeez. Callum felt his legs fold out from under him. No more. No, please, no more weirdness.

The gravel did look rather soft; perhaps this would be a nice place to go to sleep? The scary-eyed man should wake him up when the sun came up with breakfast. He looked up at him and attempted to ask for a bacon sandwich without a side order of puddle water when he caught the sight of another one of those things running towards them with the speed of a greyhound. Callum shrieked out, the shrieking intensified when he saw the other one heading straight for him, coming from the side and weaving its way through the playground equipment.

His weird friend dove to the side and rolled over to the roundabout. He didn't see the man shoot as the thing heading for Callum scaled up the slide ladders. Callum staggered back, keeping his horrified gaze fixed on the liquid, brown shape directly above him. It squawked like some huge mutant featherless parrot before throwing its shapeless body off the top of the slide. Callum jumped back and brought the blade down on what looked like a head as soon as it landed on the gravel.

A sickly sweet stench of rotten peaches erupted from the wide gash that he'd cut into the creature's thick skin. Callum stabbed it again and again, while groaning and crying. He just couldn't stop slashing at the horrible, foul, inhuman stain of creation.

Callum heard somebody's voice shouting, but it sounded so distant. Was it aimed at him? It didn't matter. All that concerned him was stopping this dirty abomination from getting back up. A pair of arms encircled his body and savagely pulled Callum off it. Before he had time to return to his job, the other man aimed and fired his odd weapon, reducing the mutilated creature into boiling, stinking soup.

The man dragged Callum over to the see-saw, pulled the knife out of his slimy hands, and threw it into the grass. He then sat on his thighs. "Enough!" The man slapped Callum hard across the cheek then pushed his other hand under the tramp's chin. "Look at me. It has gone. There is nothing left. The night has claimed its companions and the moon will show us the way to the bunkers. Listen to the silent screams of the fallen Goliath and take your joy from the knowledge that in the end, they all will suffer the same fate as the vile spawn you destroyed."

Callum heard the man's words; they made no sense at all but that didn't matter much. He took a deep breath, while listening to the comforting sound of the distant traffic, as well as the faint beat music noise drifting from the town's only night-club. It'll be kicking out time soon, meaning that his old mate, Nick Bannon, one of the town's originals, will be crawling out from under his newspaper collection and making his way across town, heading towards the one remaining takeaway. Callum looked into scary man's eyes. "It's been a fair few years since I zoned out like that, man."

Scary-eyes climbed off Callum then helped him back up onto his feet. "I am sorry. I should have taken their last human thoughts into consideration."

"Again, you're making no sense. Look, all I want to know right now is are we still going to end up dead within the next half-hour or so?"

He shook his head. "No, not if we move away from this location."

"Fine, that suits me down to the ground. I think it's time you met a couple of pals of mine. With luck, I might be able to snag a drink from one of them. When we get all cosy, perhaps you could then explain exactly what the hell is happening in my fair town?"

He nodded. "I'll try."

"Oh, I almost forgot. What's your name?"

The man smiled. Judging from the effort he was putting into the motion, Callum guessed that he wasn't used to showing joy, or anything else for that matter, apart from his standard dead face.

"I'm called Harry," he replied. The man held out his hand, "and I am pleased to make your acquaintance."

Callum nodded and reluctantly shook the man's hand. "Yeah, ain't I the luckiest chap in the whole of Brandale."

CHAPTER FIVE

The first fingers of the dawn sun crept up the captain's arm. The weak rays weren't strong enough to dry out the thin coat of birthing fluid covering his naked body. He would need to stay here, in this position, for another few hours before that happened and although the feeling of that new sun upon his skin was most enjoyable, the tasks he had to complete before his God's arrival stopped him from enjoying that pleasure.

He lifted his arm up above the table in front of him and twisted the new flesh around. Tiny wet balls of pseudo-muscle, unused from the process, adhered to his palm. He wasn't the only individual to notice the prize. Liquid grunts from his two associates hovering behind his body reminded him that they still needed finishing off. The two women desired more food.

"Go back to bed," he commanded. "We will hunt when I say."

They slinked away, each one taking different routes back to the same nest. The captain sensed that perhaps the original meat probes had not digested enough of their former host's memories when they took over the two females. It was a trivial matter if that indeed was the case. The captain would simply command one of the females to eat the other one. Their God ordered two prime foot-soldiers, but if their original minds would not cooperate, then one would have to suffice.

He paused and then grinned. His host disapproved of such wanton facial expression, but the captain did not particularly care for what the few strands of the original mind desired. He performed a mental re-wire and pushed the previous iteration of conservation of meat into a nice dark corner.

This was a new world, full of life and opportunity. Why scrimp on good building material when all the captain had to do was find another body, cut out one of the meat probes, and transfer it across.

Unlike the previous world, where their Gods had almost exhausted the supply of meat and material, the captain believed that they would not run out in this bountiful paradise for at least another three generations. The stuff was simply everywhere!

The captain pulled back the curtains even further to allow more of that glorious light shine through. He noticed the excess meat had now transferred to the curtain material. Indeed, the stuff really was everywhere. The captain carefully picked off the meat, placed equal amounts in his hands, then approached the two women, each one having taken up position on either side of the bed without actually climbing up.

As he neared, their soft growling reached his ears. The truth of the matter was that he did not want to sacrifice either woman, as both showed promise to become fine prime foot-soldiers. Even now, in their foetal stage, the two women already had the strength to beat any of the other God's prime foot-soldiers, but he suspected that the balance of power would not be in their favour for long. As already, he sensed the others; his adversaries had started to build their own armies.

"Here you go, my children," he said, holding out his hands. Their rough tongues tickled his skin. It was surprisingly pleasant. As they fed, he listened, with great delight, at his host's frustrated howling; it transpired that the original owner detested cats and their tongues brought that memory back.

Usual procedure advised on performing a total purge, removing all trace of the previous host as soon as the memory transfer was complete. The captain had never been a great follower of procedure, as his vast experience taught him that more often than not, an empty vessel only followed the line dictated by their God. Unswerving worship, devotion, and obedience were fine for the lesser creatures, but the right hand of God should, at least, possess a tiny amount of intractability.

He firmly believed that his decision not to purge this mind was the sole reason as to why his God had become the most powerful entity in all the multiverse. Also, keeping a few strands of the original mind gave him something to play with and torment whenever he became bored.

They whined quietly once all traces of the pseudo-flesh had gone, reminding him that perhaps getting these two finished should take priority. Sensing his acceptance to proceed with a hunt, both women scrambled off the bed, each one taking their place beside his legs. They were just a hairsbreadth from each other and yet neither woman had bristled up. The captain took this as a good sign that it might work out for the best. Granted, their excitement over the anticipation of their first feed had probably taken their focus away from their mutual hatred, but the captain decided to overlook that tiny omission.

"Okay, enough with the fawning. You win. We will hunt. Go wait at the door while I clean myself and dress."

The captain could only marvel at the speed in which they both traversed through the rooms of this large house. Their flexible shapes and well as the extra adaptations built into the code ensured that they reached the outside door less than a second after he had finished talking and not once did the pair's feet or hands touch the floor. They truly were a product of superb design which stretched back many thousands of years and back through hundreds of defeated worlds. His God, as well as his own predecessors, had moulded the perfect prime foot-soldier.

He turned around and walked towards the wardrobe to select some appropriate clothing for his first venture out in this glorious new world. Thanks to his host's extensive knowledge of the local inhabitants, he knew exactly where to find his companion's perfect prey. In fact, his host had furnished him with a great many weird and wonderful memories. Everything from this world's technological achievements, of which he was justifiably proud, to his prediction to how the population would react once the Gods emerged through the thousands of trans-portals, built by subjects just like the captain. He chose a rather fetching pale green summer dress, a pair of bright red tights, and his old army boots. The captain so enjoyed the memory strands screaming at his clothing while he dressed. "I am so going to enjoy being you," he shouted whilst laughing. On his way to meet his eager hunters, he stopped by the study and pulled a compact pistol off the wall. After some mumbling and weeping, the memory strands told him where the ammunition was kept.

Now ready and willing to explore this next world, the captain took his two meowing hunters out into the bright sunlight. In just the hour or so that he had awoken, the temperature had already increased by five degrees. Only small patches of birthing fluid were left on his skin, most of them under the dress. In retrospect, it might have been a better idea to dry himself before donning any type of false covering. Still, it would not be for too long. By the time his God had emerged, his own bio-armour should have pushed through this tender surface and solidified. Right now though, it was essential to maintain this human appearance while he mingled with the natives.

The captain took them up to the main gate, input the key-code, and stood back while the gate swung inwards. It took a lot of mental effort to stop the two hunters from racing across that field on the other side of the road, although he did understand why they were close to breaking their conditioning. He felt exactly the same. In the field next to this one were thirty-one cows. It had been decades since he had been so close to that amount of live meat, and although the temptation to release his mental lock and join the two hunters in the inevitable gorging, the captain just couldn't. The hunters needed to understand the first rule of the importance of self-control, of taking just enough to sustain their bodies. Of all the familiars, the role of prime foot-soldier had to be the most revered position. After his role, obviously.

He guided them away from the field, ensuring that he too avoided staring at those moving mounds of delicious, firm, meat, not the easiest of tasks when they would not stop mooing. "Behave yourselves!" he snarled. "Remember, your meat probes are not yet fully implanted. If you continue to defy me, it is I who will feed on your flesh and I will give those cows your meat probes."

With one last defiant look, the hunter once called Jenny gave the other hunter a sneaky bite on the rear limb before galloping a few metres along the road. The remaining hunter emitted a low growl but did not pursue. Instead, she waited until the captain had reached her before pushing her body against his legs. Her intention was clear enough.

He gritted his teeth in annoyance at the power play shown between the two rivals. The hunter formerly known as Maggie obviously wanted him to go through with his threat with just one adjustment. The captain shook his head and booted her in the place where the other hunter had bitten her. "Enough!" he growled. "Either you both learn to cooperate or you lose your right to exist."

She took the hint and ran over to her companion, where the hunter kept at a respectful distance from the creature who once begged Thomas Copperfield to poison the old cow. He allowed the memory strands his first view at what the meat probes had done to the two loves of his life and chuckled as screaming started up again.

"Just wait and see what these perfect examples of controlled evolution can do to a normal human."

That would come sooner rather than later as even now. The captain could hear the tuneless whistling coming from the young voice of David Hampshire, the boy who delivered the morning paper to the house. According to the memory strands, this rather pleasant fourteen-year-old boy had taken quite a shine to the captain's wife, so it seemed rather fitting that it should be her to take him down.

He signalled to the hunters to get out of sight while he took up position in the middle of the road. The captain stood motionless, his hands placed on his hips, and waited. The whistling stopped as soon as the boy saw him. So did he, in fact. A brief expression of utter terror exploded across David's face and before Copperfield knew what was happening, the kid had already turned his bike around and had started to pedal as first as his legs could go. To make matters even worse, he had the advantage of being on top of a hill.

"Get him!" he screamed. Gone were the thoughts of allowing the older hunter to eat most of the boy while the other one watched. Now it would be simply a matter of which one reached the boy first. He raced along the road until he reached the incline, interested to see which of his hunters caught the kid first.

They ran on all fours due to the meat probe shortening their legs and lengthening their arms. The simian method of locomotion wasn't exactly advantageous in this flat terrain, but the altered state came into its own in wooded or urban areas. In another couple of seconds, that kid was about to discover exactly why he took the liberty of ensuring the meat probes carry the adjusted genes within their transfer pipes before entering the trans-portal.

The weeping child vanished from his sight when he passed under the tree cover and just as he expected, his two hunters left the ground by scaling the closest trunks. The only evidence the captain saw from that point was of the branches shedding their leaves.

A short scream followed by the sound of the bike smashing against the road signalled the end of the hunt. It would be a good few minutes before he was within sight of his hunters and by that time, there would be very little left. In their foetal stage, the hunters would devour everything organic, including the bones; especially the bones, as the creatures needed the material for their own armoured shells.

Perhaps their first taste of food would contribute in calming down their mutual dislike of each other. That, and the threats he had already issued. The captain continued his journey along the road, while pondering on the immediate future of the two hunters. Right now, he did know that neither of them would be in any shape, mentally or psychically, to continue this annoying grudge, as their bodies would be preparing for their first transformation. Within the space of a few hours, the first blossoming of what they would become would be showing through their flesh. Meaning that it was now his time to feed.

He reached the spot where the hunters had taken the boy. All that remained was an off-coloured stain on the road. They had even licked the blood of the tarmac. The captain ran over to the wall and leaned over. There they were, sleeping in each other's arms. Already, tiny lumps were forming under their skins. He picked up a short stick and poked both of them. When they opened their eyes and stopped growling at him and then at each other, he ordered them to return to the house and stay inside until he got back. As they scampered past him, he realised that he still did not know which of the hunters made the kill.

He removed the gun from his dress and turned it around in his hands. This world had a bountiful supply of weapons just like this one. The memory strands had shown him the extent of progression the species had made in terms of weaponry. It took him a lot to impress him, but when he found out just how far they had come compared with the other world, that rare emotion did indeed rise to the surface.

The captain paused before he replaced the weapon. The memory strands were chuckling. They were actually displaying mirth. At first, he thought it was because of the human weaponry, that somehow their jet fighter aircraft, their tanks, and their nuclear weapons could defeat their

Gods. The gigantic beasts they worshipped might not have encountered weapons as potent as what this version of the human species possessed, but it wouldn't matter. This world, like all the others, would soon fall. This event was inevitable.

Even after explaining this to the memory strands, as well as showing just what his Gods had done to the other worlds they had conquered, the chuckling continued. "Okay, you have either gone insane, which is a possibility, or something else has happened. I could unravel them and find out for myself or you could just tell me. Which option do I choose?"

After another few seconds of giggling, the memory strands calmly informed the captain that the only reason why that boy scarpered was simply because he saw him in the dress. It seemed to please him that the captain had made such a grievous error even before he left the house, that although the monsters did catch the boy, it could have quite easily gone the other way. The memory strands then informed the captain that this world would kill them all. God or no Gods. The humans here knew how to fight and each and every one of his disgusting creatures would meet their end here. The memory strands then showed him an image of exactly what these nuclear bombs were capable of.

He stood in the middle of that empty road, listening to the birds flying from one branch to the next and hearing the distant noise of an oncoming vehicle and found, for the first time since he became sentient, almost twelve thousand years ago, that perhaps his Gods really had arrived at a world which they might never leave.

CHAPTER SIX

Not once had this disparate collection of individuals interrupted his monologue, which, by their way of thinking, must have sounded fantastic, bordering on the verge of insanity. Harry had to stop talking now as his throat hurt. He looked at the four men, one by one, almost daring them to call him a liar. Yet, he sensed nothing but sympathy from them. Did they really believe his account?

Even if that was the case, Harry doubted that he would be able to counter any holes they were likely to pick in what he had just told them. Harry couldn't remember the last occasion when he spoke for such a great amount of time, probably never.

Talking aloud and for any amount of time had never really been encouraged. Harry believed that was one of the reasons why he used to love listening to the old ones tell their many tales of life before the Goliaths. They were only allowed to speak because of the great respect and awe the remaining humans had for them, coupled with the fact that they occupied the deepest burrows, well away from the dugouts, trenches, and tunnels, close to the surface.

The familiars had devices which could pick up human speech vibration through the ground. He had known of at least two near-surface colonies that had awakened to find adapted defilers breaking into their shelters.

Callum passed Harry a clear bottle containing what he hoped was water. The bottle's lightness surprised him as did the material's flexibility.

"It's called plastic," said Callum, smiling.

He nodded, containing his continued disbelief at how far they had progressed in this world. It almost equalled his shock at how the local population threw out all this gear with such wanton abandon. Harry had come up with at least four uses for this plastic bottle. This stuff was everywhere too. It felt like he was sitting on a goldmine. Some of this material would have been invaluable to his companions back where he came from and yet here, they treated this stuff as junk.

Perhaps their attitude will change with the coming of the war? Considering what is to come, Harry kinda believed that the locals would have more important things on their minds than working out what to do with an empty plastic bottle.

Right now, all Harry wanted to do was to find other people who would actually believe the trouble about to land upon their heads. If he couldn't even persuade these chaps about what was to come, then what chance did he have of telling anybody else?

Harry shuffled to the edge of the folded-up mattress that he and Callum occupied and took the time to study the rest of his audience. The youth sat opposite Harry, looked approximately ten to fifteen years younger than him. It's odd. Of all the men here, he saw this one becoming a good fighter. He certainly had youth on his side, as well as quick movements and a keen eye. He was obviously too soft, they all were, but that would soon go, if they lived past the big invasion. The boy stood a little taller than Harry and had quite a bit of muscle clinging to those bones. Earlier, Callum told Harry that the boy used to work out back before he fell on hard times. Harry had no idea what that meant but kept that to himself. There was a lot about this world that he didn't understand.

The two other men were the leaders. That much was obvious, although how this came about was still a mystery. From what he had observed so far and taking pointers from his own world, Harry guessed that the two men had simply outlived all their potential rivals. Obviously, their lives hadn't been as tough as what they would have endured on his world, but they had lived tougher lives than the other section of this world's population, the ones who believed it was perfectly acceptable to throw plastic bottles over their shoulders and forget about them seconds later.

Callum told him moments before arriving under this huge road bridge that Malc and Dosser were the last of the town's originals. He also reassured Harry that the two guys would know what to do about the shit-storm about to drop on their heads.

They sat in identical dull-pink armchairs directly opposite Harry. The one on the last, Dosser, reminded Harry a little of his old man. They both possessed the same intense bright green eyes. When he fixed you with that piercing gaze, it felt like he was peeling away pieces of your soul, layer by layer. Right now, that's exactly what he was doing. He only broke the connection when the other man coughed.

"You've certainly given us plenty to think about, young man," said Malc. "It is, you have to admit, a fantastic account."

"No shit," muttered Dosser.

"I know you believe it." Malc stared straight at Callum. "And considering he went as white as a sheet once you told us how you two met, he believes it too. I tell you. It takes a lot to make our pal look like he's just shit his pants."

Dosser nodded in agreement. "Valid points, my friend. Trust us. We know a bullshit artist when we see one. Callum, why don't to take your new pal over to the river bank for a few minutes while we decide how to proceed." Dosser reached into his pocket and pulled out a small note.

Harry couldn't help but stare as the old man handed the note over to the boy. He remembered when he was younger than this boy, back before the war knocked the sense of wonder out of him. Amongst all the other tales of old told by the great old ones, they used to talk about money in equal amounts of love and anger. To that young boy, their stories of how people killed over little bits of paper seemed utterly alien.

"I think the sandwich shop at the top of Greenhead Lane will be opening in a few minutes. Why don't you go buy our guest something to eat?" He grinned. "Make it a bacon sandwich. If what he told us is true, then he won't know the delights of such a mouth-watering meal. Get something for Callum, and I suppose you can have something as well."

The boy nodded while grinning. The face soon changed to shock when the old man's other hand whipped forward and grabbed a handful of grotty brown jumper. "If you even think about running off with that tenner, young lad, I'll come over to your house and box your ears. You got that?"

"Yes, sir."

"Good, and I also want some change. You got me?"

He released the boy then turned to Callum. "Go on then, you two. Off you trot. We'll call you back soon."

Callum nodded to the two seated men before hurrying towards an overturned vehicle. Harry did the same, unsure whether that was protocol. The other man took him out of the other side of the road bridge and down a grassy banking. Callum grabbed his arm and pulled Harry over towards a pile of thick rubber wheels.

"Folk have been chucking these tyres over the edge of the flyover ever since I was knee-high to a grasshopper."

Harry nodded once, despite not understanding any of that. He didn't think he would ever understand their strange accent or their terminology.

"I used to love coming down here when I was younger you know." He plucked a long blade of grass and wound it around his index finger. "I shouldn't have been down here at all. Back then, this area belonged to a rival gang and if any of them had caught me in their patch, so to speak, they'd have knocked seven shades of shit out of me."

"A rival gang? You mean other kids like you?"

Callum nodded. "Yeah, there were two schools in the area, and we were always having a go at each other. It's just what you did, you know?"

Harry shook his head. "I think so. I guess if we didn't have the horrors belonging to the local Goliath hunting us down, then I suppose I would have been just like that."

"Not that any of them did catch me, mind. I was way too fast for them. Hell, even if they had caught me, what they did would have been nothing compared to what my dad would have done."

"Did he not like you fighting?"

"It's not that. See, I skipped out of school to come down here." Callum sighed. "Perhaps if I hadn't missed so many lessons, then my life could have been so much different." He laughed. "Then again, considering what you have been through, I should probably count my blessings. "Can you believe that I actually thought my time in the army had turned me into a monster?

"You were a soldier?"

Callum pulled a haunted expression. "They thought it would sort me out. It was my dad who ordered me to sign up. I didn't really have a choice. It was either that or jail time. I was a right little shit once the old balls dropped. Alienated my family and what few friends I had." He shrugged. "Looking back, maybe a bit of jail time would have been better for me." Callum picked up a flat stone and skimmed it across the river. "At first, I loved the Army. The routine, the training, the lack of responsibility, the fact of never having to worry where my next bit of money would come from. It was all fluffy blue sky and unicorns until they shipped us off to Iraq."

"You were involved in conflict?"

"While I was over there, I did as I was told, followed orders just like everybody else. I saw mates getting shot or blown up. I killed the enemy and all that time, none of what I did or saw registered. It wasn't until I came back and tried to fit back into society when the problems began to surface." He turned to Harry. "You're a soldier. You must know what it's like."

Harry leaned back and looked into the morning sky. He saw at least three aeroplanes and from the lack of noise, their altitude and size, their engines inside those huge metal beasts were more advanced than anything dreamt up by the old ones. Hundreds of automobiles sped along that road above him. The people inside their metal boxes had absolutely no idea of the terror about to befall them. Finally, he looked back at Callum, the man broken by having to murder members of his own species.

Harry shook his head. "No. We have never known anything other than war." He paused. "No, it wasn't war. Not by the time I was born. By that time, we had exhausted almost all of our ammunition, and they had decimated our population. To make things worse, if that was even possible, the things we were fighting were made from our dead." Harry was a little surprised by his subtle response. Deep down, he wanted to grab him by the scruff of the neck and tell him to pull his head out from his arse. In fact, Harry wanted to do that to those two as well. While he sat on this banking, listening to this man's tale of woe, those things belonging to the Goliath were continuing to secure their foothold upon this world.

"Christ. You really have come from a hell planet. Was it really so grim?"

Harry shrugged. "That is difficult to answer as I knew nothing else. Although, I suppose, if the Goliaths had not succumbed to their mysterious malaise, then it is likely I wouldn't be here to provide my futile warning."

Callum's mouth opened then closed without a single word leaving his lips. Even after all the horrors that man had been put through tonight, Harry seriously believed that Callum simply could not imagine what Harry's existence had been like. After a full five seconds of staring, he pointed towards the top of the banking

"I think the originals want us back. I'm sure I heard them shout."

He followed Callum back up the banking, knowing full well that the two men up there had not shouted anything. Harry had excellent hearing.

"There you are," said Dosser. "I was just about to call you back.'

The old man reached down and helped Harry up to the top. Dosser had a firm grip. He pulled him a little closer.

"Tell me something. Is your last name Scrimshaw by any chance?"

Harry's other hand instinctively tightened around his weapon. "How the hell did you know that?"

Dosser released him and chuckled. "Relax. I knew a couple of Scrimshaws back in the day. You share their features. Come on, let's go back to the chairs. There are a few points we still wish to discuss."

Harry wasn't sure whether to demand the old man to disclose more about this alternative Scrimshaw family that he allegedly knew or laugh out loud at the man's pompous attitude. Harry might not be from around here, but it was still as plain as the nose on the end of his face that he had fallen in with a group rejected by the rest of the humans who shared this location.

What right had they to act like judge and jury regarding his account? They would soon change their attitude when the others appear in the midst of their cities.

He took his place back on the mattress with Callum sitting next to him. Dosser sat back in his chair. The old man then looked at the other one before they both turned to face Harry.

Malc let out a quiet sigh. "We've known that something's been seriously wrong in Brandale for the past few weeks. The rats were the first ones to vanish followed by the cats." He looked straight at Callum. "Joe isn't the only one to go. A couple of drifters who used to bed down behind the railway station vanished a couple of nights ago."

"You never told me that."

"I'm telling you now, Callum." Malc shrugged. "You and Gavin aren't one of the originals. Granted, you are closer to being an honorary member far more than Gavin is on account of you not being an idiot. Still, though, there's stuff we don't like to share. It's just how it is. Speaking of sharing." He turned his attention to Harry. "I want you to tell us about these Goliaths. Before though, do you think the bits which fell off the mobster which chased you two will be a concern?"

Harry shrugged. "I cannot answer that with authority as there wasn't much individual life left in my world."

"You mean no animals?" asked Malc.

"Perhaps a few scattered birds and insects but nothing larger than my hand. As for the pieces of wandering flesh?" Harry shook his head. "My advice is to stay well away from anything belonging to the aggressors. Perhaps they will not actively seek out prey at least until the Goliaths arrive." Harry looked up, noticing the boy was making his way through the knee-high grassland. He carried three white packages, a red cylinder, and a beaming smile. Before too long, the only thing that boy would be carrying was a weapon, if they could find any. That is, if he survived the first few hours of the inevitable apocalypse.

"They appeared in our cities seventy years before I was born, so I can only convey the tales that I heard during my younger days, if that is acceptable?"

Dosser nodded. "Please. The more we know, the better prepared we are."

He took the packages from Gavin, and passed Harry the cylinder and one of the packages.

"It's a can of coke," he said, grinning. "Callum will show you how to open it after you have eaten your sandwich. Judging from the lack of meat on your bones, I'm guessing you're not exactly used to starting your day by stopping off at a sandwich shop before you go and battle your monsters?"

Harry shook his head while listening to his stomach rumble. The aroma that left the package when he opened the top turned the bottom of his mouth into a lake of drool. This world truly was a paradise, and it did make him sad to know that it would not stay like that. Harry confirmed the heavenly metaphor after he took his first bite from the sandwich. Harry had fallen in love and its name was bacon.

"I will recount what horrors that my old friend, Fred Davis, witnessed just days after returning from the trenches. I have heard the story so many times that I can almost imagine being there with him."

.

CHAPTER SEVEN

Of the seven hundred from the town who set out to battle the Hun four years previously, only seventy of Brandale's warriors came back, and each and every one wanted nothing to do with the celebrations that the town elders, mothers, wives, and girlfriends organised for their glorious return. All Fred craved was his comfy bed, the arms of Hilda, his wife, and to sleep for a week.

Sadly, none of that happened.

One of his fellow survivors, a man called George Hammond, actually stopped the bus before they reached the town, stating for the benefit of the others that he had nobody waiting for him so if they didn't mind, he intended to spend tonight swapping his remaining eight shillings for ale. Fred remembered several other soldiers getting off the bus at the same time. He also remembered that if his darling wife hadn't been waiting for him, Fred would have done the same. He had enough of cheering crowds back in Southampton.

Leaving the bus had just guaranteed that those seven men would be part of the few who would survive to see the next dawn.

Fred could never remember the time from stepping off the bus to the arrival of the monster. It all seemed to merge into one multi-coloured cacophony of confusion broken with kisses from his wife, bottles of warm beer pushed into one hand, and wet sandwiches pushed into the other hand.

Fred awoke to screaming. For a terrifying moment, he thought the armistice and the homecoming hadn't happened, that his tormented mind had imagined everything from escaping the horrors of the trench to falling into the arms of his darling Hilda.

The soft sheets smelling of fairy soap and sound of his grandfather's mantelpiece clock ticking away downstairs helped to put away that irrational dread of still being in the trenches, and yet that terrible screaming continued.

He snapped open his eyes and jerked up in bed. Fred realised that all that screaming was bleeding in through the shut windows at the same time as finding Hilda had left his side.

Fred threw the covers back and stared in disbelief at the sight of a thick glaze of red-streaked slime which covered the white sheet where his wife should have been. He scrambled backwards and fell onto the floorboards when he caught his foot in the sheet tangle at the foot of the bed. Fred lay on the floor, listening to the continuous manic screaming, breathing in the dust and looking at the shrivelled remains of his wife which had been pushed under the bed.

The only way to lock in the fanciful notion that none of this was really happening, and to come to terms that the war really had followed him home, was to stare at the mind-numbing atrocity that was once his wife. Fred's tear-blurred eyes followed the contours of the broken skeleton from the shattered skull all the way down to the small toes fragments, poking out from the end of the bed. "We'll meet again, my darling. That is a promise."

He untangled his feet, stood up, and wiped his eyes before covering up the mess on the bed. As the first sheet fell, some of that jelly-like stuff showed through the fine fibres. He stood there, unable to move, holding the remaining covers in his hand while the perfect outline of Hilda appeared through that single sheet. It had to be his mind hammering in one more nail into his sanity, but Fred just could not look away. He needed to see this outline move, for her shapely leg to bunch up or one of her slender arms to reach up and push that sheet closer to him.

Fred blinked which broke the spell. He dropped the remaining covers before falling back. His body crashed into the wall at the same time as his bedroom door burst open. A figure ran in, saw him then stopped dead. A fragment of Fred's rational mind, the piece which had escaped all those coffin nails, calmly informed the rest of his wailing and shrieking mind that his new arrival had just spotted the dry remains of Hilda.

The new arrival rushed over to Fred, grabbed his wrist, and dragged him out of the room. On his way past the window, he saw a flash of something huge, scaly, and grey in the distance. The mind screamed dinosaur at him, but Fred had no time for anything that useless lump of muscle told him right now.

Fred was sat on the wooden dining chair in the hallway, while the other figure slammed the bedroom door. Fred believed that the sound of that door smacking into the frame had just signalled the start of the demise of his existence, which is ironic considering he had thought that to himself at least three times since the reality of what he had been convinced to join sank in. Could it be the addition of this new arrival which triggered that stray thought? That did sound likely as the man, now pulling out a service revolver tucked into his belt, had been there when that German shell landed just yards from the dugout, occupied by Fred's section. The blast tore through the men, shredding their corporal, lance-corporal, and three of Fred's mates. Only he and the chap passing him the pistol survived with all their limbs still attached.

"I need you, old man Dodger!" He looked nervously back towards the stairs. "We all do. There's not much of us left."

The cold steel and the faint odour of gun-oil lifting from the pistol he pushed into Fred's hand helped to push back enough of the mental insanity to give him limited function. "Pardip?" He took his eyes away from the gun and gazed into his friend's expressive brown eyes. "What's happening? Who did that to my Hilda?" Fred increased the pressure on the handle, keeping his finger well away from the trigger.

"Take a deep breath, Fred, then tell me who I am."

"You're Private Pardip Basra, assigned to the Brandale Pals when some idiot from above ordered your company to charge a German defensive line. You were the only survivor." Fred winced when the building shook. "Please, what's going on?"

His friend had towered over all the over lads by a good few inches. Looking back, Fred thought that his huge height was probably one of the reasons why the others tended to keep their opinions of his colour to themselves; that and the sheer fact that no German bullet could touch him.

Pardip pulled him out of the chair. "What's going on is that we're getting out of here before Vritra turns your house into rubble."

"Before who?"

Pardip shook his head. "It's from a tale that my grandfather used to tell us as children, concerning a huge dragon which—" He abruptly shut his mouth. "Nothing, it doesn't matter. Just follow me."

Fred held on to the bannister and ran down the stairs. Once he reached the bottom, he looked up just the once and whispered a quiet goodbye to Hilda. His gut told him that it would be unlikely that he would be returning here. Why his gut suggested such a ridiculous idea bore out when Fred reached the front door. Pardip stood to the side, so he could look out at all that remained of his beloved town.

He cast his gaze across the landscape and felt his memory taking him back three years to their passing through all those nameless Belgian towns, each one flattened by artillery shells from both sides. Brandale now joined their ranks, only no gun had caused all of this devastation. The instigator of Brandale's destruction was at the far end of the town, close to the town's brickworks. Even as Fred asked Pardip if that was his so-called dragon, a limb belonging to this nightmarish beast lifted and swung to the left, catching the side of the brickwork's chimney. The structure toppled over and smashed into the ground, throwing up thick clouds of grey smoke which mixed in with the plumes already circling this massive, moving behemoth.

The surrounding cloud lessened enough for Fred to get a scale of its incredible size. Even from this distance, he knew that the creature was no dinosaur. He remembered his father taking him to the British Museum in London back when he was a child and the sight of all those huge ancient animals had blown his mind. Compared to this thing, those animals would have been like kittens to an elephant.

It took Fred a few seconds to find an animal which remotely resembled the creature now heading towards the steel works further away from the centre of town. More like an amalgamation of a couple of animals. It had the body and head of some giant beetle with eight spider legs, but those legs were a lot fatter and with double the joints.

Fred looked at the pistol that Pardip had given him and put a firm lid on the hysterics which threatened to explode out of his mouth. "Is this gun loaded with something other than normal shells, Pardip?" He glanced across at the giant monster currently demolishing a steel gantry, close to several brick chimneys. "I don't even think artillery shells would make much of a dint against that thing."

"The gun isn't for that, Fred," replied Pardip. The soldier ran over to the side of Bailey's bakery and tapped three times on the front door. "Come on, over here, man. Away from the road."

"I don't understand this. That creature is miles away now."

Pardip reached over, grabbed Fred's nightshirt, and pulled him closer. "Look, man. Look at the monster. In particular, its back. Tell me what you see."

It didn't register the last time he looked at the giant. At least, it probably did, but Fred had just assumed it was flying residue, leftovers from its continuous destruction. Now though, now that Pardip had ordered him to take a closer look, Fred now saw that the creature had friends, or parasites. Whatever they were, they moved across its hide, along its back and up and down its legs, as well as flying around the creature. "What are they?"

"Believe me when I tell you that you don't want to know."

Fred noted the undertone of fear in the man's voice and felt his own terror announcing an unwelcome return. Pardip wasn't a man to openly display his emotions, especially fright. "What do you mean?"

Before he could reply, the bakery door opened a fraction. "Paddy, is that you?"

Fred recognised that voice. He took a couple of steps closer to the door. "Arthur?"

The door opened a little wider, enough to show him that the owner of the Oak and Crown wasn't the only one to live through the destruction of their town. Arthur pulled him and Pardip inside then shut the door.

"Good to see you, young man," said Arthur, locking and bolting the door. He looked at Pardip and then at Fred. "Hilda?" Arthur's expression changed from hope to sorrow when he caught Fred's quiet sigh. "Oh Lord. I'm so sorry." Arthur pulled Fred into a tight embrace. "The bastards took my wife too." He pushed Fred back to arms-length. "We'll get them for this," he growled. "You mark my words."

Mrs. Clough, one of Fred's old school teachers, gently pulled Fred over to a chair. She sat him down and placed a white cup in his shaking hands. "Here, drink. It's tea. I popped in a bit extra sugar too. I think you need it."

"Do you think that's a good idea? You know, given our circumstances? Perhaps we should think of keeping a close eye on what little food we have left?"

Fred took a sip of the drink and gave the woman a grateful smile before turning his attention to the last member of their little group. Angus Hardy's wife, Maude, returned to her place beside the window, sat on a stool, and stared out of the window.

"I'm just saying, that's all," she muttered to nobody in particular.

"Stop your natter about provisions, woman," snarled Arthur. "Don't you think we are all aware of our situation?" He moved back to the front door and grabbed a rifle leaning against the wall. He looked through the door window before walking over to Pardip. "Mind the women while I take a look at our guest." Arthur nodded over to Fred. "You're with me, young man. You need to see this."

Fred drank as much of the teas as he could before placing the cup on the scratched glass counter, grabbing the pistol, and standing up. "See what?"

"See why we're all stuck in here, Fred, and not running through the remains of Brandale, looking for anyone else who might have lived through this." He looked across at Pardip. "The only reason I let him out is because the Indian knows how to handle himself. Now stop your dawdling and follow me."

The man took Fred over to another door. Even before Arthur reached it, Fred heard some quiet muttering coming from the direction of the window. Pardip sighed heavily before moving closer to Maude Hardy.

"You should calm down, miss. Don't worry, it can't get out."

"Oh, and suddenly you're the expert now? Mr. Basra, I will not tolerate being spoken to in that manner and to think that I allowed you all those sandwiches last night."

Fred watched the old man bristle. He then nodded over at Mrs. Clough. "Come on, Fred. Let's get this over this. Pardip, you know what to do." Arthur opened the door and ushered Fred inside. "Mind the steps."

The temperature in here had dropped significantly and dropped even further as he made his way down the stone stairs. Fred also noticed a strange smell in the air; a deeply unpleasant odour, one that had offended his nose recently, only Fred could not recall when that had happened.

"I'm glad that the boy stood his ground now."

"You mean Pardip?"

"Yeah, if he hadn't risked his life to search for more people, that woman upstairs wouldn't have stood a chance. By the time we found her inside one of the classrooms, Pardip and I had already found over thirty people." He put his hand on Fred's shoulder. "Oh Christ. I know you lads saw some horrible sights over there, but I don't think any of that could be worse than what we found all over town."

"What do you mean?" he asked, turning his head. Looking at the man's blood-drained face, Fred wasn't sure that he wanted to know either. He took a deep breath and immediately wished he hadn't. The strength of that vile odour almost knocked him out. What was that?

"Did Pardip show you the other things? Its pets?"

"Yeah, I saw them."

"Yeah, well, the giant thing had killed Christ knows how many of us, but it's the things which follow it that's killed the most." He licked his lips. "They don't just kill them, Fred, they..." He pulled his arm back. "You'll find out soon enough. Now, come on, let's get this over with, down you go."

Fred was about to do just that, curious as to why the old man had brought him down here, when he remembered why that stench was so familiar. "Oh no!" he gasped. The smell had almost woken him up last night! He placed his hand against the lime-painted brick next to him when the realisation of what must have happened slammed into him. He gave the man behind him on a higher step a pleading look only for Arthur to gently push him down one more step.

"You can do it, son. Just a couple more steps."

Fred held his nose and continued his progress down to the cellar floor. The pistol now felt like his only friend. He paused again only for Arthur to push him into the first room. Piles of old packing crates were stacked against the left wall and over a dozen wooden chairs, which looked just like the ones on the floor above, had been placed against the wall opposite, leaving a narrow gap in which to walk through and into the main room. It was from there where the stench originated.

He almost jumped out of his skin when Arthur picked a wooden box off the shelf next to him and threw it onto the floor. Its contents of rusty bolts, screws, and nails bounced across the dirty concrete floor.

"Come on, you!" yelled Arthur. "Show me your ugly face. Somebody wants to have a look at you." Arthur nodded over to the next room. "Go on, lad. It's time to see the face of the real enemy."

Fred looked into the darkness beyond the chairs and the packing crates. He couldn't see anything, but he did pick up a loud clatter and a very human-like grunt. The trepidation of encountering the unknown vanished when he realised that something which awaited him in there was probably related to whatever had murdered his wife while he slept.

"Wait, let me throw some light on it." Arthur flipped the switch then pushed Fred along the narrow gap.

Something in that room smacked into metal and made another grunt. That noise did shock him as it sounded exactly like a small boy's weep. He looked at Fred. "It did that a lot when I put it in there."

Fred stopped dead and gazed, more in morbid curiosity than horror at the dog-sized creature curled up in the corner of the cellar. They had made sure that the thing couldn't leave by walling it up with boxes full of bottles and placing a thick sheet of glass over the top. He looked into its prison, trying to figure out what the hell it was.

Just like the huge thing out there, this had eight legs but a thick black pelt covered this creature. It didn't look all that dangerous. That opinion changed when Fred tapped on the glass and it uncurled and leapt forward. Fred then saw bristling fur, razor-sharp claws, and a mouthful of needle-like grey teeth.

Arthur joined him. "We pulled this one off Mrs. Clough, seconds before that evil-looking mouth was able to fasten around her face." He pulled Fred away. "That is what we are facing. There's hundreds like that running through the ruins of Brandale." He tapped his rifle. "Hundreds against three? It doesn't take much working out to know that we won't stand a chance out there."

Fred looked into the creature's prison. "Tell me something, why did you save it? Why did you endanger yourself and the others by bringing it back here? If there are hundreds out there, it makes more to have killed it as soon as you dragged if off the woman."

"I agree." Arthur tapped the gun again. "Your notion does make sense until you consider how far the noise from a bullet travels." He walked over to the other side of the cellar, leaned against the wall, and slowly slid down. "Fred, there were eight of us who tried to rescue the teacher, and that doesn't include the Hardy woman. She was already cowering in this shop before we arrived."

Fred listened to that thing in the corner restart its child-like noises while waiting for Arthur to continue. It was fairly obvious what the man was about to tell him. After all, until a few hours ago, there were hundreds of soldiers in Brandale and that didn't include the old man opposite him. Despite wanting to fight, he was turned down due to his age. At fifty-four at the start of the war, he had no choice but to stay home. Brandale had more of its fair share of old soldiers who saw combat in the minor skirmishes in the years before the Germans got too big for their boots and thought they could take on the Empire.

"Alistair Parsons was the first one to buy a plot. Just off Fleet Avenue. Three of those things leaned out of an open window and just pulled the poor bugger inside. He never stood a chance. His screaming only lasted a second or so which, I suppose, was one mercy. Naturally, we all opened fire. It's then when we understand just what big mistake we'd just made. They must have zeroed in on the gunfire."

"Stop. Please, I don't wish to hear anymore." Fred resisted the urge to boot the boxes beside him, in the vain hope that the foul beast would stop it with that God-awful noise. "Just tell me how you plan to get us out of here."

The old man grimaced. "That's one of the reasons why I brought you down here. Away from the others. You see, because of what happened earlier, we're the only military men left in Brandale."

"No, you're wrong. There's also Pardip."

"I didn't count your friend because he isn't a local. Use your head, man. I need soldiers who know the lay of the land. Men who can help us find a route out of town." Arthur nodded over to the creature, who had, thankfully, stopped making all that pathetic whining. "I was thinking that the little demon might be useful in helping us get past all its pals. You know, like using it as a hostage perhaps?"

"A hostage?" Fred's blood suddenly ran cold. The old man had obviously lost something in the past few hours. His damn marbles, that's for bloody sure. For a start, how could Arthur dismiss his friend so easily? After all, if it hadn't been for him, Fred wouldn't be down here, listening to this loon talk about hostages. Out of respect for the man's previous military experience, he shut his mouth and decided not to explain the utter madness of such a wild idea. The damn thing was an animal. It had done nothing to even suggest that there was an ounce of human intelligence rattling about in that nasty little head.

His opinion changed in an instant when he heard the sound of human laughter. Fred glanced back towards the steps, convinced that the woman from upstairs had followed them down.

"You need to see this, son. Look to your left," said Arthur. "I had a feeling it would do this."

The man's hushed tone suggested that looking to his left was the last thing that Fred should be doing. Fred looked anyway. The creature had somehow lengthened its hind legs so it could press its face against the glass, only the face pressed against that glass did not belong there. He gasped aloud at the sight of his darling wife's distorted face with her mouth open wide and those delicate blue eyes staring straight at him while it laughed and giggled.

"Stop doing that, you foul thing!" he yelled. "I said stop it." If anything, its noise grew in intensity. Fred raised the pistol. He heard Arthur yelling at him, ordering the young man to lower that weapon, but he was having none of that. This vile thing was laughing because it knew there was nothing they could do to stop them. He listened to its teasing laughter for enough second before squeezing the trigger.

The report in such a confined space deafened the pair of them. Not that Fred cared. He leaned over. The bullet had torn it into two pieces. Blood, blackened lumps of flesh, and shattered glass now covered the bottom of the thing's prison and yet, despite the damage, the bloody thing still moved! Fred fired one more time, snarling in satisfaction as its head literally disintegrated.

Arthur grabbed his shoulders, spun him around, and ripped the pistol out of his hand while yelling into Fred's face. Not that he could figure out what he was saying. He couldn't hear a bloody thing. He pulled the pistol back out of Arthur's hand. That shut him up. Not that it mattered. Fred turned around and stormed back towards the stairs; he had enough of this. It was time to gather the others together and get out of here. For a start, Fred did not believe that everyone in Brandale was dead except for the few survivors in this shop. Fred would find them. He'd find them all, with or without Arthur's help.

Before he could reach the bottom of the stairs, a hand slammed down on his shoulder and jerked him back. The pistol fell out of his hand. Fred spun around, intending to give the old man a piece of his mind but only with his fists. Arthur moved his head to the side and was able to slap Fred's fist away before grabbing the side of his head and moving his mouth right up to his ear.

"We need to move it, you stupid little boy!" he screamed into his ear. "You shouldn't have done that. You have really fucked things up now!"

Arthur screamed again, but it wasn't from fury. The man staggered back, bringing Fred with him. The old man slammed into the wall then pushed Fred to one side before pointing at the ceiling. By now, Fred had realised that something was seriously wrong due to the amount of dust falling around them. It looked like it was snowing.

He spun around and moaned in horror when he saw a brown point push through the floorboards between two rafters. Fred dragged Arthur out of the way when that section of ceiling caved in, exposing the floor above, only now, Fred could see daylight.

The point belonged to the tip of that huge monster's foot. It had smashed it through the roof and the two floors. It pushed two more feet through the hole in the roof, curled the limbs under, and pulled off the rest of the roof. It then proceeded to do the same with the upper floor. Fred wept at the sight of three drained skeletons falling.

Fred wept when he saw so many bones mixed with the debris which rained back down. He now understood when Arthur had said there was nobody left. Hundreds of those vile creatures like the one he'd just put down had gone through Brandale while the population was sleeping and murdered his friends and neighbours while they slept.

The blue sky vanished yet again when the huge beast thrust its monstrous head through the hole. Fred gasped when he noticed the all the others cowering around the shop counter.

"We need to hide!" hissed Arthur. "Maybe it'll go away?"

Fred snatched the rifle out of the old man's other hand. "You do that," he replied, handing Arthur the other gun. "I'm going to save my friends." Fred skirted past the creature's massive leg, leapt over a pile of rubble, and managed to get to the foot of the stone stairs.

A stomach-churning moan stopped him dead. He peered through the hole in ceiling and saw the woman trying to crawl out from around the counter. Both Pardip and Mrs. Clough were desperately trying to stop her by grabbing her legs.

"What the hell are you doing, you daft woman?" he screamed. "Get back to the others." His voice went unnoticed. The woman had managed to get away from the other two by booting Mrs. Clough in the nose. Judging from the look on that stupid woman's face, she actually considered hurting the poor teacher so she could get away as some kind of victory.

Fred raced up the remaining steps and burst through the cellar door. He dropped to one knee, aimed the rifle, and fired a single shot. The creature screamed. Its body moved from side to side. He hurriedly slammed another shell onto the chamber. Had he done it? Did his last shot do so much damage? Fred aimed, eager to finish it off, but before he was able to squeeze the trigger, one of the monster's arms smashed into the front of the shop.

The woman shrieked out and skidded to a halt when both shop windows imploded, showering her with shards of glass. Fred ran towards her, trying to get this stupid woman back under cover when a flexible blood-red pipe dropped from under the creature's belly and curled around her midriff. Her screams were cut short as that pipe tightened. The end of the pipe wriggled its way out of the coils. Fred blanched when he saw the end fold back like petals on a flower and a dozen pale cream needles pushed out from the middle. The end then whipped back around and slammed into the side of the woman's neck.

He scrambled back and joined the others still cowering behind that counter. Fred raised the rifle, only for Pardip to push it towards the floor with his hand. His friend pointed towards the huge creature's head. Fury, as well as the sense of total helplessness, ran through his system in equal amounts when he saw what Pardip was pointing at.

Large bony-looking lumps had grown across the front of the creature's face. He couldn't believe it; the bastard thing must have reacted to Fred's shooting and armoured itself. What hope did they have against these monstrous abominations?

He watched that pipe lifted the woman's body up and for the first time since becoming fully aware this morning, Fred contemplated ending his life before that thing and its vile helpers could get there first.

Fred might have even gone through with the sinful deed right there and then if Mrs. Clough hadn't spotted that it was about to leave the shop. It also appeared that the other little nightmares were leaving as well. Also, he had swapped his pistol for the rifle.

...

Harry gratefully took the offered water bottle from Callum and drank the contents in one go. He listened to those automobiles travelling along that concrete bridge and glanced at his silent audience while anticipating the torrent of questions which would inevitably follow. Harry felt confident that he should be able to answer them all. The young Harry from many moons ago had milked that old man dry, squeezing out every scrap of information the man possessed.

CHAPTER EIGHT

Patrick Nolan stomped over to the bedroom window, placed his thick arms on the cluttered window sill, and stared through the dirty window. He looked past his pride and joy which that wife of his had wrecked last week. There was little movement along the bus route which cut through the middle of Harmony Estate.

The only shop open at this stupid hour just happened to be the one that he intended to visit once he had dressed, which, in Patrick's eyes was good news for him, but bad news for the cheeky fucker who should be behind that counter around about now.

As a lifelong inhabitant of Brandale's notorious housing estate, its bad name, mainly thanks to people like him, Patrick had believed that other people, the normal ones, the kind of mice who crossed to the other side of the road to avoid people like Patrick, would have the good sense not to get all cuddly with his wife.

A black Passat stopped in front of the shop. A moment later, some suited dude stepped out and disappeared inside. Obviously not a local. Not dressed like that.

Nice car. Patrick might have to have words with a mate to see if he could acquire such a vehicle for himself. This time, he wouldn't let the silly cow anywhere near it.

Patrick moved his hand a little further towards the wall, grunting in satisfaction when one of Tracy's porcelain elephants dropped off the window sill and onto the carpet.

Much to his annoyance, the bloody thing didn't break. Tracy had come home with that horrendous thing a few days ago. She told Patrick that she saw it on one of the market stalls in Brandale market and just had to buy the gorgeous-looking ornament. Tracy promised him that it hadn't cost that much, less than a packet of cigs. Like he even gave a shit. What caused him the stress, enough to ball up his fist, was that she was there frittering his money just two days after smashing up his car.

Patrick leaned close enough to inspect the damage she had caused to his car. It sat there, on their drive, like a gravely wounded animal just begging him to put the beast out of his misery.

Yeah, he so needed another car. The woman who had committed the atrocious deed then rolled onto his side of the bed, stretched her arms and legs, and started to snore.

Jesus, now he had another wounded animal in his sight. Patrick so wished that he could put that annoying bitch out of her misery. To think of the problems he'd solve if he could find a way to make her disappear.

He lifted his leg up to hip height then brought his foot down on Tracy's last acquisition. That would teach her not to leave her crap all over the bedroom. The woman had a glass cabinet in the corner of the living room for all this tat. Fifty quid that bloody thing had cost him. The fact that Tracy had already placed it there a couple of days ago had crossed his mind. It's more likely that one of the kids had taken it out and brought it up here.

Patrick crouched and carefully picked up all the broken bits and dropped them in the bin. Why one of the kids had brought the elephant in here was anybody's guess, although knowing them, they'd probably sneaked in here to root around, looking for either money or cigs.

He guessed that Emily had done it. She liked to pick up things she thought were pretty and hide them under her bed. Nobody knew why; the little witch had been doing it since she was a kid. He wondered if she was part magpie.

Sky wouldn't have taken it, not unless it was worth anything. He was another one who was part magpie. Unlike his sister, that bugger took stuff he could sell to Abdul, who owned that second-hand shop on Bethel Road. There'd been more than one occasion when Patrick had walked past that shop only to find something which once belonged to him for sale in the shop window.

That reminded him: did that lad come home last night? He'd have to have a peek in that pig-sty of a bedroom and see if he could see the no-good layabout under all the chucked clothes, discarded coke bottles, and empty pizza boxes which covered his carpet. He was another one who needed a good kicking.

Patrick picked the ceramic head out of the bin and placed it on Tracy's pillow Godfather-style before he grabbed his boots and left the bedroom, making sure to slam the door on his way out. If it woke up the lazy bitch, then that would be a bonus. Listening to her scream when she found the head on the pillow? Oh, that would really make his day. Well, perhaps the sweetener before the main meal.

He stopped by the landing window and looked out of the window. His main meal lay yonder, in the guise of that shady fucktard Raymond Custer, the man who actually believed that he was God's gift to every woman on the estate. He would be receiving a gift alright; Patrick's gift would be his big fist in the man's mush. Not too violent, just enough so Mr. Custer would need a straw to drink every meal he would ever consume.

No man tried to get into his wife's knickers, not while he still lived and breathed. Sure, Tracy had been asking for it, giving him the sly wink every time she walked past his table to and from the bar. Patrick even heard from Andrew, the part-time barman, that the dirty slag even touched Custer's knee when he went for a piss. Whether that was true was another matter. She swore up and down that it never happened when he confronted her outside Khan's Kebab Shack, but then she would say that. Patrick had never used his fists on a woman, but he had come real close. Tracy knew how bad his temper was, especially after he'd put away a few pints.

Whether she had led him on didn't really matter. It didn't excuse Custer from trying to put his hand up her skirt in the car-park outside the Dog and Goose, and that was one event which did happen. He saw it with his own eyes. Looking back, it might have been more of a case of him not knowing where his hands were going when Tracy rushed over to pick him up, but that was beside the point. The man clearly fancied his wife, meaning he needed to do something about that. It was that simple.

He checked in on the kids before going downstairs. Emily was fast on, just like her mum. In fact, that girl shared more than laziness and the ability to waste money on shit. She also looked just like her when Tracy was that age, even down to the shapely legs and soft blonde hair. Thankfully, unlike her mum, Emily had an overprotective father to stop any hormone-ridden teenage waster from trying it on with his daughter. He'd already 'had words' with five brats in the past couple of years, who thought that Emily could be another notch on their belt.

Patrick was no fool; he knew his little princess wasn't exactly the sweet naïve girl that he used to take to the park every Saturday without fail. Just living on this shitty estate soured your innocence. Having a complete brain donor for a mum didn't help either. Still, he had to try his best to keep her pure. It wasn't totally within the bounds of science fiction to think that, one day, she might fall in love with a boy who didn't sell weed on the corner of Maple Street, or spent their weekend stealing beer from the local supermarket.

"Someone like that Passat owner?" he murmured.

Emily turned over and groaned. He hurriedly shut the door and left the young woman to her dreams and walked up to the next door.

The tragedy of Patrick trying to save his daughter from the groping hands belonging to wasters just like Sky wasn't lost on him. He knew that Sky had gone into the weed selling business, and no matter how many quiet words Patrick had with the lad, he still continued to persist in defying him.

Patrick opened the boy's bedroom door and sighed loudly. There was no fear of his noise waking the lanky streak of piss on account of him not being in there, meaning that he'd stayed at a mate's house or the idiot had fallen in some alley as drunk as a lord and won't appear until dinnertime. Patrick slammed the door and stomped back over to the landing window.

Jesus on a stick. What had he done in a previous life to deserve all this bullshit? "There's always some motherfucker trying to skate uphill." Where had he heard that saying? Probably from a movie. Wherever it came from it was apt, and if the shoe fits, lace that bitch up and wear it.

While making his way down the stairs, it did occur to Patrick that just like Emily followed in her mother's footstep, so Sky was turning into a younger version of himself. Patrick had behaved just like Sky. Probably less of the thieving and more violence but still, it was obvious as the nose on the end of his face that Sky took after his daddy.

Patrick reached the bottom of the stairs, pulled out his lucky cricket bat out from behind the dresser, and walked into the living room. It was all well and good acting the outraged parent now that he'd got older and mellowed out. Hell, he couldn't remember the last time he really hurt someone. Sure, he did punch some random guy in the pub last week, but that didn't count. He only hit him once, just a touch really.

Patrick left the living room after checking Tracy's cabinet and made his way into the kitchen to snag a dishcloth from the drawer under the microwave.

What he needed to do with that kid of his was to find some way to channel all that aggression. It's what Patrick's old man tried to do to him back in the day. It didn't exactly work, mind. He guessed that's due to the daft bastard trying to get Patrick into motors. Cars and especially their engines had obsessed his dad since he was a kid and naturally, he believed Patrick would become hooked too.

That didn't happen. Patrick couldn't give a crap about cars which earned him a good hiding. Looking back, he decided that Dad's method of getting Patrick to calm down probably had the opposite effect. Then again, his dad had always been a bloody idiot.

Patrick pushed the dishcloth into his back pocket and opened the side door. He filled his lungs with the cold morning air then stepped onto the path after shutting the door.

"Shooting," he said. "I could get the little shit into that!" It made sense. Sky's bedroom walls were covered in posters showing guys with big guns blasting apart zombies. Granted, Patrick couldn't exactly pull a bunch of walking dead people from out of his arse, but he could show him what it was really like to fire off a shotgun.

His old mate from school, Jacob Dunn, now owned the farm which once belonged to Jacob's uncle. Patrick knew for a fact that Jacob did a bit of shooting, mainly rabbits and the occasional stray dog which managed to get inside his property. The lucky bastard had inherited the shotguns along with the rest of the place.

Shotguns weren't the only type of weapon that low-life scumbag kept. Thanks to copious amounts of beer, a bit of speed, and the promise of a go with Patrick's girlfriend, his old mate had once confessed to finding a cache of automatic weapons hidden under the floor inside the huge barn.

Twenty-five years had passed since that confession inside the lounge of the Dog and Gun. He doubted Jacob remembered, but Patrick sure as hell did. Just as he remembered watching that drunken oaf trying it on with Tracy in the bushes at the bottom of the carpark.

Yeah, getting Jacob to teach his boy to shoot sounded like a great idea and if that pretend farmer started to get a little shirty, then Patrick would drop just the tiniest of hints about what the fella had found in that barn.

This was turning out to be a glorious day. The sun was getting ready to peek over the rooftops, he'd managed to sort out his son, and his trusty bat was about to taste blood again. Passing his wrecked car cast a shadow upon his otherwise flawless finish, but even that was fixable. Patrick had a plan for everything.

He approached the front gate and, as this day had turned out so well, Patrick leapt over it, something he hadn't done in bloody years. He reached the curbside, waited for a lone delivery truck to pass him then crossed over. The time to severely fuck up the rest of Custer's day had arrived.

The sound of whistling greeted Patrick when he entered the shop. It reminded him more of an old-fashioned boiling kettle than some recognisable tune. He leaned against the doorframe, casually eyeing the top-shelf magazines while simultaneously watching his next victim cut the plastic strap off a pile of newspapers. The fancy knife Custer used looked expensive. Patrick decided that would be his. He needed another knife since his other one, the knife that he stole from his dad, back in the day before he met Tracy, had mysteriously vanished a few days ago. Maybe not so mysterious; he knew Sky had taken it, the thieving shit.

He felt like coughing to announce his presence, or how about smashing the bat on the counter, or his head? His next victim continued to make that God-awful noise while he bent down to grab another pile. What was wrong with the guy? Did the man not realise how badly out of tune he was? Breaking the fucker's teeth would be a blessing, at least for future individuals who could inadvertently have to listen to such racket.

Patrick grabbed a cheap toy from the shelf next to him and took it out of the box. He had to stifle a snigger when he found himself gazing at another elephant. Patrick dropped that on the floor. The whistling ceased and the man looked up from his work, and judging from the startled rabbit eyes, Custer obviously saw his immediate future involved getting twatted by Patrick's cricket bat.

The man let out a mouse-like squeak then jumped up and ran up to a white-panelled door, just behind him. In his panic and rush to get away, Custer pushed instead of pulling which brought the latch down.

As amusing as this was, Patrick didn't have the time to laugh at the man's terror. He needed to get home have something to eat before putting his plan for Sky into motion. There was also the issue with his car. He'd have to get that sorted out today as well, figuring he had mourned long enough for his old love of his life.

Patrick approached the counter, still grinning at the silly man's attempt to get away. This fool really was having a bloody seizure. Was Patrick really so frightening?

Raymond Custer spun around. Patrick honestly expected him to start begging for his life there and then; his words probably packed with a truck-full of apologies too. When the man did open his gob, Custer's words shocked him rigid.

"Don't just stand and stare, you gormless idiot!" he yelled. "Kill the bloody thing."

"What?"

Custer moaned. He picked up his knife, looked at it then dropped it back on the spilled pile of newspapers then grabbed a handful of chocolate bars and threw them in Patrick's general direction.

It's only when he jumped to the side to avoid the chocolate when he discovered that he and Custer weren't the only things moving inside the shop.

Three pieces of what looked like badly cut steaks had flopped into the shop. They moved erratically, shifting from a caterpillar crawl to a fish out of water flop. Whichever motion they chose, it didn't stop them from getting closer to his feet. He grabbed a tin of beans from the shelf next to him and threw it. Unlike Custer, his throw rang true and as soon as it hit, Patrick realised just how much danger the pair of them were in.

Dozens of thin, grey spines burst out from both sides. Patrick took a step back, trying not to panic while this thing slowly curled around the tin. Somewhere at the back of his mind, he heard that old guy's voice from all those BBC nature documentaries start to give Patrick a running narrative of what it was about to do. Oh Christ, another three more of the things had just flopped into the shop!

Patrick silently told the old guy to fuck off, as well as that mental image of an insect caught in a Venus fly trap when the thing's spines punched through that metal can. A moment later, the spines slid back out and shrunk back into the thing's grey flesh. The can rolled towards him, stopping about an inch from his foot. Cold bean juice, mixed with a pale cream fluid, ran out of the holes and where the cream liquid touched the tiles, it left a tiny smoking crater behind.

"You have got to be fucking kidding me," Patrick whispered.

"Come on, man, help me get this door open!"

He took his eyes away from the punctured bean can, glancing at the moving pieces of meat which now seemed to be all moving towards the counter before he took out the dishcloth from his back pocket. Once again, events had transpired which had made his life so much more complicated. Patrick screwed up the dishcloth and shoved it back into his back pocket. He closed his eyes, counted to three, and silently told whoever was pulling his strings to sort this shit out and put everything back to how it should be.

Predictably, when he opened his eyes, nothing had changed, except for Custer was now climbing on the counter, while threatening all those disembodied bits of meat with his stupid knife.

Patrick growled softly. This was so much bollocks. He raised the bat high, considered swinging the business end into Custer's side then, at the last moment, changed his mind. He slammed it into the slap of meat that had previously murdered the bean tin. "Yeah, thought you wouldn't like that, you freaky son of a bitch," he snarled when he heard a wet-like pop as soon as his trusty bat made contact with the thing on the floor.

He grinned at Custer, hoping that his bestial expression would frighten him enough to jump into that writhing mass of meat now directly under the counter. It would save Patrick the trouble of punishing the goon.

"Kill another one!" Custer yelled triumphantly. The man's noise quickly turned to panicked yelling when they all began to climb up the front of the counter.

The way for Patrick to leave through the front door had just become his best option. These things showed no interest in sticking their spines into his flesh. He could simply leave Custer to his fate, go have his bacon sandwich, and carry on with the rest of the day, secure in the knowledge that this clown would never bother his wife ever again.

He swung the bat into the only thing which hadn't started to climb up the counter. It flew across the air and crashed into a box of cheese- and onion-flavoured crispy snax at the back of the shop. His sudden intervention made the remaining five pieces pause. They all extended their spines.

"Okay, which one of you dirty bastards is next?"

"Patrick, get back around here!" shouted Custer. "I've seen movies. What's betting they can shoot those grey needles like sodding crossbow bolts?"

Taking advice from the very man he had intended to hospitalise felt like the biggest joke on the planet, but considering the bizarre circumstances, it had now become an option, especially since another one had just flopped into the shop. The new arrival, just like its companions, had already pushed out its thin spines. Patrick roared out like a wounded bear, furious at his inability to control this situation. He swung the bat into another one and cried out in disbelief when its spines punched through the wood like a hot spoon going through ice cream. He cracked the bat against the shelves. Bits of creature, combs, paperclips, and hair bobbles sprayed the shop's revolving paperback stand, but his violent action did nothing to stop the thing from slivering down the bat, closer to Patrick's hands.

"Fuck you, Custer!" he yelled. He refused to take advice from anybody who used to piss his pants in secondary school just to get out of doing games. He also refused to be beaten by anything which looked like a hedgehog that had been run over by a bus.

Patrick heard a whistling noise and gasped when he felt his bat become a fraction heavier. Jesus on a stick! These things could jump! One of the things on the front of the counter had just landed on the end of his bat which, by now, had begun to liquefy, turning into something which resembled paper maché.

He had no other choice but to drop the bat and run around the back of the counter. Patrick snatched the knife out of Custer's hand, resisting the urge to push the blade into the side of the man's neck before hurling his body on top of the floppy invaders, and ran up to the other door.

Unlike the shaking popsicle who panicked at the sight of a single wasp, he was not fazed by a little latch on the top of the door. Patrick popped it off, pushed the door inwards, and grabbed Custer's shirt who had taken up his cowering position beside Patrick's legs. He pushed him inside and followed the man, managing to shut the door before four of them climbed over the counter's edge and leapt towards them.

"Oh God, oh God!" Custer collapsed on the stair, a few feet from where Patrick stood. He looked up from staring at the thin buff carpet and the terrified man's gaze found him. "What the hell are those things? I've never seen anything like that?"

"Apart from in movies?" The door started to bow out and take on a spongy look. It now looked like chipboard left out in the pissing-down rain. Patrick had the urge to touch the door just to see if his observations were valid, until he remembered what that pork chop with an attitude had done to his beloved cricket bat.

He could press Custer against the wood, just as an experiment, mind. It did sound like a good idea. For a start, it would stop the clown's continuous whining. Honestly, Custer now sounded like his kids when they were younger pulling a paddy because he wouldn't give them ice cream.

"What are we going to do now, Patrick? Oh please, tell me you have an idea?"

Yeah, he'd go for that idea. Push the whinging cockwomble into the door, wait for the meat bits to turn him into Custer custard then fuck off back home, and he was buggered if he was going to ring for the busies. Not a chance was he going to be pulled any further into this quagmire.

Patrick moved away from the door and tuned out Custer's continuous annoying whine while peering down the hallway, looking for the other door. Would it be locked? The chances would be high. This guy wouldn't leave his private gaffe unsecured. Patrick spotted a top of the range Sony TV attached to the wall. No, the door would be locked and bolted. Patrick also had a top of the range TV attached to his living room wall but unlike this clown, he didn't pay top dollar for the second love of Tracy's life.

He stopped directly in front of Custer and grinned again. He wanted his demonic smile to be the last thing this sad excuse for a man was before turning into slop. Amazingly, Raymond Custer, the man who once stole Patrick's bike back when they were both ten years old, smiled back up at him. Patrick balled up his huge fists then paused.

Standing at the top of the steps and gazing down at the pair of them was a medium-sized black dog. He attempted to relax when the bloody thing began to growl. Fuck, he hated dogs almost as much as he hated cats.

"Diesel!" shouted Custer. "Hush that noise, Patrick is a friend."

Oh Christ, did this knobhead really think that? He glanced back at the door. Shit, his moment to end all this had just passed. A mouse hole now showed through the bottom of the door and the surrounding wood bent out like hot toffee. He tapped Custer on the shoulder. "We go now. Get your arse into your grotty living room and open your other door, you know, before we both get eaten by the fucking tenderloin!"

Custer glanced up the stairs then back at Patrick. "What about the dog? I can't leave him up there."

"Fuck Diesel," he snarled. "Move it!"

At the sound of his name, the dog padded down the stairs and growled at Patrick before giving Custer's hand a crafty lick. Diesel's hackles then lifted. He raced forward and snapped at the thing trying to squeeze through the small hole, the dog's jaws bit it into two pieces.

"Come back here, Diesel!" shouted Custer. "Get away from that stuff."

Patrick savagely pushed the man through the door and into the living room. "What part of leave your dog do you not understand?" Custer actually looked like he was about to strike him! Patrick put paid to any of that nonsense by giving him a backhand across his cheeks. He so wanted to punch him, but he knew that if he started, Patrick wouldn't be able to stop, meaning he'd die too.

Custer flinched when Patrick grabbed his shoulders. That was a good sign. It meant balance had been restored and from the amount of noise that dog was making, Custer's dog had covered their backs, which made him feel a little more at ease. The owner's dog was a million times braver than the owner almost and it brought a smile to his face.

By some miracle, Custer got the door unlocked. The man turned around. He pushed past Patrick and started to pat his knees.

"Come on, Diesel, there's a good boy. Come to Daddy!"

Once again, Patrick grabbed the man and threw Custer in front of him. He pushed the man forward when he tried to get past Patrick. "Leave him, you idiot. Your dog is saving your miserable life." He clamped his hand around Custer's wrist and dragged the protesting man out of the yard and into the alleyway behind the shop, hoping that those things wouldn't do in this fool's dog before he got to safety.

"Where are you taking me, Patrick?"

He ignored Custer's noise, pulled him out of the alley, around the side of the shop and across the road. Patrick couldn't believe this; where was everybody? Brandale should be waking up by now, yet he saw no vehicles or any people, not even a dog walker. He could still hear one though. That dog of Custer's was making a fair old racket. That dog had respect, unlike this little turd. He pulled the man over to his gate.

"Where are you taking me, for crying out loud? Get your hand off my wrist, Patrick. I haven't done anything to you!" Just for that second, a red mist fell like a blood curtain over his eyes. Custer must have finally realised the threat to his continued existence no longer lay in the spines of a bunch of disembodied lumps of muscle but in the hands of the gorilla holding his wrist in a vice-like grip. At least, that's what Patrick believed until Custer pushed his body into Patrick's chest and pointed towards the big man's house.

Several meat things were crawling up the side of the house, all heading for his open bedroom window. "Oh fuck, no, not this!" Patrick released Custer and ran into the house, through the kitchen, and up the stairs.

His daughter's bedroom door opened. Emily peered out. "What the hell are you doing?" she asked while rubbing sleep out of her eyes.

"Stay there!" he commanded. "Just don't fucking move an inch." Patrick ran past her and burst through his bedroom door only to find several of them had already found their way through the window. Two pieces of meat had attacked his wife while she slept. Hot tears ran down his cheeks and his guts rolled over. Patrick spun around. He slammed the door and ran over to Emily.

"What is it, Dad? What the fuck is going on? Where's mum?" She tried to pull away from his embrace. "Mum!" she yelled. "Are you okay?"

As she fought, Patrick spotted more movement below him. "No, this cannot be happening!"

Patrick grabbed the girl's head and forced her to lean over the edge of the bannister. "Look, Emily. They're all coming up here to murder us. Now, are you going to stop with the struggling?" He didn't wait for an answer; instead, he pushed her back into her bedroom and over to the door.

Diesel and his cowardly owner were both in the middle of their lawn. Patrick heard them reaching the bedroom door at the same time as opening the window as wide as he could. "Emily, go on, out you go."

"Fuck off, Dad," she screamed. "I'm not jumping out of my bedroom window. Have you lost your mind?" She ran back over to the door. "I want my mum!"

He pulled her away but not before she had opened the door a crack. Before Patrick could close it, one of those pieces of flesh slid inside and rolled under the bed. He slammed it shut, grabbed his daughter, and forced her back over to the window.

"Listen to me, you silly little girl." He pushed his face right up to hers. "Your mum is dead. Those things stuck needles into her face which dissolved her head. Unless you want to end up like that, you need to jump. Come on, the ground is soft, you won't hurt yourself as long as you bend your legs before you land."

Patrick noticed the meat thing had emerged from under the bed. He grabbed the closest object which turned out to be Jessica, Emily's favourite Barbie doll, and chucked it towards the thing. He sighed with relief when Emily climbed out, hung from her hands then dropped. He ran over and started to do the same just as the piece of meat leapt from the side of the bed and landed on Patrick's chest. He screamed out and tried to pull it off, only for those spines to burst out of the thing and into his body.

Seconds before the agony crashed into him and he lost consciousness, the man noticed something weird on the creature's back. It had a tattoo of a green eagle consuming a snake. The same tattoo which he paid for his son to have when the lad reached his eighteenth birthday.

CHAPTER NINE

Captain Thomas Copperfield shook with fury, unable to wrap the sections of the mind he controlled over his latest discovery. Even the two constructs had stopped their bickering, both acutely aware that any untoward noise or movement could result in their immediate termination. He walked along the perimeter of the trans-portal gateway into which his God would cross, still holding the offensive object which one of the constructs brought to him just three minutes ago.

Such was his fury, he could not even remember which one had brought it to him. All the captain could remember was the construct running up to him on all fours with something red in its mouth. It stopped in front of his feet, sat on the grass, opened its mouth, and dropped the object onto his clean shoes. It obviously expected him to throw it, like a rubber ball or a fucking stick. The construct received a sharp kick while he bent down to examine exactly what he'd been gifted.

Had he howled when its identity revealed itself? The captain could not remember that either. Not that it mattered. His obstructive memory strand then joyfully told him that he pissed his pants and cried like a big blubbering baby. The captain soon stilled those gloats by casually informing it that his now transformed wife once had an affair with his brother.

The captain finally reached the last corner of the now complete trans-portal, gave the two constructs another withering glare then hurried over to a dry stone wall. He placed the object on the top while wondering exactly how to proceed. He jabbed it in the middle with his index finger and jumped back, startled when both ends produced a grouping of grey needles. The captain had not expected that to happen.

This had to be the work of one of the new Gods. Only they possessed the arrogance to assume that plans which had worked perfectly for millennia could be flawed. Only they believed that uncontrolled accelerated evolution could improve the outcome of the invasion. His memory strand would no doubt call them fuckheads who had gotten too big for their boots and so needed their arse kicking. For once, he agreed with this assessment and sooner rather than later.

He nervously glanced back at the trans-portal and knew exactly how his God would react if he entered this veritable bountiful garden and found some disrespectful child had already stolen food from what rightfully belonged to him.

His God would seek out this usurper and eat its face, something which had not happened for thousands of years. This could even be the beginning of yet another civil war where the Gods abandoned all the unspoken rules and raged across the planet, consuming everything in their path. Not caring about their futures or their subjects. Without the care and attention of their God's devoted subjects, it was certain that the great beasts would die on this world. Not that the captain would no live to see the eventual outcome. He suspected that he would be the first of his God's anger.

A little melodramatic perhaps? The captain did not think so. His continued survival had always depended upon caution mixed with a large dose of paranoia. "I so don't need this at this time," he growled. The captain ripped the thing into several pieces then started to eat it while making a way back to his constructs. He threw the last two pieces to them and watched as they both gulped the bits down without swallowing. The two creatures would need far more sustenance before being ready for their final duty.

His mind was already spinning, thanks to the torrent of images which showed just how far this species had advanced in such a short time. It wasn't just these nuclear weapons which awaited the Gods when they passed into this world, using exotic-sounding devices such as wire-guided missiles. Depleted uranium rounds, fast-attack aircraft and predator drones, the memory strand confidentiality predicted that the huge invaders wouldn't last a week in this world.

The captain had to silence the memory strand by showing his own torrent of images. It began to weep moments after his brother finished with his wife. The captain allowed the memory to continue for a few more seconds, just to make sure the memory strand got the message. When his wife wrapped her naked legs around his brother's back and pushed the man's head further down her body while ordering him to 'sort her out down below,' the captain allowed the memory strand to go back to its hiding place.

When he tapped his thigh a couple of times, his two constructs ran out from under the bramble bush and stopped by his feet. "I need you to show me where you found that piece of meat."

They both scrambled down the grassy hill, heading for the road which led back into the centre of Brandale. He followed at a leisurely pace, his troubled mind not granting him enough energy to run after them. It did not matter; once the constructs had reached the spot, they would soon come back for him.

A jet-liner passed overheard. He stopped to watch this incredible feat of human technology streak through the sky and for the first time in his long life, he actually felt sympathetic towards the new God's need for change. His God, as well as all the other ancient beings, should have foreseen this, nine worlds before, when the humans started attacking the Gods and their subjects with projectile weapons. Granted, these new devices did not even scratch his God's hide and from what he could remember, the subjects were still more wary of their arrows and spears.

The devices were seen as an insignificance, nothing of consequence. Just another fad, invented by the tribes of clever apes. The genie was out of the bottle, as he discovered with the crossing to the next world and the world after that, until they found the humans attacking them with machine guns and flimsy aircraft.

Another jet-liner streaked through the cloudless sky and the captain shuddered to think what the next world would bring. "If, that is, we live through this one," he muttered. Whether the new Gods were right about changing the design which had kept the Gods away from murdering each other did not matter, at least, to him. The captain had to perform his duty with unquestioning loyalty. This meant finding out exactly who had trespassed on their territory and to eliminate the subjects who had slipped through the trans-portal before his God arrived.

It should not be too difficult a task, not if they keep leaving their discarded waste dumped in fields where anyone could find them. The captain stopped walking when he found the constructs were nowhere to be seen. Unlike them, his new adaptations had not furnished him with an enhanced sense of smell or sight, meaning he needed to wait for them to find him.

Once more, this nuclear thing sneaked up on him. He knew the Gods would probably withstand those predator drones, air-to-air missiles, and all the other human inventions but those bombs really did worry him. No matter how well armoured, no matter how large his Gods, they were still living creatures. The memory strand told him that upon impact, the immediate blast zone heated up to a temperature equal to the surface of the sun. What defence could any creature have against that kind of power? His memory strand had informed him that there had been more than one occasion in the last sixty years when the threat of nuclear wars had raised its ugly head. That had not surprised the captain in the least. The humans were a confusing and violent species, who could not stop themselves from killing anything which moved and breathed, including themselves. From what he remembered from his last body in the previous world, especially themselves, millions of young men had perished in that war. What astounded him was that, in this world, they fought yet another great war just twenty years later.

If or when his Gods had bled this world dry and move onto the next, perhaps they might not fight a technologically advanced human civilisation waiting for them on the other side, armed with weapons which even the memory strand would find fantastic. Perhaps what awaited the Gods on the next world was a wasteland devastated by a nuclear conflict? Now that thought did make his pseudo-blood curdle. To emerge into a world already drained of meat really would be a disaster for them.

How he envied the olden days, back when the human species numbered a few and only existed in isolated pockets of land. They were just a mild irritation. Nothing more than tasty bits of meat treats. The vast wandering herds of grazing beasts were the real prize. Millions of animals, each one packed with nutrition, just begging for disassembly and consumption.

It did occur to the captain that the good times could very well return once the humans had wiped each other out. The multiverse Earths had endured catastrophes far worse than this annoying evolved monkey. He just had to place himself into the mindset that lean times were just around the corner, two worlds for the humans to murder each other into extinction then several more worlds for the planet to recover. Less than a thousand years really. He shrugged to himself. It was not that long to wait.

His two constructs were returning. He watched them race each other up the hill. There were occasions when the captain envied their new behaviour modes. The new adaptations had stolen their sentience and regressed them to the point where their intelligence equalled that of a horse. Their only care was to please their master and to feed. The construct which was once the wife reached the top of the hill, waiting for the other one to catch up before turning her large head to the side. She growled and snapped at the other one which then flattened her flanks and lowered her head to the floor. It appeared that the fight for pack dominance had been decided. If only his life could be so simple.

She came up to him, rubbed her side against the captain's legs then turned, and padded back the way she came, this time at a slower pace, giving him plenty of time to keep up. The other construct followed behind him.

He followed her along a waist-high wall which ran parallel to the road. A white car passed them. The driver waved. The captain waved back. The driver probably guessed that he was out enjoying the morning sunshine whilst walking his dogs. It brought a smile to his face at the thought of that driver actually seeing what kind of beast accompanied him. Would he have crashed his car at the shock of seeing his constructs? It was likely. His short experience of being in this new world had already shown him that the indigenous population were as weak and docile as all those vast herds of beasts which once wandered the lands many millennia ago.

The construct led him closer towards the outskirts of town, past several industrial units and close to the entrance of a public park. Both constructs then stopped. They swivelled around and started to growl.

"Is it over there?" Neither responded. They just continued to emit that annoying noise. The captain sighed, while forlornly wishing that at least one of them were not so devolved, just so he knew what had spooked them. All he saw was a huge concrete flyover which, at this time, had started to fill with commuter traffic.

"Fine. So the pieces you found are over there?" He took several steps in that direction only to find the two constructs had not moved. They only moved when he stopped and glared at them. The pair stood up and bolted in the other direction and vanished through the open gates to a public park

Copperfield felt something stir at the back of his mind. He ran back to the path, crossed over the road, and stopped beside the park gates. So, the memory strand was back. It was obviously a glutton for punishment. He considered showing it some of the more unusual positions his brother bent his wife into. He then decided against it. Copperfield could always save those for another day, as he suspected that in the coming weeks, the stress of command would no doubt fray his nerves to the point of breaking. Pushing the memory strand right up to the verge of suicide was bound to make him feel a little better.

The two constructs were waiting for him when he entered the park. The creature who was once the captain's lover had caught a duck. She had bitten off its head and feet and eaten them before leaving the remaining bloodied lump, the tastier part of the animal beside the other construct.

That was so sweet. She was trying to cement their bond. That pleased him. The heretical structure was already forming. At least one aspect of this operation was performing to expectation. Knowing that he did not need to replace either of the constructs did make him feel a little happier.

As soon as he reached them, the dominant one snatched up its prize, turned, and scampered towards the playground equipment. He followed with haste as already; the captain could smell a scent which should not exist in this world. At least, not yet.

"No. This is not possible." He crouched beside a large slide and pushed a tiny fragment of jellied material out from a damp patch of smouldering grass. He scooped it into his palm and sniffed at it. This did belong to a renegade meat probe. There was no doubt. Just as there was no doubt that it had met its demise by a fleshmelta.

He stood up and surveyed the immediate area. Signs of a fight were everywhere. A worrying picture began to form in his mind. One which meant that his problems had just increased. The time of flight and conservation would already be in place in the old world. Every remaining scrap of organic material would be now making its way towards their sleeping God. Every defiler, foot-soldier, prisoner, as well as every piece of equipment, including fleshmeltas, would be used for feed before he burst through into this world. Not even the new Gods would waste valuable meat. It was something which all Gods did understand. So, as ridiculous as it sounded, the captain now believed that it wasn't only a new a God's renegade section of stragglers who had passed into this world, but a human. One of the few resistance soldiers stubborn enough not to allow themselves to be absorbed into the greater good had somehow managed to find their way into this world.

He shook his head, refusing to allow this new piece of information to worry him. The intruder would not be much of a threat, even armed with such a formidable weapon. This was a new world. One where the inhabitants lost themselves into a spectrum of fictional worlds rather than face the reality of their own drab, predictable, and boring lives. Nobody would believe he had come from an alternate reality to save them from an army of church-sized monsters. They would lock him up and throw away the key.

"Where did the survivors go?" The captain held out his hand for the constructs to smell the mess. "Show me where they went after here." They both sniffed the remains, looked at him, and growled. He stood up and wiped the mess on the side of the slide. "Well? Go on then, you stupid creatures. Don't look at me like that. Go find the remaining meat probes!"

They scampered off towards the other end of the park. This time, he attempted to keep up. Time was flying past him at an incredible speed. Thanks to this stupid diversion, the captain had hardly achieved any of his allotted tasks. The fact that he still retained this human body was proof enough that he was falling behind. Thankfully, his God was not to arrive for at least another few days, which gave him plenty of time to catch up with his work.

The constructs jumped onto a wall and disappeared. He did the same, landing onto a weed-covered path between the wall and a metal wire fence. The others had already found a hole large enough for them to fit through. The captain had to employ a more direct method. Thanks to his enhanced muscles, he simply ripped the wire apart. It was the first time he had needed to use the optional extras in this body and he liked them immensely. He had wanted to use his extra muscles on a human first. With all the excitement, he still had yet to feed; a situation which he did intend to rectify sooner rather than later.

The pair stopped in front of a metal-walled industrial unit, one of several industrial buildings in this complex. The captain reached his companions and stopped. He looked around, searching for any more evidence that the constructs had brought him to the correct place. He found what he sought in the form of utter silence, like a bubble had formed around this building into which nothing living dare approach. Nothing natural anyway. He crouched and ran his fingers along the ground. Even the grass had begun to wither and die.

The new Gods did not believe in wasting anything.

It took supreme effort not to shiver. Until this moment, the captain had not given much thought about how he should proceed if he did find their base of operations. He had heard the stories of what he might find in there. They dispensed with the tried and tested methods used by the old Gods for collecting food. What they used in their place made his own adapted flesh curdle.

He took a step back, lifted his arm, and scrutinised his tender flesh. He still had most of his human meat attached to the bones. Even compared to the two constructs, he was weak and vulnerable.

It was irresponsible of the sole representative of his God to enter an enemy stronghold without either reinforcements or the knowledge of what to expect. He couldn't die. If he perished, then so did his God.

The captain let out an audible gasp, startling both his constructs. Had he really thought such blasphemy? His God relied on no lesser being. Back on the other world, if he heard of any other subject uttering such nonsense, to actually have the audacity to believe in such fiction, then he would have dropped them into a vat full of digestive acid.

His God did not need him. He did not need anyone.

The captain called the constructs to heel. Now that he knew its location, their fate was sealed. Once the transition was over and the God's new subjects were ready, then he would send a few newly grown foot-soldiers to this place with orders to burn it to the ground. Without any of its own subjects, the new God, that dirty trespasser, would have to move to another location, to avoid a confrontation with the captain's God, a battle that it would surely lose.

Just as he turned back towards the ruined fence, his memory strand began to laugh and called him a coward. He growled and ordered it to shut its lying hole. The captain then looked to the constructs to allow them to verify that he certainly wasn't cowardly, momentarily forgetting that only he could hear the voice of the residual trace of the man who once occupied this body.

Warming to his subject, the memory strand continued his vitriol by further explaining that he was a yellow-bellied, weepy, shivering little girlpants who'd shit himself and cry for mummy if anything larger than a mouse ran at him.

"Fuck you," he snarled, turning around and heading towards the front of the building. Nobody told him what he could and could not do. Nobody at all! The captain strode along the side of the building, opening and closing his fists. He was absolutely furious with the situation and with himself. Just what was he trying to prove to himself? The captain should have flushed the memory strand as soon as he became self-aware and took control of this body.

By the time he reached a light-blue wooden door, that fire in his gut had lessened somewhat. He also felt a little foolish for allowing it to goad him into this foolish act and although there was still time for the captain to leave this place and go home, he still grabbed that door handle. He still pushed it down and he still wrenched the door open, breaking the lock as he pulled.

He waited for a moment, allowing his senses to absorb the ambient sounds and smells drifting from the dimly lit interior. His eyes had already adjusted to the low light level and informing him that nothing 'off-world' was inside the immediate vicinity. The captain didn't believe it to be cowardly to assess the environment before rushing in; just cautionary. Unlike his goading memory strand, he knew how formidable the new Gods made their guardians and although these subjects couldn't possibly have designed and built an eight-foot, armour-plated killing machine so quickly, the captain still felt it prudent to be careful.

Apart from dirty oil, a sickly-sweet fragrance, and the old scent of human sweat, his nose revealed nothing which could pose any danger. He glanced down at the constructs while wondering if perhaps they had got it wrong.

"In you go," he whispered, walking inside as well. The captain quietly padded along cracked tiles, only slowing down to allow the constructs to pass him. From how they slinked and fidgeted, neither animal seemed too keen to venture any further.

He stopped beside a rusted clocking-in machine and ran his fingers along the damp wall. Their reluctance to continue must have been contagious. The captain no longer wished to pursue this line of inquiry either. The constructs relied on his commands and their base instinct. They were not burdened with his memory strand, nor did they possess a nagging doubt, unrelated to the memory strand but still just as resolute.

It annoyed him to find that only his own base instinct screamed loud enough, ordering the captain to get the hell out of here, that he was about to walk into a spider's lair. The captain's hand reached for a gun that was not there. Once again, his arrogance had betrayed him, but then why should he need a human weapon when no other creature on this new world had the capability to hurt him?

He did not feel like an apex predator. The captain felt like a prey item. He felt like some huge beast was watching him, hidden inside this dark labyrinth, waiting for him to get a little too close to its lair so it could reach out and tear the flesh from his bones.

The two constructs vanished around a corner, leaving him alone. Ironically, the solitude allowed his frayed nerves to knit back together. It gave him the opportunity to understand that there was only one monster inside this building…him!

Obviously, his memory strand had found some way to access some forgotten area of the human psyche. The part which stemmed back to when this species was not the animal at the top of the food chain, back when it really was just another prey item for the roaming predators.

He followed his constructs further inside, feeling (a little) better as the light began to improve. "Your reign as the dominant species is over, my friend," he muttered. "You had better get used to it."

The corridor opened out into a single large area, surrounded by a dozen other smaller rooms. The captain assumed they would have been for offices, storage rooms, and areas for the workers, back when this industrial unit wasn't a hangout for the local homeless and the town's resident junkies. Not that the unfortunate wasters who had used this place we're in any position to complain on account that he believed they were dead. The captain allowed his gaze to roam across the three structures which graced the otherwise abandoned floor of this derelict building. From this angle, they looked like containers. What they contained required further investigation. At least now, he did know that his two constructs hadn't been following phantoms. Lackeys belonging to one of the new Gods had been here all right.

He left his constructs to continue with their investigation of the containers while he proceeded to check every other room to ensure they truly were alone. Moments before he reached the last closed door, the constructs resume their odd behaviour, growling and snapping while jumping from foot to foot.

"Stop that right now!" he admonished. "There is nothing here." The captain opened the last door and examined the last room, just to be sure. "What is wrong with you two?" Their irrational behaviour had calmed down, but the two creatures were still spooked. They jumped up and rested their hands on the side of the containers. They licked the container sides then and tried to dip their heads into the contents.

"Get down, the pair of you." He tapped their noses then kicked their legs when they refused to move. He understood why the constructs gave the containers a large amount of attention. The containers were made from leftovers. The lackeys had used the bodies of the original squatters to build those containers. They had fashioned the bones into a scaffolding before layering sheets of skin around the bones and sealing it all with a resin. Secreted from what, he did not know.

The captain booted one of the constructs who had found an ear attached to the bottom of the container.

"Stupid lackeys." Trust the servants of the new Gods to waste perfectly good material in making something, which, if they had looked around, would have found some perfectly acceptable barrels in those offices.

Every servant of the Gods understood the value of the flesh. To conserve the organic material meant for a more prosperous stay. Food in the new worlds always provided bountiful harvests and it was true that certainly compared to the exhausted worlds they left, the flesh seemed endless, but it was a false horizon.

Once the Gods arrived with their seemingly unquenchable hunger, the meat soon became harder to catch. There was enough material here to build three-quarters of a foot-soldier. They really did not understand anything. The captain leaned over the lip, curious as to why they spent so much valuable material in creating this container. What could it possibly contain?

The constructs whined at the barrels then turned their heads to whine at him. He sensed that they already knew what these containers held. The captain leaned closer and sniffed. He frowned. This is where that sweet smell had come from! Already, he was drooling and he just couldn't stop his hand from dropping into the cool liquid. He lifted a cupful, opened his mouth as wide as he could, and slipped the liquid inside.

Shards of unfiltered, pure ecstasy danced on every nerve ending, running from his mouth, along his tongue, and down his throat. The heavenly sensation continued for another few seconds before his taste buds settled back to some resemblance of normality.

He staggered away from the stuff, already feeling the change which he had kept dormant begin to grip his body. The stuff in those containers had the power of life; it was nectar, concentrated energy, the fluid which literally powered the Gods, and now the stuff flowed through his body. The captain dropped to his knees. He shivered violently, vaguely aware that his constructs had resumed their noise-making, only this time, it wasn't for want but for panic!

A huge shadow dropped from above and landed just metres from his changing body. Caught in the process of transition, his eyes failed to focus in on whatever had landed, only he knew with certainty that it meant harm. A chemical-like stench of ammonia and rotting fruit drifted over him and beneath the warning growls from his constructs, the captain heard another sound, a deep rumble which brought back terrible memories from thousands of years before, back to the last great civil war between the Gods. Back to when the Right Hand of God produced not only prime foot-soldiers but guardians too; gigantic beasts, towering over everything but the Gods, each one armoured with thick bone plates and possessing terrible weapons, designed to slice, cut, tear and dismember their enemies.

He crawled away from the rumble, already cursing himself for listening to that fucking memory strand. Thanks to his pride, he and his two prime foot-soldiers would not live to witness their God arriving on this planet.

The rumble changed into a shriek. What was happening? Hands, or paws, took hold of his shoulders, and he felt himself being dragged across the floor but back the way he came! That shrieking continued without respite, his notion that perhaps that huge shadow, obviously some kind of guardian for one of the new Gods, could be in trouble, soon vanished when the shrieking turned into a dying snarl after which that rumbling reasserted itself.

His body, still coping with the sudden and unwelcome transformation, was put under even more pressure when his helper lifted him up and leaned him against what could only be the side of one of those containers. More of that cool, life-giving liquid splashed against his face and body and, this time, his system knew what to expect and it opened its pores wide to accept more of this nectar.

The Right Hand of God's new eyes, designed by beings of ages past and now improved by the new God's life-fluid, returned moments after his now fully transformed body absorbed the last of the nectar. He took one look at the shredded corpse lying by the guardian's thick feet, allowed his memory strand a second of grief to mourn on the abrupt passing of the woman he once married, then launched his new, armoured form at the beast. His leap took it totally by surprise. Although more thickly muscled, resembling a bipedal rhinoceros, covered in spines to his more athletic, lightly armoured shape, the new God's guardian did not have the dexterity, speed, or experience to defeat the improved form of Copperfield, as long as he stayed out of the way of those huge arms, each one ending in a bony club, and avoided the spines.

He jumped onto its back and was able to land enough blows in one spot before the behemoth realised it was being attacked. It spun around and roared while trying to reach for him. The captain deftly leaped backwards and landed on the wall.

The prime foot-soldiers were not the only designed being with that ability.

Once the guardian of the new God turned back around, Copperfield whistled and his remaining construct lunged forward and sunk its teeth into one of the behemoths thick legs. It roared out in either surprise or pain. It probably did not expect the other one to do that, not after it had slaughtered its companion.

It raised both its club-like arms at the same time Copperfield attacked again. His last assault had cracked one of the creature's bony plates. He leapt from the wall onto its back, his claws finding purchase in the soft tissues under the edges of each plate. Copperfield slammed his own armoured forehead against the damaged plate, finding satisfaction at the sound of it breaking into several smaller pieces.

He pulled his left arm free then plunged it through the tender membrane under the plate and up towards the shrieking creature's neck. Copperfield roared himself as he sliced through the beast's insides. His searching digits found resistance within all that wet, stinking, red and black filth, and Copperfield grasped its spine and gave it a savage twist before jumping away. He ran over to the construct and pulled the creature off the behemoth's leg, seconds before it toppled forward and slammed onto the broken floor tiles.

The remaining prime foot-soldier lifted her head, those beautiful big green eyes finding his. It let out a quiet whine then lifted its head up towards the ceiling. He followed her gaze and whined too at the sight of the ceiling moving. One by one, more guardians dropped around them. He stood up and slowly turned in a circle. Copperfield now faced eight behemoths, each one as hideous as the next.

They moved as one, closing the circle and trapping him beside their fallen comrade. Their time had come, and although once they attacked, his remaining existence would be measured in seconds, Copperfield still intended to do as much damage as he could. The Right Hand of God prepared to leap and then stopped as every behemoth froze. They pulled back their huge heads and let out a soft sigh.

The construct looked straight at Copperfield and tilted her head in confusion until she did the same. He began to laugh, then cry, before finally he sighed as well.

All of their Gods had just arrived into the new world.

CHAPTER TEN

The walking stick sure came in handy. He'd snagged it from outside the back of the bus station about ten minutes ago. At first, Callum did feel a bit guilty for taking something that obviously didn't belong to him. Some old geezer had probably just forgotten about it after he'd got on his bus. He reconciled the theft by telling himself that, if Harry's words really were true, then the old guy, the bus, and most of Brandale's population would be dead when that Goliath appeared. Granted, they weren't exactly sterling words of comfort, but they had made him feel a little better.

His new prize had also just served as an alternative purpose than stopping some bandy-legged pensioner from falling on his arse. The stick had just saving Gavin from getting the beating of his short and pointless life.

Callum sat back down on the only seat in Brandale's ancient shopping centre, placed his stick next to him, and glared at his companion, just daring the thoughtless idiot to comment. Several shoppers and two assistants coming back from a sneaky smoke break had already stopped and watched with vague interest. Probably wondering how Gavin would react to some older homeless tramp pulling the kid backwards along the promenade with the walking stick handle around his throat.

"I can't believe you just did that!"

Callum just sighed. There seemed to be no other reasonable reply. Not for the first time since leaving the flyover with this cockwomble, he really wished the others hadn't saddled him with Gavin.

"Sit down, man," he hissed, very aware that the crowd had just grown. Callum's little mad voice, the one that usually stayed well out of sight, decided to come to the fore and excitedly announced that if he stood on the seat, waved his arms about and shouted that building-sized spiders were on their way, ready to eat them with mayo, he might receive enough money to buy a couple of Big Macs.

Ironic, considering that Gavin's obsession with food had gotten them into this situation in the first place. Surprisingly, the young lad did slouch over to the bench and park his arse next to Callum. The very action caused the first of the shoppers to resume their journey. Callum guessed that they were probably waiting for him and Gavin to start knocking the crap out of each other. He watched a young couple turn around and walk away, hand in hand. The boy whispered something into girl's ear which resulted in the girl punching him on the shoulder. Two more people drifted off, leaving the two employees and a new arrival, the shopping mall's security guard, still giving them an interested gaze.

"You can't believe I did that?" Callum did, in fact, want to knock the crap out of this idiot. "They bought you breakfast, man!" The kid shrugged. "And you repay them by begging on their patch?"

"Oh, come on, stop being so melodramatic, Callum. Does it really matter? If Harry is telling the truth, then we're about to enter Armageddon. You know, the five dudes wearing blankets and carrying farm implements. Earthquakes, volcanoes, and other cool shit. So I tried to snag a few quid. Big deal. If we're all going to die anyway, what difference does it make?" Gavin looked behind his shoulder before grabbing the back of the seat. "And for your information, I still think that your new mate had just spun the biggest line of bullshit that I have ever heard! The bloke's a raving nutter. Giant monsters, alternate worlds, aggressive lumps of burger meat? Come on, it's a wind-up."

He couldn't believe his ears. The king of bullshit was calling his new best friend a big fat liar.

In his mind, Callum saw himself picking up his stick and hitting this self-absorbed, annoying dickhead repeatedly around the back of his head. He did note that Gavin conveniently neglected to mention that Callum had experienced more than his fair share of aggressive lumps of burger meat last night.

The stick stayed beside him. As tempting as it was, turning Gavin into a big bag of bruised hurt was more than likely to bring plod crashing down on their heads like a ton of bricks. When the monsters did invade, he'd welcome the police and the army with open arms. Until then, they were supposed to keep a low profile. A task made almost impossible thanks to Gavin's irrational behaviour.

If Gavin's claim turned out to be just a wild goose chase, then Callum would take the stick to the gobby little bastard's lying mouth. He nodded to himself. Yeah, that sounded like a good deal. Until this unexpected diversion, Gavin and Callum were making their way through town and up to the Harmony Estate where, according to Gavin, there was this lad he knew who collected swords. To make it even better, Gavin knew for a fact that this guy was sunning himself in the south of France for the next two weeks.

Poor Harry, who obviously had no clue about the shit that Gavin came out with, said that bladed weapons would be their best option to tackle the beasts already here, as well as the familiars who would accompany the Goliath.

Moments before Gavin had conveniently remembered he had a mate who collected swords, the lad had suggested that they all just waited for the monsters to turn up then just hide and let the army sort them out with their machine guns and grenades. Both Malc and Dosser ordered him to shut his hole, which he did for at least ten seconds before coming out with the sword collector story.

"Gavin, if you drag me all the way up to the top of the estate only to find you've been talking shite, I swear by Almighty God that I will drop you."

"It's true, you have to believe me, dude."

Believing anything that came out of his gob took faith and patience. None of which he had but considering the circumstances, he had no other choice. "For crying out loud," he said, sighing. "Come on then, we'd best start making tracks. Some of the normals are getting a bit jumpy."

"That's a good thing. The more excitable they are, the more cash they're likely to throw to get rid of you. That's always been my motto."

Callum stood up and collected his walking stick. Just to make sure that the boy didn't get any more ideas about fleecing the normals for cash, he accidentally whacked his shin and glared at him until the lad finally moved off the bench. "You listen to me, Gavin. You and I are going to leave the shopping mall and haul our arse all the way up to the estate. We do not pass go and we do not collect any money. Especially the last part."

He escorted the lad past two mobile phone shops, a charity shop, and stopped in front of the betting shop window. He stopped because the normals had not calmed down. If anything, more normals were acting odd, like their behaviour was contagious. It reminded him of a Mexican wave. Several more around them now had their ever-present mobile phones clamped to their ears. Callum no longer believed that it was their presence causing the panic.

"Okay, so this is a bit freaky," muttered Gavin, his gaze roaming from person to person. "Callum. Do you think we should get out of here?" Without waiting for a reply, the lad made a beeline for the fire exit.

Callum raced after Gavin and escorted him back. "No, not that way," he said. The rising sound of panicked crying had now begun to filter in from the outside, further unsettling the few shoppers still remaining, although from the frantic looks upon their faces, they had already received enough bad news to sink a ship. From their phones, he guessed.

"I think we'd best take a shortcut through here, Gavin." Callum dragged him into the shopping mall's largest shop. The Celador store sold everything from shampoo to cutlery. He dragged the protesting lad through the open doors and down the middle of the shop, past the makeup counters

Even with the knowledge that a couple of shoppers had just run past them and through the entrance, this store already had that deserted feel to it. He pulled Gavin over a dropped shopping basket full of items previously thought to be essential to that shopper. Callum stopped and turned towards the main entrance. Three more people just raced past. Two of them were shrieking.

Gavin repeatedly tugged at his jacket while making a funny little moaning noise at the back of his throat. Had his companion caught the Mexican wave panic as well? If so, then why did he feel perfectly fine? Callum wasn't exactly ready to chill out with a few beers but he certainly wasn't running around like headless chickens like everybody else. Perhaps the foreknowledge had helped to prepare him for what was to come?

That skin lotion which cost enough to feed both Gavin and himself for a month would be staying in that basket, along with the rest of those inessential essential items forever. Nobody was coming back to put that and all the other crap on the shelves.

"Callum, you weirdo. What the fuck is going on?" He tugged at his jerked again. "Oh crap. What's wrong with you, man? We need to move it!"

"Young man. Moving it is exactly what we are doing. Oh, hang on, these will come in handy." Callum ran over to another aisle, picked a few chocolate bars from the shelf, and stuffed them in his pocket. He then grabbed a couple more and hurried back over to Gavin. "Do you know what's really funny?" Gavin looked at him like he'd lost half of his marbles. "Thing is, I should have let you continue fleecing the normals. I mean, you know with what's happening and stuff?"

"What is happening?"

"For crying out loud, man! Will you pull your head out of your arse and keep up with current events? That bloody great big Goliath must have turned up. You know, the one that Harry told us about just a few hours ago? Here, get this down your neck." He passed him one of the chocolate bars. "Maybe the sugar rush will help you put your brain into gear."

"Surely you can't be serious."

Callum grinned. "I am serious, and don't call me…"

Gavin pressed his hand across the older man's mouth. "That wasn't even funny the first time around."

Callum shrugged and pulled the lad's hand away. "At least some of your brain is still functioning. That's a relief. As for where we're going,

I figured we'd make our way down to Basin Street. No bugger goes down there. We ought to slip away easily enough."

Gavin eyed the chocolate then looked back at Callum. The kid was obviously having trouble processing this utterly fantastic information and judging from the distraught expression spread all over the kid's ugly mug, he wasn't doing very well.

Callum simply grabbed his wrist and pulled him towards the back of the shop. He had no time for niceties. He reached the stairway which led to the ground floor, the underground carpark, and the way out. "We're almost there, Gavin. We've just these steps to go down and we'll be at the fire exit."

Gavin released another one of those weird noises when the three lights which illuminated the stairwell flickered twice before going out, plunging the area into darkness. The only light now came from behind them and from the twin spears of white light coming through the doors below them.

"I think that's our signal to get the hell out of Dodge," he said while wondering how long it would be before the other lights followed suit. Shit the bed, now that would be terrifying. The normals who spent their hard-earned cash on buying crap like scented clay designed to smooth out your skin and shampoo containing argon oil had no clue how terrifying it was to be stuck in a pitch-black enclosed environment. Gavin would freak out. That much he did know. Especially if... Callum shut his mind to the very thought of the other—things, Harry mentioned. No, that just had to be fiction.

He raced down the steps, reached the next set of doors, and peered through one of the windows. Even in full light, the very thought of the other part of Harry's prophetic warnings turned him cold, and it took a great deal of effort not to burst out laughing at such absurdity.

So he was quite happy to believe that a huge monster had arrived from a parallel reality all set to turn Brandale into rubble, but he couldn't get to grips with man-sized monsters, despite already almost dying at the claws of smaller versions that were just as nasty. What was wrong with him?

"You've got it all wrong, dude. It's probably a bomb threat or something. Yeah, that sounds about right." Gavin patted him on the shoulder. "Dude, it's a bomb threat. It's got to be."

That kid's sense of denial was far greater than his, that's for damn sure. A bomb threat? Oh yeah, Callum would just love this to turn out to be something as benign as a bomb threat. Hell, even something more insidious like a bunch of terrorists shooting up the mall with Kalashnikovs would be preferable to stand here, looking through this stupid window, and checking for signs of any man-sized monsters that he didn't believe in.

Callum pushed the door open wide enough so he and Gavin could squeeze through. "Don't make a single sound," he whispered and, to his utter shock, the kid actually nodded in agreement. That one action caused his heartbeat to quicken. Did that mean Gavin no more believed that this was a bomb threat than he believed that the Goliath's familiars had already infiltrated this store?

He sneaked across the cream tiles, heading for the clothing section. Callum decided that cutting through was preferable to following the designated route. It was much quicker for one thing. His companion stayed a couple of paces behind. The lad sounded more scared than he should be for just a bomb threat. Gavin then grabbed Callum and forced him down to the floor. He nodded over to a large shoe display.

It took him a second or two to see what had spooked the lad.

"We are so fucked!" moaned Gavin.

Callum rested his hand on the younger man's thigh and squeezed gently, hoping he'd take that as a comforting gesture. He did not want him to panic. That would get them both killed.

The display sign proudly announced that the Lin Tau trainer had lightweight cushioning and a visible air-sole unit which Callum couldn't work out what the rest of the display said due to a segmented insectile creature, the size of a domestic cat, clinging on to the sign. It wasn't quite man-sized, but it still posed a significant threat. Those hooked claws on its feet kinda told Callum that it wasn't a grass eater. This was a hunter alright, and it was down here searching for a new three-piece suit.

Callum reached up and took a blouse off the rail.

"What the hell are you going to do with that?"

"Shut up." Damn, the beast must have heard them! It clambered down from the sign and disappeared behind a shop-floor mannequin. He held the blouse in one hand while gripping the wooden coat hanger with the other. "Stay close," he said before moving closer to the tiles. Perhaps he should have followed the route after all. At least this way, nothing could jump out at them.

He stopped. That thing skittered through the other side of the clothing, knocking down trousers and nighties. He spun around and pushed passed Gavin. "Get back to the door!" he said. "It's coming right for us." A carousel holding sale price clothing toppled over just as the little beast leaped from the floor towards Callum's face. He yelped, threw the blouse at it then smashed the hanger on its head. It squealed then vanished again. Callum turned and saw Gavin hadn't moved an inch. "Do you still think it's a bomb threat?"

Callum didn't receive any reply; the lad just stood in front of him, shaking like a leaf.

"Hey, calm down, Gavin. Don't look so worried. It's gone now and I doubt it'll be back." Frigging hell. If the kid was going to freeze up at the sight of that, how would he cope when they got out of here? "Come on, Gavin. We still need to make tracks. I don't think the lights are going to stay on for much longer."

Gavin shook his head. The kid then reached into his inside pocket and pulled out a kitchen knife. It still had a price tag on the handle. He'd swiped it from here.

"I hope you're not thinking of using that on me."

Gavin shook his head again. "Look behind you, man," he moaned.

Callum turned to find another two were swerving through the clothing racks. These were larger, much larger. He remembered the description Harry gave them and found it fit these creatures exactly, and all he had to defend himself was a stupid coat hanger! The creatures moved apart and approached them from opposite directions.

He threw the coat hanger at the monster coming towards him then pelted towards the double doors, hoping to God that Gavin was right behind him. His worst fears were confirmed when he risked a glance over his shoulder to find the kid hadn't moved an inch. To make matters even worse, more creatures were heading towards the kid now and he stood there, holding out that little knife of his, like that was going to save him.

"Gavin, get over here!"

"No, save yourself, dude. I got this."

"You fucking idiot," he snarled, running back toward him. Callum grabbed a bunch of glass reed diffusers as he passed a scented candle display, thinking they'd have to do for missiles. He threw the first one just before he reached his companion. The glass canister arced through the air and smashed on the monster's back.

The overpowering scent of apple pumpkin blasted into their nose along with the stench of what smelled like burning meat. The monster jerked to a sudden halt, screeched out in agony, and dropped to the floor.

"You've got to be shitting me!" gasped Callum. The stuff inside the glass had melted through the creature's armoured plate, bone, and muscle like strong acid. A low growl then reminded him that there wasn't just one of them. He turned his head and yelled out in shock when he saw the other one charging straight for them. All the reed diffusers fell from his hands in panic.

Gavin dropped to the floor and scooped up two of the unbroken ones. He then flung them at the charging creature. One broke against its face. The result was terrifying as well as spectacular. The liquid ate through everything organic, leaving it without a head. It collapsed and fell into a pool of the stuff.

Callum picked the lad off the floor. "Harry and the others need to know about this!"

Gavin nodded. "Yeah, too right. God, what a blast! Hang on, let me get some more. You know, just in case." He raced over to the shelf. "Callum, what do you think, lemon lavender or clean cotton?"

"Seriously, does it fucking matter? Just pick some and get back here." Callum eyed the rest of the room for signs of any more of those things while watching those lights, sure that a couple of them had just flickered. It wouldn't matter how much of their new secret weapon that carried. If the lights did go, the pair of them wouldn't stand a chance. "Come on, man! There's other places in Brandale which stock them, you know. Get over here!"

He snatched one of the diffusers out of Gavin's hand, ripped it out of the box, and wrapped his fingers around the glass. He had to admit, it did give him a small amount of comfort. Callum hurried through the clothing department and headed straight for the fire exit. The need to get back into the fresh air going more urgent as it became obvious that the lights down here really were flickering.

"Callum, I think I can hear something."

"Forget about it, man. We know this stuff kills them. Stop looking for more targets." He turned around to find he'd been talking to himself. Gavin was already rushing towards the baby section. "Get back here, you dickhead! The lights are about to go out."

Gavin paid no attention to his yelling and continued to run across the floor. Callum heard him shout something intelligible before he let a surprised yell and vanished from sight. The vision of several monsters lying flat against the thick dark grey carpet and pulling the lad down to the floor and ripping him into tiny pieces refused to leave his mind. Callum glanced at the fire exit, now almost within reach to where Gavin had vanished. "Why are you doing this to me, you shithead?" he growled.

Callum took a deep breath, kissed the reed diffuser, and ran along the tiled route while praying to God that his wild imagination was wrong. He caught movement in the corner of his eye. He stopped and looked to his left. He wanted to run there and then, to get the hell out of here and forget this stupid heroic gesture. Callum counted nine more monsters clinging to the wall, right at the back of the shop. They were looking right at him too. "Gavin!" he shouted. "Get your arse back here, right now!"

He spotted more movement, this time from the floor, next to a section of new baby clothes. Gavin lifted his head up, grinning like a bloody idiot. He even had the audacity to give Callum a little wave. His fury at the boy acting like an arse vanished when he noticed Gavin wasn't alone. A grey-haired middle-aged woman held Gavin's hand. She wore a pale green Celador uniform.

"Miss, can you run?"

She nodded.

"Good!" The creatures were now scuttling along the walls, heading straight for them. "Then fucking run!" Callum raced straight for the fire exit, well aware that those things were gaining on them. He heard Gavin shout out a warning. Callum then felt someone push him to the side just as one of the monsters dropped from the ceiling. Gavin smashed one of the reed diffusers on it before picking Callum up.

The three of them reached the fire exit just as every light in the room died, plunging them into darkness.

"I can't see!" shouted Gavin.

Callum felt his way up the side of the door, trying to locate the bar while listening to the sound of coat hangers falling to the floor as those monsters ran towards them. He found the bar and pushed it down. Weak yellow light took away some of that impenetrable darkness but only enough for Callum to see the two of those monsters had already reached them!

Gavin saw them too. He rolled onto his back and kicked out, his boots smashing into the face of one of those evil-looking fiends. Callum grabbed the woman's wrist and tugged her to safety. "Gavin, move it!" He threw the glass canister at the creatures. It detonated and sprayed them all. The resulting howls of agony were music to Callum's ears. He helped his companion through the open door and slammed it shut.

"Are you okay, miss?"

She gazed into his brown eyes and simply shook her head.

"Gavin, help our new friend up." He ran over to the doors which led outside and pushed them open which filled the room with sunlight. He heard Gavin complain that he'd lost all of his grenades. He also heard the woman tell both him and Gavin that her mate, Stacy, was still in there and they had to get her out. Callum just gripped the metal bar and cried in horror at the sight of the gigantic, horrific creature rising over the city's rooftops, its six massive legs holding up a body longer than an oil tanker. Callum sank to the floor, his own legs giving out on him. He gazed in utter terror while this living nightmare's head snapped down and bit through the side of an apartment block.

"Come on, man," said Gavin, helping him up. "Don't lose your cool now. We need to get back to the flyover while we still can."

Callum watched it rip off more concrete, the rubble plummeting to the ground and landing on the parked cars, while the flying things around the huge monster all flew forward and into the damaged building. Even from this distance, Callum heard the screams as the flying things dragged the people out of the building and threw them into the air, only to be caught in the Goliath's open mouth.

CHAPTER ELEVEN

Malc did not want to be the bait this time. The old man had made that quite clear, but Harry would not take no for an answer. After a minute of grumbling coupled with Dosser going over exactly what Harry had just said, the old man resigned himself to the task and got into position.

Malc reluctantly handed his pride and joy to Dosser.

"For crying out loud, man. Stop it with the sad eyes! You'll get it back."

"In one piece?"

"Scouts honour. Anyway. That wasn't my fault."

"Sorry, I know. Well," replied Malc, "it's just that she doesn't like anyone else touching her."

Dosser sighed. "It's just a rifle. It isn't your wife."

Harry could understand the man's reluctance. He would feel the same. Only for him, the difference was more practical. His fleshmelta wouldn't respond to anyone else.

"Yeah, well. Just look after it."

Dosser gave the man a mock salute before taking up position behind a blue automobile.

"Do not worry, Malc. Now that the Goliath has moved away, I am confident that their numbers around this part of the city will diminish."

Malc took off his hat and scratched the side of his head. "I know," he said miserably. "So are the people. It doesn't take a genius to work out why. At this rate, they'll be nobody left to hide in the tunnels. That is, if we even get to them without ending up as dinner."

"That will not happen, my friend." He flashed the man a rare smile then turned and ran over to his position. He crouched next to the corner of a brick building, in sight of his two new friends. Harry lifted his fleshmelta and nodded over to Malc. Everybody was ready to face the monsters.

He checked on Dosser to see if he was ready. The old man waved the gun. Harry suspected that, despite the last unfortunate encounter, of the two old men, it had to be Dosser who had taken to this new style of existence easier than his companion. Harry found that a little strange as Malc had previous military experience whereas Dosser told him that during the troubles in Northern Ireland, he had been a salesman in a computer store. Both men had to explain what the troubles were and what a computer did.

He lowered himself when the familiar noise of another collector reached his ears. Thankfully, Harry wasn't the only one to hear it. Dosser had already gotten ready to blast it. He waited, unable to stop his heart from speeding up. The last time, Dosser had almost died when Malc fired and only wounded the creature. The only reason why the man escaped with just scratches was his quick reactions and the realisation that the rifle could be used like a club. Dosser had managed to disable his attacker before Harry could run over and turn it into mush. Seven of the collectors had attacked them on the last occasion. Harry hoped the number would be lower now. He hoped so. His fleshmelta had yet to recharge fully.

Three of the beasts charged over the top of the hill, heading straight for the only visible target, Malc. To his credit, the old man didn't turn tail and run away. Harry wouldn't have held it against him if the man had done that. These things looked nothing like the other creatures they had killed. The bastards were twice the size for a start and faster. A lot faster.

They had already passed Dosser. He too must have realised their plan would not work as he broke cover, ran into the middle of the road, and fired in their general direction. The shot obliterated the rear end of the middle creature. Despite its grave injury, the beast still managed to spin around and launch its broken body at Dosser. The man fired his last cartridge which, thankfully, tore it apart, but now the remaining two had taken interest. Dosser ran for his life. He jumped onto the front of the automobile, turned, and calmly broke open the weapon to reload. Even from his position, Harry knew that the old man wouldn't stand a chance of killing them both.

Harry jumped up and ran from his position while hoping that these vile beasts didn't employ the same technique as the things before. He was still too far for his hits to count. At this distance, if he fired, he was likely to cook them all including Dosser. They were almost on him! Harry tapped into an energy reserve he didn't realise he had and pelted forward another few metres. Harry lowered the fleshmelta and fired two shots.

The tarmac immediately below the running beasts turned into a pool of steaming fluid. All three beasts screeched in agony as they sank into the black muck, the boiling hot tar burning the soft flesh off their bones. The time gave Dosser enough time to reload. He shouted out in rage then fired twice. The shot destroyed two of them, leaving the remaining beast meowing in agony while it attempted to drag what remained of its damaged body out of the cooling quagmire. The creature pulled itself away, leaving most of its dissolved legs stuck in the gelatinous tar.

"Harry!"

He saw them a split-second after Malc's panicked yelling. Another four more of the larger beasts were galloping towards Malc, coming from another direction, just like their previous encounter.

"Go on, man," shouted Dosser. He had only just broken open the shotgun. "Don't worry about me. I'll catch up."

He ran towards Malc who saw him coming and attempted to close the gap between him and Harry. The beasts were faster, much faster, and the first creature had almost reached Malc. It leapt towards the running man. Harry could not fire without killing the man.

"Get down, you daft old git! On the floor, Malc."

Dosser's urgent shout had the desired effect. The man dropped onto the road and rolled to the left, giving Harry his target. "Die, you vile monster," he snarled. A stream of energised plasma particles slammed into the approaching creature, reducing it to liquid in an instant. He fired again, only to discover the weapon's energy resources had dried up. "Dosser, I need you now!"

The three other monsters were not as eager to charge to their deaths. The beasts slowed down then jumped onto the roof of another parked automobile. The three creatures looked straight at Harry. The largest animal opened its jaws and roared. It was the last action it would ever do. A blast from Dosser's shotgun turned its head into of red and black wet lumps. His other shot took out the other beast, leaving just one.

"Harry, kill the bloody thing!"

"I can't," he replied, desperately squeezing the trigger. "It'll be at least another minute before the weapon can fire."

"We don't have another minute and I'm out of shells!" gasped Dosser.

Sensing triumph, the remaining animal slipped off the car roof and onto the bonnet. Dosser had already turned the gun around, but Harry knew that even brute force would not save them, not this time. This monster was too well protected.

He pulled out his knife. "You are not going to kill me so easily!" he growled.

The animal matched Harry's growl then slid off the car. It lowered its head and jumped straight at them. Both men staggered back and fell onto the road. Harry yelled out in rage, knowing that he had failed, but before those serrated teeth could rip into him, Harry heard the sound of shouting, followed by another gunshot.

The beast screamed when something punched through its side. Harry shuffled backwards then helped to pull Dosser back towards the curbside. More gunshots followed and the creature skidded across the road before it collapsed. The gunfire continued and now Harry saw the originator of their rescuer. The tall, grim-faced man with very little hair and wearing a black uniform ran towards the dying creature, still firing. The man only stopped when the gun dry-clicked. He stopped by the beast's head, calmly ejected the clip from the pistol, inserted another, and pointed the gun straight at the creature's head.

"This is for Dennis," he said. The new arrival fired one more time.

Harry reached for his own weapon then got back on his feet. He helped Dosser up then walked over to the animal still alive. It had crawled away from the now solid road and its detached hind legs and took up shelter under the wheels of a large van. It hissed at Harry when he approached. He heard his two new friends thanking the new arrival for intervening and after ensuring the damaged animal was no longer a threat, he returned to the others.

It shocked him a little to discover this man belonged to the city's constabulary. From the uniform and the presence of body armour, Harry had first assumed he was part of some military force.

"That's some wacky-looking gun you have there," said the new arrival. He held out his hand, which Harry promptly shook. "I'm Paul, by the way. Pleased to make your acquaintance."

"I am Harry," he replied, "and the feeling is mutual. The addition of another armed man will make our mission a little easier."

"Right." Paul glanced at Dosser and then at Malc. "Okay, so what's going on here, guys?" His eyes finally rested on Dosser's shotgun after one more curious glance at the weapon cradled in Harry's arms. "This is a bit of a change for you too. You're normally skulking inside the shopping mall, annoying the locals." He then gave Harry a detailed scrutiny. "And what's your story, and what the fuck is that in your arms?"

"It's called a fleshmelta."

"Yeah, obviously. So what's it do?"

Harry briefly wondered if this new arrival had any mental health issues. If that was the case, it would explain why he wasted so much ammunition on killing that beast when a single shot to the skull sufficed. "It melts flesh," he replied. Unlike the humans on his world, Harry was not used to wasting anything, including words. He pushed past the constable and walked back over to the parked van. He placed his foot close to the front wheel and waited. As expected, the beast's need to devour overpowered its need for self-protection and it crawled out from under the vehicle. Harry took three paces back, aimed the weapon, and fired.

"Holy shit!"

"Indeed." Harry walked back over to the reaming corpse. He raised the gun only for Dosser to push the gun down.

"Wait a minute, Harry." He looked over at Malc who joined them. The constable stayed where he was. "What are we dealing with here, man? This thing is so different to the other bastard things!"

It was clear from the man's tone that this new thing had seriously spooked him. "It is a collector," he replied.

"A collector. So you've come across them before?"

He shook his head. "No, Malc, this is the first time that I have encountered such a beast."

"So how do you know what they are?"

He crouched beside the corpse and used his weapon to pull back one of its forelimbs. "Observe that the legs appear to be larger than such a creature needs, and do you see that? There is a flap of membrane which runs down its belly. These animals have the ability to store a huge amount of material. They expand like a balloon. Judging from the size of these, they have just returned from emptying themselves and were about to restart the process, only they had the misfortune of running into us first." Harry stood up. "These creatures are part of the next phase." He looked at Malc. "You were correct about the lack of people." Harry sighed. "We may already be too late."

"Too late? What the hell is that supposed to mean?" The constable took a step back from Harry. The man blinked then aimed his pistol at Harry's face. "Put your space gun on the floor, sonny, then place those hands on the top of your head. Also, if you don't mind, I want you to shut your bloody hole. I've heard enough bullshit to last me a lifetime."

"What are you doing, you silly twat?" shouted Dosser. "This guy is on our side."

"Yeah, man. Quit being so excitable." Malc walked up to the constable then placed himself between him and Harry. "Come on now, if we don't all work together, we're never going to survive this nightmare. Lower the popgun."

"Why do you think it's too late, Harry?"

The constable still hadn't lowered his pistol. Harry found the man's behaviour a little disturbing but understandable. His uniform suggested that the police in this world were trained to deal with situations far more violent than the stories he had been told of their type from his world over a century ago. He snapped the fleshmelta back into its cradle, guessing that its absence might help the man relax. After all, the constable was more likely to be better trained in subduing armed civilians than dispatching monsters from another world.

He gently moved Malc to the side and wrapped his fingers around the pistol barrel then moved it up to his forehead. "Dosser's shotgun is now empty. Your clip has probably ten rounds left in the magazine. Nine, if you shoot me and the weapon on my back will only respond to my touch." Somewhere in the distance, the sound of an explosion made the man holding the gun jump. Harry could hear human screaming. They were not far off. The collectors they had just killed were obviously not the only pack operating in this area. "How long do you think you and these two will last before the collectors catch you and turn your bodies into food for that Goliath?"

Malc reached for Paul's gun and pulled it away from Harry's face. "He's got a point there, Robocop. Do you not remember your prime directives?"

"Christ, Malc. I told you not to call me that." The constable slipped the gun back into its holster. "Forgive me, I guess I'm not thinking straight. I've not had the best of days."

"Understandable, Paul," replied Harry. "It is not every day that monsters from another Earth invade."

Paul looked him up and down. "Another Earth, you say? An Earth that, perhaps, you came from?"

"Come on, man," snapped Dosser. "What do you think?" He gave the shotgun back to Malc. "See, told you I'd look after it."

"Not much use to me now. Not unless we can get some more ammo for it."

Harry nodded. "Normally, I would agree as right now, if I die, then we all do. Time is against us. If we do not reach these tunnels, then it will no longer matter how much ammunition we carry."

"Wait on," said Dosser. "What did you mean earlier about it being too late?"

"There's a sports shop opposite the shopping mall, on Basin Street. They stock shotgun shells." The constable gingerly booted the collector. "After how easily this fucker took my bullets, I could probably do with an upgrade too."

"The city landscape had changed considerably since I arrived. Gone are three of its tallest buildings and black smoke covers much of the landscape. Right now, the Goliath appears to be heading for the tower blocks on the outskirts of the city and moving in a clockwise direction. It would not be long before it re-enters the centre of the city. Once that happens, none of the humans still alive would stand any chance of surviving. The familiars that accompanied the monster will see to that." He stopped then turned to stare at the corpse. "That isn't why it is too late. I believe that there is more than one Goliath."

"What? No way, we'd have seen it," cried Malc. "I mean, come on, they're not exactly hard to miss."

Harry shrugged. "Its absence is mysterious, but the evidence fits. With such a large amount of available meat, phase two should not be happening for another few days. My guess is that both creatures are stocking up before they run out. Remember, they are like cows. The Goliaths will never stop eating. The only way to stop them is to take away the grass."

"Protect the innocent," murmured the constable. "These tunnels, you mentioned. I take it you mean the abandoned sewer outflow, a few streets from here?"

Malc nodded. "Yeah, we once used it as a place to bed down until some of the local kids decided to start organising their dealing there."

"Then we had better get started. Harry, don't you think you had better have that pop gun in your hands? Wait, does it ever run out?"

Harry shrugged. "It hasn't yet. I do not know how they work. Nobody does, only that it is effective."

"Have you ever used it against a Goliath?"

Harry paled. "No, Dosser. Nobody has been able to get close enough to try."

"Come on, we're wasting time. Harry, take the rear. I'll lead. You two just keep your eyes peeled. They will come at all angles."

"No shit," muttered Dosser. "Like we don't already know that."

The old man looked quizzically at Harry. He wasn't sure how to act. He shrugged and held out his hands. "Dosser, the man is a constable, are you not supposed to do what they say?"

"Huh, until he gets us killed, you mean?"

Malc sighed. He grabbed his friend's sleeve and pulled him away from Harry. "Come on, man. Let him play the brave police captain. Does it really matter? Now come on." He glanced at Harry. "Both of you, the copper's almost out of sight."

Harry followed the others as they ran through the deserted streets. He could still hear those screams but they had become more distant. Harry hoped that the remaining population had found secure places to hide. Could he be correct about the addition of another Goliath? After all, Harry might know more about these beasts than anybody else on this planet, but he did not know everything about them. Only the Goliaths knew that. Still, it did make sense, although he had accused the people of this world as soft and weak, they were still human, and even the most subdued individual will fight for their right to exist.

Right now, they were only fighting products belonging to the Goliaths. The invaders have not had the time to begin the construction of creatures built from human parts, meaning their numbers should be few. The locals were plenty and, as Dosser and Malc had demonstrated, were more than eager to fight back.

If two Goliaths had arrived here though, that meant twice as many monsters. The fighting humans would not withstand an assault from familiars belonging to two monsters, not even with help from people like Paul. Harry looked to the skies and hoped that everything the two men had told him earlier on was true.

He ran along the middle of the road, seeing signs of the passing of collectors but no bodies. He did see a few human weapons. Everything from Dosser's shotgun as well as pistols similar to the one carried by Paul. Harry also spotted knives, axes, as well as garden tools. The humans here had done their utmost to avoid being taken but, Harry guessed, the overwhelming numbers of collectors had made short work of any resistance.

Harry stopped dead when he spotted movement from beyond a window to his left. "Hello, is there anybody in there?" He looked straight at Dosser and pointed to the floor, hoping he would understand then ran over to the stone building. The door swung inwards when he pressed upon it. "Hello?" he repeated.

The sound of someone or something moving above him told Harry that he had not imagined a presence within this dwelling. He had to throw caution to the wind. Leaving Dosser out there alone was so irresponsible, considering the man had no weapon. Harry was just hoping that as the collectors had already scoured this area, they were unlikely to come back.

Harry raced up the stairs and proceeded to check each room. It took him seconds the reach the last room. Harry pushed open the white door and scanned the interior, trying not to marvel at the vast amount of material possessions scattered around the large bedroom. He saw teddy bears, books, and dolls, but no sign of any human. That changed when Harry moved further into the room.

A spool of cotton fell from the top of a wooden wardrobe. Harry's eyes darted up and saw something bright scoot back towards the wall. "It is okay," he said, keeping his voice level. "I am here to help."

Harry heard another sound from behind him. He spun around to find himself staring into the face of a young boy who had stuck his head out of the bottom of a sliding cupboard. The boy looked at Harry then his eyes darted up to the top of the cupboard and he released an ear-shattering scream. He swivelled around and gaped at the sight of five irregular lumps of moving flesh clinging to the wall just above the wardrobe. He fired and liquidised two pieces. The other three moved at incredible speed along the top of the wall, heading straight for the cupboard where the boy had been hiding.

He had no other choice but to drag the shrieking boy from out of his hiding place and sling him over his shoulder. The boy's teeth sank into Harry's fingers but still, he held him tight. He ran over to the door, knowing he had to get out as quickly as possible. Holding this struggling infant rendered him helpless, as there was no way to fire his weapon.

Not that it mattered. The pieces of flesh didn't appear to be after him or the boy. "Oh no!" gasped Harry when he saw the open window. He ran along the hallway and raced down the stairs, desperate to reach Dosser before those things landed on his head.

Harry stopped before he reached the door and pulled the boy off his shoulder. He wiped his bleeding fingers against a black coat hung up beside him while watching those things fall from the window. He saw no sign of Dosser. Harry turned the boy to face him and lifted his head. "I am really sorry for what you must have been through, but right now, if you are to continue to live, it is essential that you do everything that I say. Do you understand?"

In response, the boy tried to bite him again before he wriggled out of Harry's grasp and ran out into the street. "Wait!" Harry ran after him. He saw the boy head straight towards Malc. He breathed a sigh of relief to see both Malc and Paul were stood beside Dosser at a comfortable distance from the house.

Harry dodged through the pieces of flesh and ran over to them. "The boy, he…" Harry looked at his damaged hand then sighed heavily. "It does not matter. Paul, we had better hurry."

"I was almost there until I noticed you'd taken a diversion." He smiled at the boy. "Are you okay, son?"

To Harry's surprise, the boy smiled back.

"S'ok, it's just past that last row of houses." Paul took out his baton and gave it to the boy. "Here. Can you take care of this for me?" He held out his hand. The boy ran from Malc and took the constable's hand.

"I take it you don't have kids?" asked Dosser, smiling.

He shook his head. "Our children are kept deep underground. They are the future of humanity so they are more precious than anything else." Harry walked past Dosser while wondering what happened to the ones he left behind. Were they safe now that the Goliaths and their vile familiars had crossed into this world?

"Harry, down here."

He stopped beside a wooden fence. While being so preoccupied with his own thoughts, Harry hadn't noticed that the others had gone. How could he be so negligent during a mission? There was no greater crime.

"Hey, don't look so down in the mouth," said Dosser. "They're just down here. Come on. I'll show you how to get down." Dosser pushed his way through the wire fence then held it up so Harry could squeeze through. "We used to come down here all the time until one of the locals rang the police. Do you see the end house, number twelve. The black door?"

Harry nodded. He also saw numerous signs that the collectors had already been through here. He just hoped that these locals had taken precautions and hid. He remembered the old ones telling him that the familiars took just as many humans as they did when they first arrived. The familiars knew exactly where to look. Those vile creatures tore up floorboards, broke through wardrobe doors, and broke into cellars. He didn't think this time would be much different.

"Mrs. Dyson used to live there. Lovely old bird she was too. Now, Mrs. Dyson didn't mind some of us kipping down in the tunnels. We did nobody any harm. Hell, thanks to our presence, none of Brandale's resident burglars ever came round here." He began to climb down some old stone steps. "She had a daughter did Mrs. Dyson and that where the problem stemmed. See, this young thing had this habit of undressing right in front of her bedroom window." Dosser coughed. "Some of the other guys hadn't seen a young body, at least in the flesh for years and, well, I reckon you can slot in the rest of the jigsaw pieces for yourself."

Harry nodded, astonished that the man could spout out such irrelevant rubbish at such inconvenient times. He did not comment, guessing that perhaps everyone else in this situation would have done the same. The old ones were similar in that aspect. To look back to a time when their lives were not so fraught with the fear of imminent death must give them an enormous amount of comfort.

"Tell me something, Dosser. Why did you send Callum and Gavin away?"

The man did not look so comfortable anymore. He obviously had not expected Harry to ask that question.

"Honestly?"

"That is usually the best way."

"Don't get me wrong, he's a great kid and we love him, it's just that... Well, he can be a little erratic and..."

"And you felt that if you had to look after him, you would not be able to commit to looking after yourself as well as your friend, Malc?"

"Yeah. Something like that," replied Dosser. "Don't you worry about your pal, Callum. Believe me, he'll do alright." He patted Harry on the shoulder. "Come on, we'd better catch up with the others."

Before he could reply, Harry was thrown to the floor as the ground beneath him shook violently. He jumped back onto his feet and launched himself at Dosser, catching the old man before he fell down the rest of the steps.

"What the hell was that?" cried Dosser. "We don't have earthquakes in England!"

Harry stayed silent. He had his suspicions; instead, he scanned the horizon. Harry stopped looking when he reached an area directly opposite where the apartment blocks once stood. Dosser had not seen it yet so Harry helpfully turned him around.

"Oh my God!" Dosser looked at Harry then down at the others who had climbed out of the sewer outlet. "We are so dead. One was bad enough but two? Harry, what chance do we have against two of the monsters?"

Harry tuned out the man's understandable panicked cries; instead, he focused on the new creature. So far, he saw one huge limb reaching towards the sky it was easily as tall as any building still standing. It waved like a single stalk of grass in the gentle wind. A collective gasp broke the silence as another limp joined it followed by two more and finally another two. The body then slowly rose above the buildings.

"Look at the size of the thing. It's even bigger than the other one," murmured Paul. "It's like a cross between a spider and an octopus."

"No Goliath is alike. They are as different as snowflakes. It sickens me to know I was correct. No good can come of this."

"Don't speak too soon, Harry. Look!"

He followed the direction of Malc's finger and saw four specks of light rushing towards them at high speed, just above the clouds.

Paul pulled Harry down the steps. "Come on, we need to get under cover!"

Harry followed the others into the sewer outlet while trying to keep an eye on those approaching blips. He remembered the old ones explaining aircraft to him back when he was young, and he found it so hard to believe that humans had built machines which flew through the air higher and faster than any familiar. Callum had tried to tell him exactly what these jet fighters could do, but it was just too much for him to take in.

In some aspects, Harry could understand why most of the humans in this world were so obsessed with such trivial rubbish. If they actually stopped and attempted to conceive how much their species had accomplished in the past century, their brains would probably overload.

"You're going to see something spectacular now, Harry. Those buggers won't just have your bog standard machine gun strapped to the cockpit." Malc chuckled. "What do you reckon they are, Dosser?"

"Tornadoes, I guess. They have more of them than the F-35. They'll be using those buggers in London and the other large cities."

"I bet they'll use a couple of Brimstone missiles. Believe me, Harry, pretty soon those two big bastards are about to be turned into burger meat. Once they are out of the way, the Army will either fry or shred all of their nasty little pets."

Harry wished he could share their confidence, he really did, but bitter experience taught him long ago that only fools expected miracles. He slammed his hand over his mouth to stop himself when screaming when a large portion of the sky flashed a violent red. Harry blinked away the after-images and stared at where the flash had been. Seconds later, another flash of red lit up the sky. Two more red flashes lit up the sky coming from the opposite direction.

"What the hell is going on?" cried Paul. He ran over to the edge and stared straight forward just as what sounded like continuous thunder blasted out. "Oh no. Oh fuck. Please, this can't be happening!" He spun around, his face as white as milk. "They're still there. Your bloody Goliaths, Harry. They're still in Brandale, carrying on as if nothing as if happened."

"What?" Dosser joined him. "But we all saw the explosions!"

"Yeah, we did," replied Paul. "Only all of our missiles smashed into some kind of invisible wall, an energy shield."

Harry stood behind them and watched as the first Goliath slowly turned around. It was making its way back towards the centre of the town. The blips, those fighter jets, had already veered away. "They have adapted," he murmured. "Improved upon their design."

"How the hell can they have a bloody energy shield?" demanded Paul. "You said they were nothing but cows."

"I do not know," he replied truthfully. "I also do not know how they can travel from world to world and yet they still do this."

Malc leaned against the tunnel and slowly slid to the floor. "What do we do now?"

"Nothing has changed," said Harry. "We save as many people as we can and we fight." He glared at every adult. "We fight until either they are dead or we are."

CHAPTER TWELVE

The Right Hand of God had absolutely no desire to relive his nightmarish experience inside that enemy stronghold. Just the fact that he and the remaining constructs were able to journey back to the place where he once considered home to retell a condensed version of what he had undergone should be enough.

Judging from his recent despicable treatment, the evidence showed otherwise. The new arrivals, the deviants now holding him against his will, had demanded his total and complete surrender of mind and body. After his previous distress, the temptation to show these interlopers exactly who they were dealing with almost got the better of him. Only his base instinct to serve and protect his God stopped him from turning these eight pathetic creatures into flesh confetti.

He allowed them to shackle his now completely transformed body to the side of the house. Their thoughts were closed to his mind. All he could sense was the mind of his remaining construct. His last act before the hidden wire-vines snagged him just before he reached his home was to order her to run and hide in the woods. Copperfield could also sense his memory strand and it was as confused as him. It felt strange to have that remaining piece of the previous occupant as his only ally.

The only creature to vocally communicate with Copperfield, a slinking piece of pale pseudo-flesh which clung to its crystal bone body, had already told him that it intended to dump the contents of Copperfield's Earth experiences onto a memory spool for later examination. It had also refused to answer any of his questions.

In retrospect, Copperfield really should have slowed his frantic journey back to the house. His God's early arrival should have told him that something serious had happened in the time between transferring his conscious into that memory probe and discovering one of the new Gods had infiltrated their territory.

Their territory. How bitter those words sounded now. This lump of excrement acting like the lord of the manor was the lowest of the low. Back on the old world, its only job had been to clean the bottom of the empty flesh tanks in their meat factories. To think that something that he had made, put together from discarded pieces of foot-soldier and bone-dissolver, had the power of life and death over him made his teeth itch.

Could this have something to do with what he had found back in that warehouse? As unrealistic as it sounded, perhaps while he was gone, the new God really had found some way to convert his God's creations to work for him. No, that was just too fanciful to take seriously. Even if that was the case, then surely Copperfield's God would not be here at all!

He needed more information. Copperfield knew that would not happen while he was still attached to this wall. The excrement left the company of the foot-soldiers, walked up to him, checked the shackles were secure then ordered two of its companions into the house to collect several large containers.

The creature moved back a metre then lowered its body to the ground and wrapped its four flexible legs around its midriff.

No matter which direction he approached the enigma, he could not understand how such a low-status beast, an animal not even worthy of the term sentience, could be doing the task specifically designed for Copperfield. It sat there in front of him, looking like some anorexic toad, acting like the whole planet owed him a life, thinking it was the emperor of the castle. If he was capable of being sick, Copperfield would be on his third bucket by now. He then had to calm his nerves when he remembered exactly what those foot-soldiers in his house were looking for.

Its slimy mouth, solely designed for scraping away the build-up of dried organic stains from the bottom of those stinking vats, altered its shape. Copperfield would have laughed if this whole situation hadn't been so tragic as well as fatal. This abomination was actually trying to smile, an expression it had obviously never tried to emulate until now.

"They talked in fear of you. The foot-soldiers, the ones which came to fill the tanks did. I am not sure of the others. I only heard about four or five of the same voices over and over. That was thanks to you. Yes, thanks to you, I saw nothing but the foul shit which I was forced to eat, day in day out."

It adjusted its position.

"I heard them talk often. Oh, they knew I was in there and did not care. Why should they? Who was I to tell if their dialogue strayed close to blasphemy?" It lifted its head, that awkward smile still there. "Strange how when our glorious God gently lifted me out of my prison and deposited me on dry ground, I believed those foot-soldiers had decided to have me killed. Do you think that aspect of paranoid thought was a product of your conditioning? Not once did I wonder why the greatest being in the universe had demeaned itself to associate with something so worthless as me. I did not even ask that question when our glorious God dropped a living human child in front of me."

The creature unwrapped its legs, stood up, and shouted something intelligible to the remaining foot-soldiers. They all left the front of the house and ran towards the main gate. "Do you see how they jump to my every command?"

It walked a little closer. As it approached, Copperfield attempted not to frown. This clearly was not the same creature that he designed.

Something, or perhaps himself, had lined its outer legs with cartilage. This had to be a recent addition as the stuff had time to harden. Surely, it could not have performed the improvements alone?

Copperfield could not scrape away the image of how those foot-soldiers shivered and bowed around this piece of excrement. They lacked the knowledge, skill, and steadiness to do it, that's for sure. The closer it got, the more Copperfield saw how it had changed. Everything from the subtle additions of armour plate down its chest, to the enlarged spine growth down the middle of its back. The sight of those things released quite a few millilitres of chemicals into Copperfield's system. This was no self-improvement treatment. Nor had any of the gibbering idiots serving as its muscle had anything to do with it either.

What are the buckets for?

He ordered the memory strand to shut its imaginary gob. The last thing Copperfield needed at this juncture was that annoying fly distracting him. The excrement was almost nose to nose and at this perspective, he now saw the larger brain-casing at the rear. Oh fuck. It really was telling the truth! The bastard thing really had been touched by their glorious God.

"I see you're admiring my new look."

Its proboscis attempted another smile and failed. Not that it mattered to Copperfield. He just wasn't capable of becoming more terrified. It wasn't because this walking collection of discarded body parts was trying to act like the cock of the manor. Copperfield's reign truly had come to an end. He now was the secondary option, the walking collection of discarded body parts. His God had decided for whatever reason, Copperfield was superfluous to requirements.

Tell me what the buckets are for!

Copperfield should not feel the way he did. It was not his place to question the will of his God. If his glorious God wished to throw him onto the rubbish heap, then that would be the outcome. They were nothing but insignificant fleas in the eyes of their glorious God.

"We are going to take this new world, just as we have taken the countless worlds before it."

It then had the audacity to actually touch Copperfield. The excrement started to stroke his nose while continuing to practice the smile. It was beginning to get the hang of it.

"Of course, you're not going to see it happen." It paused. "Perhaps you will, in a sense. You really do possess a remarkable set of eyes. I think I might have those after we have retrieved the required information." The bastard then flicked the tip of my nose. "So, it is not all bad news, my friend."

Copperfield sensed that the memory strand was going to try one more attempt to reach him. He gave this vile creature the dirtiest glare he could muster, a look that once would have sent any other minion scuttling into a dark corner.

The containers are to hold my liquefied flesh. It's how this thing will extract the information it needs. It is going to take each container and slurp the contents through that mouth and literally taste my memories. It will know everything that I know and, I ought the mention, everything you know as well.

My God! Don't you think you should do something about it?

Oh, you think?

Now that the excrement had finished playing with him, it retreated to its prior position. Copperfield's existence was about to close. He heard distant explosions and saw the shape of one of the Gods close to the horizon. It was a sad state of affairs to finally understand that his sense of importance had been a big sham. The Gods will go on without him. Copperfield wouldn't even be a footnote in the history of their species. The specks of dust floating in the air had more importance than him. That piece of excrement looking like the maid who'd just stolen a cream cake had more importance than him. Right now, it had. At least it did understand what it meant to be the lowest of the low.

Look, are you going to continue feeling sorry for yourself or are you going to get us out of here? I don't know about you, but I'm not too partial to becoming blood soup for anybody. Come on, soldier. Do something!

Copperfield heard the house doors opening. It appeared that the foot-soldiers were returning with whatever they could find. It didn't shock him to find they had raided the kitchen. The lead foot-soldier carried the washing-up bowl and the largest pan in the house. Another foot-soldier joined him. That one carried a colander. During his reign as the Right Hand of God, no foot-soldier would ever make such a stupid mistake. Perhaps the excrement's grip on the muscle was not as firm as he previously believed.

He joined the memory strand in the harmonic sighing when the third one brought out a white ceramic bowl. That had come from under the bed.

Do something, you fucking big goon. There is no way that I want to end my life by being drunk out of my wife's piss-pot by some armoured stick insect.

Judging from the excrement's loud bellowing, it had sensed Copperfield's extreme discomfort. Perhaps now really was the moment to show exactly who was in control here? He now recognised which God was close to the horizon, and it wasn't the one which turned him into the Right Hand of God. Yet, should that even matter?

He tugged on the chains. The sound of the metal smacking against the brick did not drown out the excrement's giggling, nor did the noise blank his memory strand's frantic urging. Copperfield closed his eyes and located his remaining construct. The beast was lying beside the thick trunk of some old oak. She lifted her head when he re-established contact. Through her eyes, Copperfield saw the remains of a large animal. The beast had killed another cow and dragged the carcass under the shelter of the trees to consume it in peace.

If Copperfield did not escape, then it would surely die.

The giggles now turned into gasps of surprise mixed with a small amount of indignation. The chain was too strong for even Copperfield to break, but that could not be said for the bricks. Even after a few moments of pulling, he felt something give.

The ratio of surprise and indignation swapped. Copperfield could not help but to be insulted that this so-called enhanced creature had not begun to express fear.

One of the bolts dropped to the floor.

Perhaps their God had stripped that emotion out of the furious piece of excrement? More likely, it still believed Copperfield's actions would prove pointless as it still commanded the foot-soldiers. Even now, they dropped the containers and reached for their fleshmeltas.

Copperfield roared in triumph as the shackle holding his left-hand came away and now, he sensed an iota of unease slipping into his inferior replacement. All the foot-soldiers had their weapons raised and yet none of them had fired. Copperfield looked at that colander rolling around in a tight circle and wondered that perhaps their transition was not as tight as the excrement believed?

What have you stopped for? Do you seriously want to be turned into a fucking milkshake? Get us out of here!

Copperfield brought his left arm around in an arc, bunching up his fingers, a moment before it slammed into the wall next to his waist. Several bricks fell into the house cavity. He pulled his other arm out of the shackle then slammed them both into the wall.

"Kill him, you idiots. Don't just stand there!"

It ran up to the closest foot-soldier and tried to snatch the weapon out of its hands. It succeeded after the fourth attempt. By the time it had figured out how to fire the fleshmelta, Copperfield had already made his way through the inner wall. He dived to the left and fell against the dining room table, narrowly missing a jet of super-heated plasma melting a large hole through the opposite wall.

He pushed away the splintered pieces of polished wood and ran for the door, fully aware that both the excrement and the foot-soldiers were running towards the hole he had just created. Copperfield did not believe that he would get a second chance. He believed that he had just used up whatever loyalty the foot-soldiers had for him. Self-preservation was a powerful notion. Lesser creatures like those did not possess the notion of sacrifice embedded into all the higher creatures, created by their glorious God.

His memory strand seemed to find that hilarious and then attempted to explain to Copperfield how religious dogma, as well as political rhetoric, worked. He blanked out the nonsense words and focused on the task of staying alive, a job made more difficult by the appearance of a large shadow moving along the far wall of the dark living room, opposite him.

Copperfield heard a quiet moan, realising a second later that the noise came from him. He gripped the wooden banister and moaned again.

The huge shape, still hidden from view, shuffled a little closer. Even without seeing it, Copperfield knew that the impossible had happened. That familiar smell had already confirmed that. He unwittingly moved back, his body armour colliding with the bottom of the first step. It moved closer and now, the light streaming through the hallway window illuminated the top of its own armoured features.

Did it really matter how one of the new God's guardians ended up inside his house? Copperfield climbed onto the first step. Knowing the answer would not stop this monster from killing him if it did manage to rest those huge claws upon his shoulders. He had been lucky the last time. Right now, thanks to using up most of his energy reserves escaping from those chains, Copperfield doubted that he now possessed the strength to even cause it any permanent damage, let alone kill it.

The monster's movements changed from slumberous shuffling to a lightning-fast dart. It charged through the doorway, ripping off the doorframe on passing. It almost had him. Copperfield hadn't a clue that any of them could move so quickly. It was only his decision to climb onto that one step which saved him from almost certain death. He did not hang around to thank his unintentional foresight, as the behemoth was still moving!

He raced up the stairs, fully aware of his pursuer's own movements just inches behind him. Despite its bulk, the guardian was faster and more agile than him. How could that possibly be? The things he had encountered before were terrifying, but none of them were in the same league as the nightmare racing up the steps just behind him.

Copperfield slammed through the closest door and ran straight for the window. He only had one chance, and a slim one at that, to get away from this vile creature, and he fully intended to take it, despite the obvious dangers. He placed his brain into neutral then leapt at the closed window.

Pieces of glass and shattered bits of the wooden window frame followed him down and three surprised-looking foot-soldiers looked up as he crashed into their bodies. Copperfield silently took one of their guns and raced down the garden path, towards the main gate. None of the foot-soldiers had run after him. Copperfield resisted the urge to look over his shoulder as the sound of their horrific screaming had already told him why none of them had given chase.

It appeared that the foot-soldiers were not the only constructs having trouble with their behaviour. Nobody had bothered to tell the guardian of the new God that they were on the same side now.

He reached the gate and scaled the metal while listening to the distant shouts and screams. *Had that really happened? The thought that the Gods, both old and new, were now working together just could not be. This was not how it went. There had to be the division of classes otherwise the equilibrium would cease to be, meaning war would surely follow.*

I can't believe you thought that, and you went on at me for spouting political dogma. Why don't you face facts? Is it more believable that some brain-dead pool cleaner just kidnapped the biggest boss in the block and stapled him to a wall? Admit it, buster. There's been a regime change and you didn't even figure in the equations. Christ on a bike. I think I preferred it when you were eating cake at your own self-pity party. Then again, maybe you are right. Maybe your pool-cleaner pal made his own guardian? Yep, the tossbag who can't find his arsehole with both hands created it. Makes perfect sense.

Have you finished?

Copperfield threw his body over the top the gate and raced for the tree cover. A blast of super-heated plasma turning the ground a metre to his left into a smoking puddle helped him confirm his suspicion that he would receive no more assistance from his former foot-soldiers. He darted to the right and took shelter behind a bunch of large rocks before peering around the side.

Several foot-soldiers, as well as that piece of excrement, were now pulling the gates open. It appeared that they were not about to lose their quarry so easily. Perhaps it was time to show this jumped-up little bastard the best reason why he should have climbed back inside that tank when the God lifted him out.

Three foot-soldiers ran ahead, following the direction of the road. They would pass this spot in a matter of seconds.

What the hell are you doing? You're free now. Get out of here!

Shut up.

Copperfield waited for the last one to pass him before running out from behind the rocks. The ones closer to the gates saw him and started shouting and yelling. He was fine with that, as long as they did not start to shoot. Copperfield believed the triggers would stay untouched due to the proximity of him to their comrades. At least, that is what he hoped.

They all turned as one, but none of them had brought their fleshmelta up. This is a movement which should be instinct. Copperfield would have still prevailed even if these idiots had followed the instructions drilled into them over and over. Their decline of discipline just made his task easier. He ripped a gun out from the grasp of one of the foot-soldiers, turned it around, and smashed the butt into its owner's face. By now, the other two's training was beginning to kick in, but it was still too late for them. Copperfield dropped to his knees and fired the fleshmelta once, aiming for the point between them. The energy turned both their shoulders into syrup.

He collected their guns and threw them as far as he could. Copperfield did not have the heart to destroy them. His inner self suggested that the fleshmelta, as well as these foot-soldiers, were now an endangered creation. Nothing was going to be the same from now on.

The remaining foot-soldiers and that dirty pretender were not far behind him, but Copperfield did not particularly care about them at this moment. If they were intent on killing him, they would have done so by now.

There was no need to transmit a mental call to the construct as she was already heading towards him. Copperfield eagerly awaited the reunion. Having her by his side might help to refocus his jumbled thoughts. With a clear head, he could then establish a workable plan to pull him out of this chaos.

A workable plan? There's nothing left, you idiot. You're stuck on another world and alone. You've been betrayed by your own kind. Admit it, what possible future could you make from this mess? Even if my kind do stop your Gods and win, there's nothing left for you. I mean, come on, looking like that, it's unlikely that you'll be able to blend back into society.

Copperfield did not even bother to reply to the memory strand's obvious gloating, even if there was a grain of truth in his words. He just needed to prove himself. To show his God that he could still be the Right Hand of God and the impostor, that pointless collection of worthless body parts, was no match for his skills, something that Copperfield had already proven. If the shoe was on the other foot, there is no way that the excrement would have been able to escape.

He jerked to a complete stop and raised the fleshmelta when he caught the sound of a snapping twig. It had to be his construct returning to his side. When that happened, Copperfield would feel almost complete. Once more, he envied their lack of sentience. She would not care about the apparent duplicity of the Gods.

Copperfield lowered his gun.

You bloody fool! That's not her. You're going to get us both killed.

He dropped to the floor and rolled to the right even before the memory strand finished screaming the warning. Copperfield saw dark grey skin, as well as the tip of another fleshmelta, hidden behind the foliage seconds before the position he previously held was obliterated. He fired and missed. Copperfield scrambled to his feet and ran straight at the hidden foot-soldier. He dropped his fleshmelta and dived on the creature, their combined weight caused them to crash into the soft leaf litter.

He did not even give the foot-soldier time to grasp what was happening. Copperfield pressed his hand against the creature's neck and slammed his fist hard against its forehead, three times in quick succession. The third blow achieved the desired result of caving in its crystal skull.

The creature would not return. Its demise grieved him. After all, it was only following orders, but he saw no other option. Copperfield stood up, still gazing down at the mess he had made of its face. The head now resembled a dropped melon.

"He was my friend," muttered a stranger's voice.

Copperfield's head darted up only to find another fleshmelta pointing at his chest. Now he understood why the others had not run into these woods. Why should they when they already had a patrol stationed in here? There was no telling how many more foot-soldiers were hiding around trees. Not that the numbers mattered. It only took one fleshmelta to kill him. "I had no other choice," he replied. "I did not wish his existence to end."

The foot-soldier shook his head. "I do not believe a word you say. Everything which comes from your mouth is going to be a lie. You are only concerned with saving your own worthless hide. Nothing else matters to you." It raised the fleshmelta a little lower. "I know this because our new Right Hand of God has said it is so."

"Your new Right Hand of God? Oh, how that makes me laugh. Your new Right Hand of God is a joke. Some rancid piece of disgusting flesh which shouldn't even have been allowed to do the job it was created for." Copperfield attempted to calculate the chances of him reaching his dropped fleshmelta before the foot-soldier fired. Even if he had been ridiculously optimistic, Copperfield wouldn't have gotten within a foot of the weapon before dying. "Your new Right Hand of God was supposed to freely give up his existence before our glorious God made the journey to this world. Just like your friend should have." He sighed. "Just like you too. Now put that weapon down."

"Tell me my colleague's name and I will ensure your death is quick. Otherwise, I shall remove your limbs one by one."

Any ideas of what to do now?

You're having a laugh. You're asking me for advice now? Oh God, that's hilarious. My advice? Easy. Don't get shot.

"I am serious. Put down that weapon."

"Fine, prepare to learn how to hop," it replied. "At least until I melt off your other leg."

Copperfield took a single step backwards and slowly lowered himself. "Wait. Just wait a moment. I do know his name. I know all your names. How could I not know that? I am the one who trained you. I am the one who showed you how to fight. How to be soldiers. You are all like family to me. Why else do you think I did not want to kill him?"

"Tell me his name!" screamed the foot-soldier.

Copperfield nodded. He then picked up the corpse and flung it at the other foot-soldier then dived to the side. He heard the weapon bark once, followed by a scream. He swivelled his head and saw the foot-soldier's leg clamped in his construct's huge jaws. The fleshmelta was on the floor. He ran over to his faithful creature and scooped the weapon out of a clump of nettles.

"Release him." He pushed the tip of the fleshmelta hard against the foot-soldier's head. "I was serious when I said that I wish you no harm." The distant sound of his other companions reminded Copperfield that his benign intentions would be no way reciprocated if he allowed the others to get any closer. "Go," he growled. "Go now and do not look back. Believe me when I tell you that I might not shoot you, but my construct is still grieving over the loss of her partner. She will easily run you down and end your existence before the others reach you."

The remaining foot-soldier took off. He walked backwards while watching the fleeing creature. It would not take it long to reach the others but by that time, Copperfield would be long gone. Thanks to the memories he retained from the captain, he knew these woods like the back of his hand.

Well done, you're still not dead. What do you intend to do now?

You mean after or before I purge you from this body?

CHAPTER THIRTEEN

The two boys were to call her Mrs. Howden and nothing else. She did have a husband at home, as well as two rather mean and protective sons living there too, so the two boys weren't going to try any funny stuff. Mrs. Howden also had a cat, called Trevor.

At first, Callum believed the woman they'd saved was only gobbing off due to the shock. He'd seen soldiers doing exactly the same back in the day; troopers who never usually said much about anything, suddenly telling anyone with ears they complete life stories after almost getting shot or blown up.

Thankfully, the noisy woman kept that ever-loving gob shut whenever the minions showed their ugly snouts. One second, Mrs. Howden was banging on about how she thought young Charlotte Brown was helping herself to the makeshift and possibly even the painkillers, as everyone knew that the camera covering aisle three hadn't worked in three years, the next second, the woman went as quiet as a mouse.

Her uncanny ability to sense their enemies freaked the hell out of him. Callum didn't comment on her radar-like talent, he was just glad they'd found her. Mrs. Howden had saved their arse twice now and he suspected the number would rise the closer they got to the town centre. Not that he was able to get a word in.

Both Callum and Gavin helped the woman over a broken wire fence which once separated a haulage company office from a pale cream brick building that had dozens of wooden blue pallets stacked against the wall.

When he was sure Mrs. Howden wasn't going to slip, he looked at Gavin, nodded once then pointed to the pallets and the wall. He then made a circle with his thumb and forefinger. Callum hoped the boy would understand what Callum's elaborate sign language meant. Not that he particularly cared.

Judging from the boy's panic-stricken expression, Gavin would have done anything to avoid being alone with the woman. Right now, she continued to explain to the boy why every supervisor wasn't worthy of the name and, in her opinion, should spend at least five years working the shop floor before even attempting to advance their careers. She knew every department inside out. She knew more about the shop in her little finger than any of those clowns would ever know.

Callum hurried over to the stack of pallets and began to climb while wondering how long it would be before Gavin told her to shut her pie hole. He carefully navigated around the protruding screws and wood splinters as he climbed. Callum reached the last pallet and rolled on the top. He then stood up and leapt onto the flat roof.

He hoped that the elevation would help Callum locate evidence of Harry, Malc, and Dosser's passing. Callum knew that none of them would still be under the flyover, not with all this happening.

Callum wasn't totally sure what Dosser and Malc would have done. If he was them, he'd have probably found somewhere to bed down, to stay out of the way of the walking nightmares which Harry so gleefully described. The fellow from the other world wouldn't have done any such thing though. Not him, not a chance.

Nothing moved down there, not even signs of the enemy. Callum sat on the edge of the building. He had spent the past several years trying to void the memories of the war from his head. Since his wife kicked him out of the house, Callum had tried every narcotic and pharmaceutical product he could get his hands on. Nothing had numbed him enough or wiped away the horrors that he'd witnessed and participated. Some of the shit he'd taken had even exacerbated those painful memories, made him relive them, over and over. In the end, Callum had gone cold turkey, believing time alone would eventually sort him out. Callum's heels banged against the top of a window. If he whacked the glass hard enough, he might even be able to break the glass. There was bound to be something worth swiping in there.

That idle thought brought a smile to his face. Here he was, in the middle of another worldly invasion, and still believing that nothing had changed. The truth of the matter was they were all like him, on the edge of buildings. Unlike Callum, every person clung to the edge by the tips of their fingers.

"We're all going to die," he whispered.

To think that he had done his best to run away from the hurt only for it to crash back into his life. Callum believed that there could be a joke in there somewhere, if he looked hard enough.

He really did want to smash the window by his feet.

"Do you mind if I sit up here with you?"

Callum bit his bottom lip to stop himself from shouting out. He shuffled away from the edge, turned around and glowered at Gavin. "What the hell are you doing up here? I thought you were supposed to be keeping an eye on the woman."

"Sorry, I didn't mean to scare you, man. To be honest, I kinda thought you had heard me. It's not like I sneaked up on you or anything." He moved closer to the edge and looked over. "Jesus. It's a long way down there." Gavin jumped back. "So, have you seen anything?"

The boy stood directly in front of Callum's face looking like some annoying brat, asking his dad if the steam trains were ever going to show up. Right at that moment, he so wanted to punch him hard enough to turn his face into a question mark. At the back of his mind, Callum kinda knew that the fury he now felt wasn't strictly all Gavin's fault. The anger stemmed from his frustration of not having the balls to face up to the simple fact that he should have at least attempted to piece his existence together, just after leaving the forces, if not just for his sanity but for the sake of the woman who once loved him. It was difficult to accept that he'd ruined his fucking life.

"Go on, man. Go back to her. Just give me another few minutes, Gavin."

"Do I have to? Come on, can't I stay up here with you? She's proper doing my head in. The old bag won't stop banging on about how everyone she works with can't do their job right. I'm telling you, she has some serious problems."

Callum grabbed the boy's shoulders and squeezed hard enough for Gavin to let out a sharp yelp. "Listen to me," he growled. "The poor dear is in deep shock. She's doing everything she can to hold onto the familiar and comfortable. The woman's gone through what is possibly the most traumatic event of her life. Right now, she needs a sounding board and until I say otherwise, that is you. Now do as you're told and get back down there."

"Fair enough, I guess you're the boss. There is this girl who works with her, she's called Shelly Crabtree. I'm sure I know that name. The old bag doesn't exactly paint her in bright colours but still, she does sound nice. Maybe she knows where the girl lives? She seems to know everything else about her."

"Are you done yet?"

"Yeah, sorry."

He sat back down in his old spot and continued to scan the deserted streets, looking for any sign of movement. Callum vaguely wondered if Mrs. Howden recognised him. It's not like she hadn't seen him before. Jessica Howden lived a few doors from the off-licence over on Alpine Street. The woman had already told the two of them in no uncertain terms that their task right now was to escort her home, to make sure that her burly son and handsome but strong husband were there.

The woman had no husband or son; she lived alone in a tiny two bedroom terrace house. Callum knew because she'd passed him numerous times on her way to buy her lotto scratch cards. She did this every Tuesday morning at nine in the morning without fail. Callum wasn't joking when he told Gavin that the woman lived for her strict daily routine. She had even dropped a pound coin into his hands the one time she won more than a tenner.

The normal people, the ones who lived in little houses and spent most of their time obsessing over their fellow workers, usually went out of their way to avoid people like him. Thanks to the dust plumes and the recent lack of care about their appearance, the normals all now looked pretty much identical to Callum and his fellow walking companions. Perhaps this was the reason why she hadn't put two and two together.

His pondering came to a sudden halt when he spotted movement below. Callum rolled away from the edge and got on his front, without taking his eyes from the spectacle now moving out of a side street on into the main road leading into the town.

"What is this?"

Callum had to blink a couple of times just to make sure he wasn't seeing things. It didn't matter that he'd already witnessed the ease in which these monstrous invaders would warp, squeeze, bend, and distort living tissue and transform it into anything they desired. Watching another completely different batch of melted freaks turn into the middle of the road still made Callum want to cross himself. They progressed along the road, keeping in three lines.

Were the ones on the outer edge protecting the ones in the middle? Judging by the layers of corrugated bone plates running down their flanks and the five curved horns jutting out of their faces, it seemed like a reasonable assumption. Were they some weird biological equivalent to heavy tanks? If that was the case, just what exactly were they protecting?

He squinted his eyes. Unlike the other things, the ones in the middle were harder to work out. From this distance, they looked like little old men, carrying half-full paddling pools on their backs. "You bloody idiot," he whispered when he remembered a little more of the account that Harry told them all last night.

The soldier told them the Goliaths relied upon the creatures they had designed to help protect them and to bring them food. That's exactly what this was. A food convoy. It didn't take a genius to figure out that those sickly yellow flesh sacs were not full of tomato soup. God, he'd give his right arm for his old rifle around about now. Okay, perhaps his right leg. He would be able to fire his rifle with only one bloody arm.

The two leading living tanks jumped forward then bunched up. The other tanks all stopped too. They all turned outwards and their bodies stretched up and bent over the creatures they were protecting. Had something spooked them? Callum risked lifting his head to gain a better view. He couldn't see anyone around, but he did hear a brief shout coming from behind Brandale's old newspaper print building.

Two shots rang out.

"Shit," he gasped, flinging himself back against the flat roof. Those two gunshots signalled the start of what sounded like a full-scale riot. It annoyed the hell out of him that he couldn't see what was going on, but he dared not risk it. If it were tooled-up civilians down there, then there's no telling where all their bullets were flying.

Callum stayed close to the roof surface and crawled back to the pallets. He peered over the edge and saw his two companions flattened against the wall. As expected, Mrs. Howden wasn't saying a word. He decided he liked her best like this.

They were alone down there, but Callum didn't think their apparent solitude would stay like that for much longer. This unexpected onrush of people, filling the streets with small arms fire, would doubtless end in misery. He hoped the invaders would be the losing side, his wish no doubt shared by the other humans, but Callum had been in many a battle and knew a lost cause when he saw one.

He hadn't heard the invaders respond with weapons fire of their own, but he knew it wouldn't be long in coming. Harry's mysterious rifle had already proven to Callum that these invaders could fight back. What hope did any of the good people of Brandale have against anything like a fleshmelta?

If he didn't find some way of pulling them back, every single one of them would be dead. Callum climbed down, his stomach seizing up when beneath the noise of the gunfire, he picked out his first human scream. His prediction was coming true. There'd be no sound of enemy gunfire. Harry had already told them all that every weapon used by the Goliaths and their ilk made no noise. The only evidence he'd know that they were fighting back would be the screaming voices becoming fewer and fewer.

"You two, get up on the roof and stay there until I get back and make sure you keep your heads down."

Mrs. Howden looked at the pallets, glanced at Gavin then returned to glare at Callum. "No. I am not going up there. I'll end up with splinters in my fingers. Not to mention that it doesn't look very safe."

She planted her hands on her hips. The pose suited her. Callum guessed she did that a lot when the woman decided to get her own way.

"What's going on, Callum? Who's shooting who, man?"

He grabbed the woman's shoulders and pushed his face up against hers. "You would be dead right now if my associate and I hadn't saved you. Those creatures were about to tear off your skin, Jessica Howden." She flinched when he casually dropped her first name into his dialogue. "Well, guess what! They're back, loads of them, and they're heading this way." He released the woman then pushed her towards the stack of pallets. "Your choice, Mrs. Howden. Stay here and die or climb and live." He spun around and stalked off.

"Where are you going?" shouted Gavin.

"To save more people," he shouted back, if there were any of them left alive. Callum ran alongside the building, aware that for each scream he heard possibly meant that the invaders had claimed yet another victim.

It didn't escape his attention that he was heading straight into a fire zone without a weapon. Callum might as well paint a big bullseye on his face. He skidded to a halt when he reached the corner of the building and dropped into a crouch. The screams were now getting few and far between.

He looked around the bricks. Several men and woman were still alive. Most of them were cowering behind a red Ford Mondeo. Two young men were still out in the middle of the street, crying and swearing while dragging a young blonde-haired woman along the floor and back to where their friends were hiding.

Callum saw nobody else left alive, just evidence of their passing. A dozen pools of steaming scarlet slop were all that was left of the people who'd gone up against these nightmarish creatures. The first line, consisting of twelve armoured living tanks, all moved in unison, pivoting their bodies a couple of degrees to the left. Now that he was at ground level and a good deal closer to these things, he now understood better why anyone not armed with anything smaller than a Browning M2 50 cal. would stand any chance of harming these monsters. There were a few pistols scattered around the road. He saw a couple of hunting rifles and even, what looked like an air pistol. Christ. What the fuck were these idiots playing at?

Thick bone-like plates covered their stubby legs, chest area, arms, and head. Only the gun mount, situated in the middle, appeared to lack any serious protection. Appearances could be deceptive. Harry had told him that these things had been on their world for a hundred years, so they would have had plenty of time and experience to work out any kinks.

From the mess they had made with eliminating any threat to their charges, Callum assumed that those organic cannons must belch out a corrosive fluid, something which ate through almost anything it touched. His theory received added weight when he noticed two melted side windows on a green van parked on the opposite side of the road. The closer he looked, the more he discovered that somebody must have hidden behind that van. A single boot with the limb still inside leaned against the front tyre. The fluid must have gone straight through the glass before landing on the unfortunate bugger who'd decided to take shelter behind it.

The monsters shifted a couple more degrees to the right. Oh shit, they were tracking the people still left out in the open! He raced out from behind the building, picked up one of the dropped weapons, and threw it straight at the armoured line. "Move it!" he shouted. "Get her out of the way." He paled when only five of them swivelled towards his position. All the others guns were still trained on the group to his left. Callum ran straight at them, just as a terrible high-pitched whine filled the air. Before he reached the group, several monsters jerked backwards a couple of inches before a narrow jet of pale orange fluid spurted out of their cannons. The acid-like substance washed over all three individuals, reducing them into puddles of lumpy goo in less than a second.

Another terrible high-pitched whine followed. Callum screamed himself. He raced towards the other survivors, jumping over the remains of the people he was trying to save, and dived into the group huddled behind that car. Callum landed hard. He gritted his teeth in pain when he felt something in his hand crack.

"Who the hell are you?" growled a deep male voice.

Callum looked at the speaker, a gorilla wearing a ripped sports top, black jeans, and scruffy beard, caked in dried blood. He ignored the gentleman's polite request to introduce himself and got onto his knees and gazed through the car windows. The monsters were pivoting again; this time, he just knew that they would fire in this direction.

He stood up, keeping his head below the car roof. "Come with me if you want to live."

"Fuck off, tramp!" replied the gorilla. "Yeah, that's right, I've figured out who you are now. I've seen you in town, searching through the bins and…"

Callum didn't even bother to stick around to listen to any more of his crap. He picked up the smallest member of the group, a young boy aged around eight, and raced back towards where his left Gavin and the woman.

A dog was the next one to follow him, then two more people. After a couple more seconds, another man ran after them. Callum reached the safety of the brick wall and put the boy down, hoping he wouldn't try to run back to the car. He sighed in relief when he saw the boy was more concerned with fussing over the dog than running over to that car.

None of the others had followed them over. Why could they not see that they weren't safe behind that car? Or was it more to do with the gorilla ordering them to stay put? "Come on!" he yelled. "Hurry up while there's still time." Only their time had just come to an end.

That horrible whine filled the air yet again. "Cover the boy's eyes. I don't want him to see this!"

Unlike the last time, there was screaming. Lots of screaming. The monsters fired off their volleys of corrosive liquid which, as he expected, turned those car windows into thick, clear glutinous slime. Some of the glass fell inside the vehicle but most of it liberally coated the people crouched behind the car. He watched the gorilla throw himself backwards and roll across the ground, both hands frantically beating against his skin. Two more stumbled out from behind the car and attempted to run towards Callum only for the monsters to fire again. Thankfully, their screaming ended the moment that orange fluid engulfed their bodies.

He slammed his palm over his mouth and nose in a vain attempt to stop the acrid stench coming from their dissolving bodies. Callum blinked away tears and wanted to turn away or at least close his eyes, but the shock of witnessing this slaughter wouldn't allow him to do either.

Three were left alive. Two teenage girls had escaped the worst damage. They must have moved back, away, towards the rear of the car just before those windows melted and showered their companions with the corrosive mixture. They were huddled together, their eyes fixed on the remaining man. His rolling had moved his body away from the car and out in the open. That whining assaulted his ears one more time, and moments later, two of those armoured tanks put the gorilla out of his misery.

Callum stood up and tried to leave the safety of the building only for the two men to drag him back. "Let go of me!" he growled. "I can still save them."

The younger man slammed his body into Callum's chest. "Don't be an idiot," he replied. "They're both dead already. You can't save them."

He stopped struggling when he noticed movement behind the girls. Two more living tanks had moved away from the column they were protecting and were now just a couple of metres away from them. The girls finally took their eyes off the remains of that last man and slowly turned around. The men pulled Callum further back, just as the whining filled the air again. He didn't hear either of them scream out.

"Thanks for saving us," said the girl. She pulled him out of the hands of the men and brought him closer. "Here, let me have a look at that hand. Looks like you've badly bruised it, but I don't think you've broken anything." She smiled up at him. "I'm Emily, by the way."

He nodded back. "Callum," he replied.

"I'm Raymond," said the younger man. "The old fella is called Ben and the dog's called Diesel. We don't have a clue what the kid's called. He hasn't said anything since we found him."

Ben shook his hand. "Thanks. Thanks for showing up went you did. You truly are an angel sent from God." He grinned then placed his hands on the other man's shoulders. "Did I not tell you that we would be saved from the demons?"

Raymond sighed. "Sure you did, old man. To be fair, you've said that a few times already."

Callum turned to the girl. "I'm truly sorry about the others."

She shrugged. "You don't have to be sorry. You did what you could. I'm just glad you were here at all. We'd all be dead if it weren't for you, Callum." She looked back towards the devastation. "To be honest, apart from Linda and Alice, I didn't know any of the others."

He guessed the girl to be around fourteen, perhaps fifteen. She'd be around the same age as Callum's own daughter. Oh Christ. With everything that had been going on, he hadn't paid a single thought to Kylie! What sort of a father was he, for God's sake? Callum felt the tears starting to flow again.

"Hey, are you okay?"

He nodded. "Yeah, sorry. Lots of extreme emotions flying around. My heads a bit mashed up, I guess. Shock and adrenalin. Beats vodka and crack hands down." Callum did even know where Kylie and her mum had moved to. He knew they weren't in Brandale anymore. That much he was sure about. Visiting their old home was the first action he'd undertaken once Callum's head was back into some kind of order. Callum didn't think they'd still be there and he wasn't disappointed. The new owners hadn't been much help. A large man, armed with a cricket bat, had run out and chased Callum down the street, threatening to call the police if he ever showed up again.

His next stop found him at Brandale's small library, located on the edge of town. His search there proved just as fruitless, but at least the nice old librarian hadn't chased him off the premises with a cricket bat despite his rather unpleasant body odour emptying the building in ten seconds flat. Callum hadn't really been too bothered about his smell while drinking himself into oblivion or abusing his body with whatever narcotic he was able to get hold of. That changed once he'd left the library after the nice lady patiently explained to Callum how to use the Internet to search for people, a skill he'd never even known existed twenty minutes previously.

"Are you sure you're okay, mister?"

The sound of Emily's worried question pulled him back to the present.

"Yes, sorry. I was miles away."

"Wish I was," she replied. "Where were you going? If you were thinking of going back into the centre, then I'd seriously think about choosing somewhere else. The streets are full of those bloody monsters, not to mention that I think the big one's coming back." She looked at the others, her gaze landing on the older man. "Anywhere away from that Bible-bashing tosspot would be nice as well."

The question of where to go next had plagued him since the arrival of those monsters too. If that column had come anywhere near Harry, then Callum would have bet his back teeth that the soldier from another world would have tried his best to blast it back to hell and unlike these Johnnies, Harry would have probably succeeded too. "Emily, have you seen anyone else on your travels? Three men. Two older than me, the third one a bit younger. That third man carried this weird-looking rifle."

She shook her head. "No, apart from the ones who you saw a minute ago. I didn't want to join up at first, 'cos the big guy in the black leather jacket would stop staring at my chest, but the kid and the dog seemed to like each other." She shrugged. "Dunno, maybe I'm a soft touch. Besides, if the big guy had tried anything, he'd have received a swift kick in the bollocks. Kinda feel a bit shitty about thinking all those horrible things about him now. You know, with him being dead and everything."

"Don't let it worry you, Emily." He left her alone and hurried back towards the corner of the building, hoping the monsters had moved off now that they had eliminated the threat. Callum choked back a terrified sob when he found one of the living tanks almost touching the outer wall. Thankfully, it faced the other way. Despite the terrible danger, Callum inched a little closer. He wanted to find out what they were doing. When he looked over the top of the beast, he immediately wished he hadn't. The living tanks were still protecting the other creatures.

They were busy sucking up the lumpy sludge deposited across the street. So much for them moving off. There's no chance of them sneaking back that way. He wasn't even sure his new friends would want to go back the direction they came.

What was he going to do now? Callum turned around and hurried back to the others while keeping his body against the wall.

When he returned, Callum found out that where they were to go next had already been decided. Both Mrs. Howden and Gavin had climbed off the roof and were already introducing themselves to the newcomers.

Gavin had already made a beeline towards the pretty girl and judging from her strained expression, the boy was trying out all his best chat-up lines. Unbelievable. You couldn't make this up. They were in the middle of the possible extinction of humanity and that fool was thinking with the contents of his trousers.

He walked over to Mrs. Howden who had caught the old man. She didn't look all that concerned that a couple of minutes ago, Callum had been so close to losing it with her. Then again, looking around the group, it looked like only he was showing the strain from their dire situation. Well, him and the kid. Maybe the others were better at hiding their feelings than Callum? He sighed. More than likely, they were just relieved not to actually be dead.

"Callum, I would like you to meet my minister. Thanks to you, our church will live on."

"Was it not the guiding hand of Jesus who showed him the way, Jessica?"

The woman nodded, like she'd just heard the most profound answer ever uttered by man or woman. Callum took a step back and wished Harry was here. That guy would soon knock some sense into these clowns. He wasn't though, and no matter how freaky their beliefs, they were his responsibility. He wasn't too sure how that came about, but it did feel like the right thing to do.

"Well, there's not much point in going home now," said Mrs. Howden, "now that my minister has returned to me. Perhaps we should all take shelter in our church? Minister, what do you think?"

Callum decided to stay silent on the big husband and burly son lie.

"I agree. The demons will not enter a place of God. That much, I am sure of." The old man looked to his right. "And it came to pass, when the children of Israel cried unto the Lord because of the Midianites, that the Lord sent a prophet unto them."

"Yeah, right. Look, is the place secure? You know, big heavy door, stuff like that?"

The old man nodded. "Of course. Thanks to the generous donations from the flock, we have the most up-to-date security. It seems that it is not only Brandale's unsaved who we have to keep out now."

Callum turned around and gathered the others around him. "This guy has a church not far from here. I think if might be a good idea to rest there and regain our strength. Perhaps have something to eat or something?" He felt relief at the collective nodding. He wasn't sure what he would have done if half of them decided they'd rather face the monster than listen to any more crap spewing from the gob of this Bible-bashing weirdo. Still, the one good takeaway of saving his arse is that Mrs. Howden won't be bothering anyone else now.

"Okay, Minister. The floor is yours. Lead the way. Preferably, away from the things behind us."

The old man nodded. He smiled at Mrs. Howden then began to walk north. The old man's posture had changed dramatically. He no longer looked like he was about to fall apart. Callum grabbed Gavin as he passed. "How many diffusers do you have left?"

He shrugged. "Not sure, about ten, I guess."

Callum stuck his hand out. "Give me a couple."

"Why, what are you planning?"

"I think she likes you, Gavin," he said, changing the sentence. "Come on, pass them over, dude. Hurry up, she's getting away from you."

"You're not coming with us, are you?"

Callum shook his head. "Don't worry, Gavin. I just need to try something out. I'll catch up. I know where you're going." He took off before Gavin had a chance to reply. He did feel a little guilty about leaving them to fend for themselves, but he believed it was worth the risk; besides, the church was only about a ten-minute walk from here.

The infusers that he had taken from Gavin were honeysuckle and morning dew. Callum wasn't sure that the last one was even a smell. He took a tentative sniff and immediately wished he hadn't. The stuff in the glass was just vile. "And people buy this shit?" he whispered. Callum then found himself thinking about all this parallel words stuff and wondered if there was a world where he didn't join up and consequently destroy his life. He saw another version of himself walking into his wife's house, kissing his daughter's forehead, asking what was for tea. He sighed. Even if such a duplicate did exist, Callum knew without a doubt that the other version of himself would think the liquid in here smelled like arse as well.

He looked over his shoulder and saw the others had already gone. That made him feel a little better. Callum didn't think he would ever be comfortable around people, not after being on his own for so many years. He reached the end of the building and looked around the corner. The convoy had already moved on, taking with them the puddles of dissolved people. They won't be too far. Callum didn't think they could move very fast.

Perhaps it might have been a better idea to climb onto the roof first? He shrugged to himself. It didn't really matter. It shouldn't be too difficult to pick up their tracks. Callum ran over to the car the others had sheltered behind and leaned to the right so he could glance down Edward Street. There was no sign of them down there. He ran over to the truck on the other side of the square and grinned when he noticed movement. "There you are!"

Callum raced after them. He got the vial ready. The first monsters in the column turned into Grandford Road. "This is for the ones you've just killed!" he yelled. Callum stopped, flung his arm back, and chucked the vial. It arced through the air and smashed against the armoured shell of the last tank in the line.

Nothing happened. The foul-smelling liquid just flowed off the surface and dripped on the floor. "That's not fair, you bastard," he shouted. "You're supposed to dissolve!" Was it the armour? Maybe it only worked with the soft parts? He ran forward and only stopped when he almost collided with the last monster. Callum threw the remaining vial, whooping when it smashed into the walking containers. Again, nothing happened, apart from the armoured monsters finally noticing human burger meat standing next to them. Two of the living tanks began to pivot.

"Oh shit!" Callum spun around and ran as fast as he could, heading back towards the alley in between the two buildings. That dreadful whining had already started. He dived to the left and smacked into the side of a black-panel van. He moaned in terror, fully aware that if he didn't get out of the way, he'd be dead!

Callum dropped to the floor and rolled under the van, a split-second before a stream of corrosive liquid gushed past the side of the van. He suppressed the urge to vomit then rolled out the other side. Surely, nothing else could go wrong?

Why hadn't he tried this whilst on the rooftop? Oh no, not Callum. Why not sneak up on them and just hope for the best? He managed to get back to the alley without any of the living tanks following him. Perhaps it was a good job he sent them off without him. At least that way, he wouldn't have put any of them at risk.

Without him around, they were so much safer. It made him wonder why he was so eager to catch up to them.

Callum only slowed down when he caught the sight of the dog. As he turned into Benson Street, Callum saw the rest of them all grouped up outside a bus shelter.

He couldn't understand why they had stopped. The church was only across the road. Unless they were waiting for him? If that was the case, why weren't they hiding in the shelter?

The closer he got, Callum noticed something weird about the air, a couple of metres from the shelter. It was like gazing into the distance on the boiling hot day. Everything beyond the effect rippled and gyrated. Is that what he was looking at? A curtain of heat?

The minister pulled away from Mrs. Howden's grasping hands. He put his arms in the air and started to walk towards the phenomenon while singing at the top of his voice. Callum stopped dead. He clenched his hands into fists while attempting to control his jittery guts. "Turn back, you silly bastard! Turn back…"

Before he could finish the sentence, the minister walked into the barrier and burst into flames.

"Things surely can not get any worse," he murmured, "and don't call me Shirley."

CHAPTER FOURTEEN

The several survivors were all huddled at the far end of the damp cave. Their quiet conversations drifted over to where Harry sat. He felt uncomfortable for thinking it, but the people he had managed to save now reminded him of well-fed hens, all huddled together, all equally anxious while hoping the foxes and dogs outside do not discover their hiding place.

In his world, the dogs and foxes, as well as most other four-legged mammals, had died out decades ago, but they still had hens, as well as 'other' predators which preyed upon a terrestrial creature stupid enough to venture outside.

After a moment's contemplation, Harry decided that it wasn't harsh at all to compare them to such a simple animal. The humans in this world, with the exception of the first few homeless individuals that he encountered last night, were all so ill-equipped to cope with this traumatic disaster. Quite frankly, the sheer fact that even a few of them had managed to stay alive for more than a couple of hours after the Goliaths invaded surprised him.

He tore his gaze away from the setting sun, casually wiping some of the cavern moss from the palm of his hand and onto his blanket before turning his head. The six men, women, and one teenage girl behind him, all huddled together at the rear of the cave, were quietly talking amongst themselves. Strangers before the traumatic events a few hours ago, now becoming fast friends, all together because of the two Goliaths and their familiars, currently hunting down every human in the vicinity.

Harry's keen hearing picked out a few words from their conversations. The teenage girl grieved the loss of her mother. Something took the woman while she was in the bathroom. She heard the window smashing, followed by a long-drawn-out shriek. The teenage girl told the assembled audience that seconds later, she heard what sounded like screaming coming from every other person on his street.

If he hadn't heard movement from above his head when Harry had searched that particular house, then it is likely that the girl, now being comforted by an older woman would now either be dead, taken by the type of creature which took her mother, or wandering the deserted streets, looking for anyone to help her.

Now that Caroline had finished her tale, the others were either shaking their heads in sympathy or reassuring her with false hope that perhaps her mother may have gotten away with whatever had pulled her through that window. One of the other survivors, a middle-aged woman, took Caroline in her arms and gave her a gentle hug while asking her if she had anyone else.

Caroline explained that her younger brother was with her dad. He always went over to his flat every other weekend. Dad took him to the match. Little Pete so loved his football. It was supposed to be her turn to go see him next weekend. Dad had promised to take her to see the latest Disney movie.

The older woman cracked a faint smile. She ordered the girl to keep telling herself that before she knew it, Caroline would be back in the arms of her dad and her brother. The woman looked over at Harry and gave him a soft smile before turning back to the girl and telling her that perhaps her dad and Pete were in one of the other groups.

Harry nodded at the pair of them before turning back towards the cave entrance. The evening sun had almost touched one of the few remaining buildings not destroyed by the two Goliaths. When the light vanished, Harry would feel a little easier to move his chickens and join up with the others.

Once he had rejoined the others at their temporary base, Harry fully intended to find somewhere safer and a lot deeper underground for the remains of this town's population. This tiny pocket of humanity needed to survive, and Harry was prepared to do everything in his power to ensure that it did.

He had already sacrificed too much recently to allow the familiars and their Gods to finish off this town. Harry looked across at Caroline who had begun to relax, still in the arms of the older woman. Was she dreaming of a possible reunion with the rest of her family? It saddened him to know that the reunion was never going to happen. He knew for a fact.

The house had shown Harry a glimpse of another individual before he eventually discovered the girl hiding under her bed. From the description which Caroline gave to the woman, Harry could only assume that the mutilated corpse that he fell over in the living room was the girl's little brother. How he got there without Caroline knowing was a mystery which would never be solved as Harry never intended to reveal the truth to the girl. He feared that news like that could send her over the edge.

They all needed time to recover from their individual traumas. Harry knew that many would not fully mend, but hopefully the mental scar tissue they grow over the wounds would be at least thick enough for them to contribute to the new existence which now lay ahead. A life where the monsters would rule this world for another one hundred years.

He decided that perhaps he was being too harsh on them after all. It would just take a little longer for them to adapt to their new way of life, certainly far longer than the likes of Malc and Dosser. Harry found himself stroking the surface of the blanket, once again, marvelling at this world's incredible ingenuity. They still had a few blankets left over from the time when the Goliaths invaded his world, but none felt as luxurious as this one.

The blanket's softness so reminded him of his surviving humans. Soft, a little plump, and obviously used to a more sedate lifestyle. Just like the hens, he remembered from when he was a child.

They kept their numerous food storage bunkers a few klicks away from sanctuary and well away from any known concentration of their enemies. In his lifetime, they had managed to increase the number of bunkers from six to nine. Their bunkers were now able to feed and provide for almost forty families all through the year. From what he heard, the elders now believed that their sanctuary was the largest one on this mainland.

Each one stored, grew, and kept a few animals, mainly rats and chickens, as they were the easiest to feed. They used to keep cats too but gave up after a couple of years as they were a nightmare to feed. It seemed stupid to give food to something which could feed a human.

Harry used to so enjoy visiting the stores back when he was first allowed to start patrolling with the older men. It helped to reinforce the stories that the elders used to tell him from the time before the arrival of the monsters when animals like these were able to roam across the land without fear of becoming another part of an enemy defiler or an extra food source for a foot-soldier.

He never told anyone else, but Harry loved stroking the chickens and the rats. He even imagined how cool it would be to sneak one of them back and keep it as a pet.

Harry shook away the reverie and glanced back at the survivors. Apart from Caroline, they were all sleeping. The girl looked too frightened to shut her eyes. He was about her age when they finally allowed him to start patrolling above ground. Is that what this little girl had to look forward to? Assuming they even survived this initial invasion?

Harry froze. He grabbed his fleshmelta, frantically gesturing to the girl to move back to the far end of the cavern before he crept closer to the edge of the cave. From his vantage point, Harry could see all the way up to the edge of the city. Lush green fields, full of waist-high plants, separated this cave from a stretch of thinly placed trees. It was the plants that he stared at. Something was running through those plants and heading for him at high speed. Harry lifted up the fleshmelta, took aim, and prepared to fire.

A grubby hand poked up through the dense foliage, followed by a head. "Wait!" cried Dosser. "Don't shoot. It's just me."

Harry reached down and helped the older man up. It took a lot of self-control not to shout at this thoughtless idiot. "I almost killed you," he whispered.

The other man nodded, trying to catch his breath. "I know and I'm really sorry for not following your detailed recognition instructions. I just didn't think." Dosser looked back towards the field then stared straight at Harry. "Oh man. Malc is in trouble! We so need your space gun!"

"Where is he?"

"I'll take you."

Harry grabbed the man's wrist. "It might be better if you tell me where he is, Malc. I don't think it's a good idea to leave these people without a guardian."

"But you don't know where anything is!" he cried.

"There's a red brick three-storey building, decorated with stone dragons near to where the edge of the town ends."

"The library, yeah."

Harry raised his eyebrows. "Oh right. Well, Dosser and I found three kids sheltered behind the back of a supermarket, near to that library. They, I mean the invaders, surprised us when we were running across the road." He took Harry's arm. "They're hiding in a shop with a bright blue shop front." He drew in a deep breath. "You need to hurry, Harry, I don't know how long they're going to last."

Harry climbed down and jumped into the king grass then sprinted through the vegetation, heading straight for the red brick building. He looked back just the once to find Dosser and the little girl gazing back. Caroline gave him a brief wave. Dosser looked so worried and Harry did kinda echo the emotion. He so hoped that Malc was okay. Harry gave the girl a wave then increased his speed, needing to find Malc as soon as possible.

It did feel a little odd to find himself being worried over another human being. He guessed it was because only Harry really knew what these evil creatures were capable of. It didn't help to know that he still believed that everyone in this world, even the homeless, lived a pampered existence, none of them knowing what true hardship really was.

Harry flattened his back against the red brick building and peered around the corner. The road opposite did appear empty, but Harry was far from convinced. Dosser had just ran past here at high speed, meaning the patrolling familiars, if any were close be, would now be on alert.

He bent down, picked up a squashed tin can, and threw it as hard as he could in the opposite direction to where he wanted to go. The can landed close to a curb and clattered along the side of the road until it came to a stop beside the front tire of a small blue car. A moment later, a thin tentacle-like appendage burst out from a grate, wrapped itself around the can, and pulled it under the road. It took it less than two seconds.

He scanned the surrounding area, looking for more grates and finding another three directly in his path. Harry scooped up another piece of rubbish before he ran across the road. He stopped next to the corner of a bank and attempted to get his bearings. He sighed silently. His trek seemed so clear when he had the advantage of height. Now, down here, Harry feared he would get lost in this labyrinth of buildings if he took just one wrong turning. Perhaps he should have allowed the older man to accompany him after all.

Harry spotted movement out of the corner of his eye. Something just slithered under a car, close to him, probably another one of those tentacles. He moved backwards two paces, watching his shadow as it passed over one of those grates. A moment later, that tentacle shot back down. It wasn't just noise and movement. A sudden change in light activated those things too. Harry imagined the older man by his side, jabbering on non-stop, and shuddered. No, he was best where he was, in those caves. Harry would be dead by now if he had brought Dosser.

He threw himself into an alcove moments before three foot-soldiers ran past him. Harry didn't need Dosser after all. The best way to find his friends was to look for the largest concentration of familiars. Harry emerged from the alcove and followed the foot-soldiers at a discreet distance. Sure enough, two minutes later, the patrol joined a larger company. Even from where he stood, Harry saw several more foot-soldiers and three collectors crowded around the front of the shop with the bright-blue sign over its door. This had to be the place.

A single shotgun blast blew out another window, showering two foot-soldiers in glass. The pair of them jumped back and almost fell off the edge of the curb. They weren't going to last much longer in there. The gathered freaks might be reluctant to storm the shop right now, but the stand-off won't stay like that. Harry risked being spotted and climbed onto the roof of a black car. Just as he thought: two bio-tanks were slowly making their way towards the shop. There was no way of shooting his way through the front, not now; there were too many. There had to be another way inside though. He shifted his attention to the edge of the building and spotted a gap between this shop and the next. That had to lead to the back. There was his route.

He climbed down, crouched behind the car, checked for any grates then raced across the road. One collector noticed his appearance and started to sound the alarm. Harry shot it in the face for its trouble. He reached the gap between the buildings, and checked to see if it did actually lead somewhere before he walked backwards down it, keeping his aim fixed on the way in. No more were following him. Was the collector the only creature to notice him? It seemed that way. The remaining collector and the foot-soldiers probably thought a stray bullet from somewhere else in town downed their colleague. At least, that's what he hoped.

Harry wasn't sure how he was going to get Malc and the survivors he'd collected past the assembled monsters at the front of the shop, but he decided not to dwell on that right now. He needed to get them out of the building first.

His boot heel scraped against the side of the wall. Harry glanced down and spotted movement reflected from the small puddle in between his legs. He threw himself to the floor, a moment before an energy bolt from a fleshmelta passed over his head. He gritted his teeth and moaned in pain when the heat from the bolt singed his hair. He rolled onto his back and fired once while sitting up. His bolt hit home, a single foot-soldier standing in the courtyard behind the shop.

He jumped to his feet and raced out into the courtyard. He fired another two shots, turning the other foot-soldier into a puddle of stinking gloop. It wasn't the only foot-soldier out here. Harry spotted the last one trying to scramble over a five-foot stone wall at the back of the courtyard.

"Oh no you don't," he growled. Harry ran over, viciously pulled it off the wall, and slammed the side of the creature's head against a flagstone. The satisfying sound of its crystal skull shattering told him he'd killed the vile creature.

Harry dropped the corpse, grabbed his weapon, and spun around, getting ready to fire again when he thought he'd miscounted.

"Don't shoot!" cried Malc. "It's just me."

Harry lowered the gun, clipped the weapon on his back then ran over to the old man. Two strangers were helping him through a broken window. He nodded at the three young men and two women before he crouched beside Malc's blood-soaked trousers. "Can you stand on it?" Harry tore away some of the material but couldn't see much of anything in this dim light.

Malc slowly nodded. "I guess so."

"That's not good enough." Harry looked straight at the blond-haired man to Malc's left. He ignored the offered handshake. Harry grabbed the man and moved him forward a couple of paces. "You look strong enough. I want you to take charge of this man," he said. "Help the others get him over that wall then carry him, the best you can. Do you understand me?"

The man nodded.

He turned to Malc. "Get these guys back to Dosser then see if anyone there can take a look at your leg." He unclipped the fleshmelta. "I'll keep the creatures busy while you lot get away." A terrible whining filled the air followed by a tremendous crash coming from the other side of the shop. The bio-tanks had arrived. "Why are you still here?" he hissed. "Come on, move it." It took the small group a couple of moments to cross the courtyard. Harry waited until most of them were over the wall before firing a couple of shots into the dark shop. Harry doubted he'd hit any of the advancing creatures, but he just needed to slow them down for a bit longer.

Every member of the group had now vanished. He fired a couple more shots into the shop then he picked up the dead foot-soldier. "You have one more duty to perform," he whispered. Harry held it in front of him and ran back through the gap between the two buildings. All he saw when he peered around the corner was a single collector. All the others must be inside. That was not good. Malc's leg injury would slow them all down; they'd be easy pickings for the creatures if they followed their route.

Harry dropped the corpse, pulled down the fleshmelta, and fired a single shot at the collector's expanded sac. The remains of countless liquefied humans spread out across the road. The collector released a long, drawn-out bird-like screech before keeling over.

"Be gone, vile creature," he snarled. Harry picked up the corpse, held it up, and waited. Sure enough, two foot-soldiers ran out from the shop. They saw the dead collector then saw the corpse that Harry hid behind. Their posture suggested caution but not alarm. As he hoped, they thought the collector had been cut down by sniper fire. He waited until they were right on top of him before he threw the corpse at them and opened fire. Harry killed them both before either of them had a chance to go for their weapon.

Three more foot-soldiers ran out of the shop just as Harry got to the other side of the road. Unlike the first two soldiers, these three burst out of the shop, already firing their fleshmeltas. Harry had to throw himself into an open doorway to avoid one of the bolts removing his head. Harry stayed close to the floor and scuttled around a display full of cereal boxes.

The foot-soldiers had followed him inside. Once they were all through the door, the foot-soldiers split off and ran in opposite directions, with one of the creatures heading straight for him. Harry shuffled closer to the metal shelving. He waited for it to reach his position before taking out his knife and thrusting it up through its jaw and into the base of its brain. Harry caught it as it collapsed and gently laid the thing on the floor beside him.

He could still hear crashing and plasma fire coming from the shop on the other side of the road, meaning some of them were still trying to locate Malc and his group. What a dilemma. Harry desperately needed every enemy, including the bio-tank, to converge in the building, but he wasn't all that keen on actually dying. He had no other choice but to compromise his cover to draw the rest of them in here. Harry ran towards the bank of checkouts, keeping his head down. He grabbed a tin off one of the shelves as he passed and threw it as hard as he could at the shop window.

The glass didn't break, but the tin did leave a spider crack in the middle. Harry ignored the shouting coming from somewhere behind him and picked up one of the swivel chairs from behind a checkout bank and threw that at the shop window. The additional weight easily finished off the job started by the food can. It also almost got him killed. Two plasma beams cut a path through the computer screen next to his chest. Harry dove forward and rolled to the side, just as another shot turned the floor next to his foot into a pool of molten rock. He scurried towards the exit, noting that a whole bunch of creatures were now running out of the shop opposite his. Every single one was heading towards his position and they all carried a weapon of some kind. His plan worked alright but too well. Harry could not see any way of surviving the next couple of minutes.

"It's better odds behind me then out there," he said. Harry jumped onto the checkout belt. He drew a bead on the shocked foot who was sneaking up on him and shot it through the face. He jumped down, shot at the other one, and missed. The surviving foot-soldier fired at the same time. Its bolt slammed into the wall directly above Harry's head, causing a cascade of tins to fall on him. The sudden weight caused his knees to buckle. He crashed onto the tiles and his fleshmelta skidded across the floor.

The foot-soldier sauntered over to Harry, booting his weapon under one of the fixtures as it passed. The creature raised its own fleshmelta and uttered something it another language. Harry assumed it was mocking him. Not that it mattered. He was going to die here, but at least the others had gotten away. It said something else in its own language. Harry glowered at the foot-soldier, refusing to allow it to see fear in Harry's eyes.

"Go on then, you vile fucking piece of shit. Go ahead, kill me."

It laughed at Harry just as something arced over from the next aisle and smacked into the side of its head. It was a tin of beans. Harry watched, fascinated as it dropped onto the floor and rolled under the fixture, coming to rest beside his fleshmelta. Another tin hit the creature. Harry crawled out from under the tins and rolled towards the fixture. He pushed his arm under, listening to a human voice call the other foot-soldier a variety of colourful insults. His fingers curled around the fleshmelta. He pulled it out, took aim and fired, melting the back of its legs.

A pair of hands grabbed Harry and pulled him up. "We do meet in odd places, Harry," said Callum. "Come on, let's get you out of here." He pointed to a back room door, next to a wall of chest freezers. "That's our way out, man. Let's get out of here!"

CHAPTER FIFTEEN

They were trying to corral him into what his memory strand knew as an old market hall. It didn't take a genius to realise it was a trap. The place was bound to have over a dozen foot-soldiers, as well as a bio-tank or two ready and waiting for him. It made total sense. It was really the only way to exterminate such a dangerous foe as himself.

Their plan was doomed to fail. How could it not? It had been him who had trained them in similar operations. It probably explained why he now had two guardians on his tail, attempting to run him into the ground. They were succeeding too, despite their huge bulk, the huge monsters faster than him.

Take the next turning, said the memory strand. *We can hide in that car showroom. At least until you have got your breath back. If you carry on like this, those things will run you into the ground.*

I don't need any advice from you, he growled, taking the turning anyway. The memory strand was correct. The bone armour which had grown across most of his body, although excellent for deflecting bolts from energy weapons and bladed weapons, was not great for running.

The captain raced down a narrow side-street then threw himself on the ground and shuffled under a white van parked on the corner. Sure enough, the two guardians ran past the van. He wasted no time in crawling out the other side of the vehicle and running back towards the showroom. It wouldn't take his pursuers long to realise that he'd tricked them. He slowed down when he reached the edge of the showroom and vaulted over the chain-link fence.

Are you sure this is a good idea?

Trust me.

The captain wasn't sure he liked that tone of voice. He couldn't further inquire as the annoying memory strand had already named every make of vehicle in here even before Copperfield was able to enter the building. He ran past several cars and pushed through the glass door and sighed with relief as the cool air washed over his sweating bulk. The captain wanted to close his eyes and enjoy the feeling. He also wanted the memory strand to stop quoting car statistics in his head.

Silence, fool, or be silent forever.

Yeah, about that. Thing is, I don't believe you are able to do that. I mean, if you did have this mythical ability, why haven't you already done it?

The captain growled quietly while shifting his position to ensure one of those two guardians didn't see him. This is your last chance.

I still don't believe you. Admit it, you need my expertise.

Sure I do, because you spouting out the engine specifications of a Jenson Interceptor is really going to stop those two guardians from tearing me into wet lumps, small enough to fit down a grate

What are you blathering on about, you idiot? Your guardians aren't even here. We lost them, remember? Thanks to my advice and help, obviously.

The captain so wanted to slap the smug bastard. Was he really so naive? He hurried over to the back of one of the cars, ignoring the memory strand's predictable gabble of car statistics, and settled down behind it. From his position, he could clearly see the new God striding closer to this place as well as the appearance of a few foot-soldiers. The captain so wished he could share in the memory strand's naive thinking, but sadly, that could not be the case.

He heard a distinctive sound of something hard scraping along the concrete floor. So, he wasn't alone in here. The noise came from somewhere behind him. He didn't bother turning around to see what it was or, more to the point, who it could be. The scent of human had already filled his sensitive nostrils. From the faint scent of flowers hidden under sweat, fear and meat grease, the captain perceived his hidden guest to be a female. He didn't bother informing the memory strand that they were not alone, nor did he try to find some way of punishing it. There was no need. The memory strand would no doubt be crawling under a metaphysical stone to hide in shame.

The two guardians were back, and even from behind do this car, he saw they were early in the best of moods. The captain instinctively jumped when the pair crash through the plate glass windows.

Don't panic. They don't know we're in here. Try to stay calm. Don't move and they'll be gone in a few moments.

His memory strand's annoying naivety was back and in full force too. Was it really that idiotic? *They've just smashed their way through the window. Of course they know I'm in here.* Maybe it wasn't just a lack of brains. He suspected it was more to do with the memory strand's basic personality. The human had gone through his entire life expecting others to bow down to him and not ask questions. Ironically, the man's arrogance had been one of the reasons why he'd decided to attach himself to the man. Being so full of itself clearly had not diminished the memory strand's perceptiveness. It was correct about him being unable to flush it out of this host's mind. He had left it too long. The memory strand was well and truly embedded in now. Not that he was too concerned. If it started to get too big for its boots again, he could always show it a few more scenes of his wife coupling with his brother.

It smashed the glass in order to make you jump, to startle you. It is standard procedure. Make a sudden, loud noise in order to flush out the prey. Standard search techniques, that's all. Now calm down, stop twitching, and be patient.

The two guardians stopped moving. He almost believed it. That last about three seconds when it became clear that the new God was indeed striding towards the showroom and bringing along its associated familiars. The guardians were waiting for extra eyes. The flyer would swarm through the smashed window, circle the ceiling, locate him, and transmit his coordinates to the rest of the familiars. The captain gripped the fleshmelta and slowly pulled it towards him. The weapon was useless against guardians, but it was devastating against a bunch of flyers.

We need to get out of here! He brought up the fleshmelta and aimed at the ceiling. The creature might be immune to the weapon's energy, but the material up there certainly wasn't. If he could bring the ceiling down on them, it might buy him enough time to get out of here!

Don't you dare. You can't lose your nerve. They're about to leave. You need to trust me on this.

The power of the memory strand's belief almost made him wonder if it could be right after all. That changed when the captain heard another noise. He glanced up. It was coming from the ceiling. It sounded like running feet. He moaned in annoyance and desperately looked for a better place to hide. It wasn't the ceiling but the roof! It must be foot-soldiers, what else could it be?

He ignored the memory strand coming up with a ridiculous excuse as to why another aspect of the new God's familiars were almost on top of him. The captain took his gaze off the ceiling and the two stationary monsters and turned around. A pair of bright blue eyes stared at him through a gap between two cars. He ignored the human and focused on the back wall.

When he spotted the first foot-soldier scrambling through a narrow gap, close to the ceiling, he so wanted to shout out in triumph just to reinforce the fact that, as he said all along, his memory strand knew fuck all about anything. Common sense got in the way and instead, he took aim and turned the creature into a dirty red wall stain. As expected, the two guardians reacted in typical fashion. They both released ear-popping roars followed by them charging towards the source of the fleshmelta blast, casually tossing aside any vehicle while got in their way. He scurried across the floor and dived behind a sturdier vehicle.

Two more foot-soldiers had managed to clamber through the gap while he'd been occupied. One jumped onto the flat roof of the showroom office and lay flat while the other one hooked an arm through a hole in a vertical girder. The captain managed to liquidise the bastard before it could bring up its own weapon.

Still think they're going to pass us by? He so wanted to gloat but it now seemed pointless considering the slim chance they had of getting out of this in one piece. His last shot helped to triangulate his position. At this rate, the guardians wouldn't need the approaching flyers.

You need to take out that spotter!

I'm so lucky to have you in me, he replied sarcastically.

It's not just you anymore. You have to save that woman too.

You really are insane. I'm not saving any human. The best she can expect from me is a quick death. That is, if I decide to eat her face. Perhaps, I should do that? The energy I'll receive from consuming her flesh might give me the much-needed boost I'll need to get out of this situation alive.

It's time for you to choose whose side you're on. Why can't you admit it that your own kind have betrayed you? They'll never accept you back.

Shut up. I'll deal with you and my current dire situation when I'm out of here and safe enough so I can work out what happened. As far as I'm concerned, the only one to betray me was that piece of excrement. By trying and failing to do the job that he alone was built to do.

You're wrong, man. Can't you see that? Come on, you must have been human once.

Something deep within him shifted when the memory strand said that, another memory strand, this one long forgotten. One that should have been purged thousands of years ago. He cannot allow the new strand learn of its existence.

Why do you even care about what happens to the human race, Copperfield? You hate nearly everybody, including your wife. Do I need to remind you yet again of how you used to treat that poor woman?

The two guardians charged into the heavy vehicle at the same time as two more foot-soldiers cambered through the hole and started to crawl down the wall. He wanted the rage and scream. Foot-soldiers were not designed to do that. Only his personal fighters should have that ability. This was yet another example of their meddling.

"Enough of this," he growled. The captain moved away from the vehicle and ran towards the wall, running straight past the cowering girl who doing her utmost to squeeze into a gap half her size.

You didn't stop to snack on her face. I suppose that's a start.

He leapt onto the wall and clamoured up, heading straight towards the closest foot-soldier who had made the fatal mistake of stopping in order to unclip the fleshmelta off its back. He roared before swinging his right arm out in a low arc. His long claws caught the fleshmelta's stock. He pulled it out of the foot-soldier's grasp and dropped it.

"Your kind don't belong crawling up and down walls," he growled, scuttling towards the terrified creature. He grabbed its neck and pulled it off the wall. "Did your new master give you wings as well?" He released his grip and followed the screaming foot-soldier as it plummeted down. Its scream abruptly stopped when the creature smashed against the concrete. "I guess not. What a shame."

His memory strand's urgent shouting reminded him of the foot-soldier's companions who were, even now, getting ready to take him out. He scuttled closer to the roof of that office then slowed when he saw the remaining foot-soldiers suddenly clip their fleshmeltas on their back and run over to the edge of the roof and jump off it. What the hell were they doing?

He found out the answer to that one when the roof on the other side of the showroom collapsed. The Goliath had arrived! One of its enormous legs slammed through the roof, its foot flattening one of the cars. Several flyers swooped through the hole, two of them heading straight for him while three flew towards the screaming female. He pulled up the fleshmelta and killed the two approaching flyers. Why won't that annoying human stay quiet? Her noise had already attached the attention of the two guardians.

Instinct told him to use the distraction to get as far away from here as he could. That gap which lead outside was just seconds away, but no matter how hard he tried, the captain could not do it. He moaned in frustration and fury when he finally realised why.

The memory strand had located and dug up the other memory strand, the one that he should have purged all those thousands of years ago when he too suffered the fate that he unleashed upon Copperfield. He was close to blacking out. If that happened while still inside, then he really would die. Did that memory strand not understand that if he died, then so would he?

The captain leapt off the wall and onto the roof of a car. A single fleshmelta bolt almost ended him right there. He glanced to his left and found the two foot-soldiers hadn't left after all. The bastards had taken up position at the other side of the showroom.

Those two guardians had already boxed her in. She wasn't going to survive this if he didn't do something drastic. He jumped off the car roof, clamped up the Goliath's leg then threw himself onto the back of a guardian. He dug his claws in and, with his free hand, punched a sizeable hole through the creature's armoured carapace. His strength had increased tenfold since their last encounter. The guardian flung its head back and the bone stubs positioned around the base of the creature's neck slammed into the captain's forehead. He growled at the sudden pain and lost his grip. He had to roll away to avoid the furious guardian from stomping on his head. He scrambled to his feet, ran through the other guardian's legs, and squeezed between the two vehicles which shielded the woman from the monsters. "Come with me," he growled. "We don't have much time."

The ungrateful bitch responded to his help by shrieking even louder and trying to get under one of the cars. "I so wish I could leave you here to die." He grabbed her leg, pulled the struggling woman back to him, lifted her up, and punched her hard in the face. Her body immediately went limp. The captain threw her over his shoulder and ran for the wall, fully aware that they were all after him how. He tried to keep at least one of those guardians between them and those foot-soldiers. That worked fine until he leapt onto the wall. He scaled the wall, while dodging from those two foot-soldiers. Just as he reached the hole, one of those bolts caught his left foot. Both the captain and the memory strand screamed as the superheated plasma turned bone, muscle, and plate armour into stinking red slime.

He pushed the woman through the hole and followed her out, both landing in long grass behind the showroom. Although both he and the memory expected the pain of losing his foot, the process started by that interfering memory strand could not be halted. His long-buried memory, the remains of who he was back when he too was human, could not be stopped.

The captain unclipped the fleshmelta and placed the stock under his elbow then threw the woman over his back again then hobbled as fast as he could away from the back of the showroom. He reached the tip of a hill at the same time as he saw the Goliath move forward. Rough land, wild trees, and thick vegetation covered the floor below.

A thick grey fog rolled across the landscape of his mind. The captain pulled the woman from his back and dropped her down the slope. He threw his fleshmelta down too. He had run out of time. He threw his body forward at the same time as that long-buried memory strand finally burst free.

***

Tirok Nar held up his muscular right arm, made a fist then spread out his fingers. The rest of his hunting party dropped to one knee and waited for him to issue the next command. He picked up a handful of the reddish dirt, rubbing it between his thumb and fingers before dropping the stuff. Tirok gave his digits a cautious sniff. The faint smell of old spoor on his fingers. This pleased him greatly. This land wasn't as dead as it looked.

There were no tracks, other than the tell-tale signs made by the demons. Tirok gritted his teeth. What made him fall into the trap of calling the new plague of stranger predators demons? He was their leader, the only one capable of leading his people out of this supposedly dire situation. That was not going to happen if he started thinking the plague were a curse brought upon the tribe from some vengeful God.

The plague could have taken all the animals just like those vile creatures ate the Keeshar tribe, as well as half their own tribe, but Tirok refused to believe that the land was completely divided of all life. He knew that was not true anyway, his scouts had already reported back that there still was life beyond the caverns and this corroborated their reports. This spoor was no more than a couple of days old.

One of the hunters shifted their position. He gritted his teeth in annoyance. Was it so difficult to stay still for such a small amount of time? Tirok did not need to turn around to know who could not stay still. His second-in-command, Bailin Cun, coughed. What had he done in a previous life to deserve such an incompetent waste of skin?

He was fully aware that Cun had been doing everything in his power to undermine Tirok's authority. He even had the nerve to announce to the selected hunters that leaving the safety of their cavern was a bad idea. He had also told anyone willing to listen that the Gods were still angry over their tribe invading the land belonging to the lesser men, and the plague were in fact demons, sent by the Gods as punishment.

The man had the heart of a rabbit and the tongue of a snake. If the position of second-in-command hadn't already been given to Cun by Tirok's father before he died, then Tirok would have pushed the man off a cliff long ago.

The man had been sowing the seeds of unease even before the arrival of the plague. What could he do? Cun was, according to tradition, right to voice his doubts. It was the way. Their tribe believed in the spirit of balance, of harmony.

He unclenched his fist and stood up while keeping his gaze fixed on the horizon, ready to flee at the first sign of the return of the plague. Bailin Cun and three of the tribe's finest hunters stood up. He was aware of Cun's muttering but chose to ignore it. He had much more important worries to consider without having to admonish the man for breaking the rule of silence. The other hunters wouldn't listen to him anyway. Tirok had purposely chosen men loyal to him alone.

Tirok lead his men along the track until he reached the marker which once separated the two territories. The weather-beaten wooden pole still had the skull belonging to one of the lesser people. Cun muttered something about turning around and going back before the demons discover them. He ignored him; the man knew nothing. Tirok bent his legs until he was level was the skull. The lesser men were smaller than his tribe, but what they lost in stature, they made up in pure physical strength. Even their women were stronger than any of his men. He wondered if there were any lesser people left in this world.

They probably thought that his tribe were Gods when they invaded this territory two seasons previously. Despite their superior strength, the lesser people were still no match for their tribe, not when it came to hunting. The lesser people hunted their prey by creeping up on them, preferring to tackle the prey close up. His hunters were skilled in the use of spears. They were able to cut down the hunters belonging to the lesser people without losing a single life.

Perhaps it had been a poor decision to invade their land. If the lesser people had still been here, their presence might have slowed down the advance of the plague enough to allow his tribe to traverse through the mountain range and get far enough away to start anew. Alas, that had not happened.

One of hunters gasped. He spun around, expecting to see the plague bearing down on them. Instead, he found himself staring at the largest pile of meat that he had ever seen in his entire life. A large herd of long tusks had just emerged from within a large forest. He tightened the grip on his spear and unconsciously massaged his rumbling stomach. They couldn't hope to bring down an adult, not with so few men, but any young ones within the herd would prove to be easy pickings.

Cun had already started his tiring speech, saying that this was a bad idea, that taking food belonging to the Gods would curse them all, that it was better to leave them and find food elsewhere.

Thankfully, none of the others took any notice and followed Tirok through the long grass, towards the long tusks. They were only halfway across when Tirok had to slam a hand over his mouth when they stumbled over the corpse of a small long tusk.

It took them just a couple of minutes to slice off enough meat to stop the remainder of their tribe from starving when the freezing began. He was already planning to return with more men when Cun began to moan in distress. He was close to giving him something to moan about when his own eyes bulged as a conical spear pushed up through the earth beside him and punched through the tender flesh between one of his hunter's legs.

Tirok dropped everything and backed away from the carcass, fully aware that the ground was now shaking everywhere. The two remaining hunters and Cun fell to the floor, each one wailing and begging the Gods to spare their miserable lives.

Several more spears pushed through the earth followed by their owners. Tirok stopped moving when he became aware of at least two or the creatures had taken up position directly behind him.

So these things were their Gods? They looked like a cross between a lesser and a human but covered in thin leathery plates. The largest individual pushed through the middle of the hunters and stood in front of Tirok. It took a great deal of will not to fall to his knees and start begging for mercy like his companions.

The creature opened its huge mouth to display a set of teeth which belonged to a carnivore. "You are one unique individual, Tirok Nar," it said. "Hunger has forced you to show yourself, as hunger often does." It looked down at the small pile of long tusk meat lying at his feet. "Perhaps we can come to an understanding, an arrangement? If you surrender yourself to us, your companions can go free. We will even allow you to keep the meat that you stole from us."

The captain's eyes sprang open. He gasped out in shock and sat up, while he attempted to bring his mind back from the distant past.

Relax, man. You're safe. The things never even bothered giving chase.

The girl, where is she?

Ran off into the woods. Not that I blame her. So, come on, tell me what happened next? Obviously you did take this hybrid up on his offer.

I had no other choice. I was the tribal leader. It was my duty to keep them safe.

So what happened to Cun and the other hunters?

Once they absorbed me, I killed them all. I then led a unit of foot-soldiers back to the caverns and slaughtered them as well.

Jesus. Man, you need to help anyone left to stop this madness. Do it for yourself, for your old tribe. Do it to save your soul!

CHAPTER SIXTEEN

The air around here did not smell right. Callum placed the shotgun beside him, fished out a filthy tissue from his side pocket, and cleaned out some black gunk that had collected around his nose. He took another tentative sniff. It still didn't smell right.

Malc grabbed his shotgun and pushed it against his chest. "Don't let go of this, you idiot. Remember what Harry said about all the stuff that's out here."

"I do know that, for crying out loud. Stop it with the mothering." He kept hold of the shotgun anyway. "Does it smell weird to you?"

His colleague sighed heavily before scrambling further up the slope. When Malc reached the top, he laid on his front and gazed at the reason why they were here in the first place. Like he needed him to tell him how to react in this situation. Callum, unlike Malc, had served his duty for queen and country. He had taken note of everything Harry had said about what could be lurking out here but, no insult to their new friend, his information was out-of-date.

The way Callum saw it, this was the main assault force, tasked with snatching as many humans as they could. This was why they had to find as many people still alive as possible before the things that Harry had warned them about, like the traps, could be manufactured and deposited. If they couldn't find some way through that fire curtain, then this section of the town could well end up being their permanent home. He shuddered to himself at the thought of having to pick their way through an organic minefield every day, while desperately seeking out anything edible.

He crawled up the slope and lay next to Malc, making sure the old man saw the weapon. "Anymore movement?"

Malc shook his head. "There was a shadow moving about, a couple of minutes ago, but that's about it." He turned his head to face Callum. "This doesn't feel right at all. I say we leave them and go back."

Rising eight storeys above the blackened earth stood the only tall building left in town. Palladium house, the only surviving building from a collection of eight tower blocks which once housed the majority of the town's less affluent residents. Callum agreed with Malc. It made no sense as why only one should be left, virtually untouched while the mounds of rubble which was all that remained of the building's companions lay around it. Just as it made no sense that anybody could still be living in that tower block, acting like nothing had happened out here. Yet, he couldn't deny what he saw. Seven floors up, he saw a pair of drawn curtains and behind that thin red fabric, Callum could see shadows of at least two people inside. It even looked like the bloody TV was on!

"Drugs? Maybe even drink. If they were utterly wasted when all this happened then, as long as they don't peer through the curtains, they won't have a clue that anything is wrong."

"Sorry, I'm not buying it. Even if what you say is right, it doesn't explain why the two Goliaths left that tower block alone." Malc reached into his pockets and brought out a pair of binoculars. He pressed the lenses to his eyes. "If there is something weird going on, I mean, even weirder than this, our three volunteers might be able to find us some answers."

Harry had pleaded with Callum not to leave the safety of their makeshift sanctuary, telling him over and over that the risk was too great, that even if anyone was left in the town, their fate was sealed now, and we could do nothing for them.

Both Dosser and Malc shared this feeling; they too tried to make Callum see sense. He just looked across at the forty-three people they had managed to save from the jaws of the beasts out there. Before their arrival, this town boasted a population of over fifty thousand and Callum was sure that his daughter and ex-wife were still somewhere within that number.

He couldn't explain his desire to keep looking. The others wouldn't understand. The two old men would call him selfish, that he was throwing his life away for nothing. Probably continuing by saying nearly everyone that they'd saved had lost somebody too. That he ought to count his lucky blessings.

None of them stopped him from going. Harry only gave him a single sad nod before he extended his arm and telling him to be careful out there. Malc and three young men ran after him, a couple of minutes after he'd left them. Looking back to that moments, he couldn't decide whether he was overjoyed at having somebody else to watch his back or guilty for thinking that perhaps Harry had been right after all and these four men were going to end up dead because of his selfish urges.

Malc passed him the binoculars. He saw them alright, picking their way through two overturned cars. On the journey here, while listening to two of the men, he found it amazing to discover that these guys used to work at the carpet mill, which was located right on the edge of his patch. In fact, it was highly likely that those individuals might have even tossed him the odd pound over the years. Callum kept this information to himself, believing that if it became common knowledge that the guys in charge were a bunch of filthy tramps, they might not be so receptive to any future commands.

The other guy owned a newsagents opposite the housing estate. He appeared to be smitten with the girl they found him with. Callum discovered she was the sister of the big lad who attacked Callum a couple of nights ago.

He groaned. Two nights, was that all it was? It felt like two years. Callum didn't want to think where any of them could be in two years' time, if they were even still alive. God, and to think that this time last week, Callum would have done anything to change his life.

"What's wrong? Are they okay?"

"Yeah, they've gone around the block perimeter and have crouched behind a transit van. Everything looks okay." He passed the binoculars back to Malc. "Come on, we had better join them."

"Don't forget the shotgun."

He saw the glimmer of a smirk upon the old man's face but kept quiet while waiting for Malc to hit him with the punchline.

"And make sure your scented candles are secured. We wouldn't want any of them to explode and spray me with the stink of mulberry and fig."

"Funny man," he said while making his way down the other side of the grassy slope. "They're infusers and they might well save your skin."

"So you say."

Callum reached the road and checked both directions as well as up before running across. He didn't stop running until he reached the next piece of cover, a brick compound which held the wheelie bins belonging to one of the tower blocks. He waited for Malc to join him. "Yeah, so I say. Look. I know how mental it sounds. but they did work. The stuff was like strong acid to them. You heard Gavin's account of what happened."

Malc ran over to the edge of the compound and peered around the corner. "Come on, Callum. It's Gavin you're talking about," he said after he'd returned. "Gavin's the biggest bullshit artist in town. He once tried to convince me and Dosser that he was the forgotten son of Charlton Heston." He placed his rough, callused hand on Callum's shoulder. "I'm not calling you a bullshit artist, guy. I'm just saying it's a little hard to believe."

Callum removed the old man's hand. "We'd better join the others." Malc nodded and set off towards where the others were hiding. He waited for a moment before following. The lingering memory of one of those infusers shattering over the thick armour of that huge monster and having no effect made a nasty reappearance. What if Malc was right and the infusers had nothing to do with those other creatures melting. They could have just stood in something on the floor for all he knew.

He slowed down and watched Malc join the other three men. The newsagent obviously had something to say by his animated actions. Callum unzipped his coat and pushed his hand into the inside pocket. He had three infusers in there, along with his lucky knife and a packet of mints he'd found earlier. No way could Malc be right. Those infusers had melted the creatures in that shop, there could be no doubt about it. He just didn't know why they didn't kill that huge armoured tank thing.

"Nice of you to join us," said Malc. "Our new friend here, Raymond Custer, is also of the opinion that something around here doesn't smell right."

The man nodded. "It doesn't, I know that smell too. It's the same smell I caught back when they first invaded the shop." He shivered violently. "Jesus, I don't want to go through anything like that again." Custer pointed at the open doors. "It's coming from there. I think we should turn around and look somewhere else. This place gives me the creeps."

"There's another way in," muttered one of the other men. "We noticed it on the other side of the tower block. Looks like something's hit the wall with a canon or something."

Both Malc and Custer shook their heads.

"Come on, Callum. How many different ways of wrong does it need to be before you listen to us?"

"You didn't have to follow me, Custer," said Callum. He made sure the shotgun was loaded before setting off towards the side of the tower block. He so wished Harry was here. "You stay here if you want, guys, but I'm going inside."

He slowed down when he got to the corner, aware that the others were still behind him. So much for turning around. Callum didn't blame them for wanting to turn back; he wanted to do the same when Custer said he'd recognised that smell.

What if it was a trap? Harry had told them about how he found that portal which took him to this world. Who's to say that this isn't like that?

"Oh fuck!" cried Malc. "Will you look at that?" He tapped Callum's shoulder. "Look up, man!"

His gaze followed Malc's pointed finger and spotted a blonde-haired teenage female leaning out of a window on the seventh floor.

"Bloody hell. There is somebody up there!" Malc took a couple of steps back. "She isn't alone either."

Custer joined him. "They must have been hiding in there all this time."

Could it really be his daughter? The age would be about right. Even if it wasn't, Callum couldn't leave them up there! He ran past the two men only for Malc to grab him.

"Custer's right. Look. There is somebody else."

Callum skidded to a stop and looked up again. "Oh my Lord. It's her! It's Caroline!" There was no mistaking that face. "Hold on!' he shouted. "I'm coming."

He ran around the corner of the tower block, his heart and mind racing. The two men from the mill flanked Callum. He reached the hole in the wall and was about to climb inside when one of the men grabbed his left shoulder.

"Wait, I think I saw something."

Callum pushed past him. "It's nothing, probably a rat or something." Nothing was going to stop him from reaching his daughter, including some mangy old rat.

He hurried through the middle of the living room, trying to avoid looking at the flat screen TV, black leather three-seater sofa, and all the other luxuries denied to him for all these years.

His family was here, right under his nose, and he didn't have a single clue. Callum reached the door which led into the communal hallway. The layout of their apartment couldn't be much different from this one, minus the huge hole in the wall, obviously. That concept of Harry's parallel earths raised its ugly head again. So, somewhere, on another world, a version of himself was no doubt living in Palladium House with his beautiful wife and daughter, blissfully unaware of the plight of his alternate self. "You lucky, lucky bastard," he whispered. Callum grabbed the handle, twisted it, and pulled.

Two foot-soldiers reacted to the door swinging inwards by firing two fleshmelta blasts into the apartment interior. Callum's lightning reflexes saved him. He shouted out in a combination of alarm and horror while dropping to the floor.

He fired the shotgun. Either by luck or design, the blast hit them exactly in the middle, shredding their sides and shoulders. "You dirty, sneaky bastards!" he cried. Callum scrambled to his feet, stumbled over to the two creatures, not caring at all about the danger he was putting himself in. Not that they were able to react to his presence.

The foot-soldiers were in too much pain to notice him. He slammed the gun stock into one of the creature's head, growling in satisfaction as the wood smashed through its skull. He pulled the gun up and wiped the thick grunge off the sides before turning to the remaining foot-soldier, but the other one had already died.

He leaned against the wall, panting heavily.

"You did this," growled a voice from the side of where he was.

Callum turned back to the doorway and saw only three men. Custer and Malc were standing up, staring, white-faced at the mess of lumpy sludge spattered across the floor. The men, kneeling down, looked straight at Callum. "This is all your fucking fault. Why don't you ever listen?" He turned his head back to the floor.

Callum saw that not all of the man had melted. His colleague held onto part of an arm. "We need to keep moving," he said, gently.

"No, no way," said Custer. He tapped the kneeling man on the shoulder. "Come on, Dave, let's get out of here."

"Wait," shouted Malc. "We need to stick together." He looked at Malc, shook his head then followed the other two. "Come back, at least wait for me!"

Callum walked back to the doorway and watched them reach the hole in the wall. The three men climbed back out of the hole then a couple of seconds later, climbed back inside. The four foot-soldiers running after them explained their abrupt change of mind. Callum spun around and raced back out of the apartment. He climbed up the first flight of steps and stopped beside the next door. He could clearly hear the other three shouting and running up the stairs almost as clearly as the sound of somebody or something sneaking around in the apartment next to him. He broke open the shotgun, fished out another shell, and placed it in the breach.

So it was a fucking trap. Those bastards had been waiting for them all along. The chances of all of them getting out of this alive had slipped down to practically zero. Callum brought the gun up to his shoulder and stepped sideways. He was going to make sure that he took as many of them with him. A single foot-soldier ran towards him. It was unharmed. He turned the gun around, ran into the room, and smacked the stock into the side of its head. It dropped like a stone.

The other three men joined him. Malc already had his gun ready. Another foot-soldier popped up from behind a brown sofa. Malc spun around and took it out. Callum spotted movement coming from the kitchen. Another one ran into the room and took cover behind its dead companion. Callum shouted and fired, blasting a huge hole in the middle of the sofa.

"Did I get it?" he shouted.

In answer to his demand, the foot-soldier stuck its head up from the top of the ruined sofa. It brought up a hand-gun version of the fleshmelta and fired. The blast travelled straight in between both Callum and Malc and hit Dave in the face. Custer screamed.

"Kill it, Malc, for crying out loud!"

"I can't," he replied. "The damn gun is jammed!"

Callum ran at the foot-soldier, took out one of the infusers, and smashed it into its face. The result was instantaneous. The creature emitted a pain-drenched scream and leaped backwards and fell into a glass cabinet. Its hands clawed deep grooves into its now sponge-like flesh. Callum searched through his pocket for another shell. He managed to place it into the breach and bring the gun up to his shoulder. Malc slammed the palm of his hand against the barrel.

"Don't waste ammo on it," he snarled. "Let the bastard die noisily. It might make the rest of them more cautious in coming after us." He grabbed Callum's arm and pulled him out of the apartment. "Come on, we still have to find those people up there. We can't allow the deaths of our comrades to be in vain."

Malc took the lead, followed by Custer. Callum couldn't help but notice that the newsagent had dropped the airgun that Gavin had given him and scooped up the revolver which Dave had brought. Callum followed them up the next flight of stairs, listening to the dying screams coming from that foot-soldier. Malc had been right. The things that had followed them through the hole were nowhere in sight.

Unless…unless they didn't need to follow them? Callum shook away the paranoia. He needed to keep his head clear. Thinking about what else might be up here waiting for them would end up screwing with his mind. He patted the inside pocket. At least he still knew the infusers worked. More importantly, the others knew it too. That had to be one good thing that had come out of this.

"Stop!" hissed Malc. "Oh no, oh fuck. What the hell are we going to do now?"

Callum ran up the next flight of steps and found both Custer and Malc staring out of a window. He joined them and felt his own guts roll over. One of the Goliaths was heading straight for them and down on the ground, near the overturned cars, was a column of foot-soldiers. Thirty heads were looking straight at them!

Callum pushed past both of them. "It changes nothing." He ran up the next two flights of steps and pushed open the door which led onto the floor where his wife and daughter lived. Callum knew exactly which door it was. He stopped outside a red painted door, checked the shotgun then pushed the door open.

Across a thick-pile maroon carpet, he saw a single chair beside the window. Thick purple root-like tendrils hung down from the chair, trailed across the carpet, and vanished into the next room. There were two torsos attached to those roots. The heads turned simultaneously, gave him a lop-sided smile, and winked.

153

"No, oh God. This can't be fucking happening!" The gun fell out of Callum's hand. It fell onto the carpet. One of the closer tendrils unwrapped itself from the main group and slithered towards the weapon.

"No you don't!" shouted Custer. He pushed passed Callum and fired at the single tendril. The reaction from the two human-like structures was instant and deadly. The stomach cavity of the creature which had taken on the rough appearance of Callum's daughter cracked open. Skin and muscle folded back like petals and a tight knot of pale cream tendrils flew out of the hole, straight for Custer. Before he could react, they all fastened around his head and pulled the man closer to the pair of creatures. The other creature, the one who was supposed to look like Callum's ex-wife, had already prepared for Custer's arrival by peeling back its face to reveal three sets of serrated, hooked, bone-like implements.

"Hello there, Callum McGuire. It's so good of you to join us."

Another figure had appeared from out of the darkness. Callum tore his gaze away from the vile-looking monstrosities which were supposed to look like the only people he had ever truly loved and glared at the new arrival. It looked like a cross between a human and a foot-soldier, only much larger. The creature was easily seven feet high and built like an Olympic body-builder. It saw him go from the gun that he'd already dropped and chuckled.

"I didn't even have to disarm you. Thing is, Callum, as much as I'd so love to digest you and your annoying band of rebels, my other friend thinks that you can be of some use." It lowered its head and moved out of the kitchen. "I'm one of the Goliaths by the way. Well, part of me, anyway. This body is just something I've thrown together in order to have a nice little chat with you. Do you like it?"

"Fuck off."

It laughed again. "Oh my, you really do have an attitude! I like that, I really do. Now, this is what I am going to offer you." He looked at Malc and grinned. "Not that you have much of a choice. Callum, I want you to join us, become part of The Cluster. If you do so without a struggle, then I will allow your friends to live, even the one who's having so much difficulty in breathing. We'll even allow all the meat which you stole from us to live. We do know where they are, by the way. They'll die if you don't accept this proposal. I ask you, Callum. Do you really want all their deaths on your conscience?"

Callum reached into his inside pocket. He took out one more infuser and ran over to the thing holding Custer. He glared at the huge creature in the corner. "How about you eat this!" Callum smashed the glass against one of the creature's bony plates. The liquid spread out from the source, sizzling and steaming as it ate into the soft flesh. He rubbed his hand into some of the liquid then ran over to the other creature and wiped his palm across its face. He spun around and saw Malc had already pulled the other man out of the room. Callum ran out, pausing to scoop up the shotgun. "What now?"

Malc pointed up. "It sounds like an entire army is charging up those stairs. There's no other route to take."

He nodded, grabbed Custer's other arm, and helped him up the next flight of stairs. Callum reached the next landing first. He peered through the small rectangular door window and saw more of the things waiting for them. "We have to get to the roof."

They reached the top and pushed through the last door. Cold air buffeted Callum's face. He and Malc pulled Custer away from the door then slammed it shut before bolting it.

"Oh Jesus," said Malc. "We really are in the shit now."

"So what else is new?" Callum walked over to the edge. Malc joined him. "We can't say we didn't try, Malc."

The older man sighed. "Do you think it does know the location of the others?"

"Who's to know."

"I'm sorry about before, Callum. About not believing you about the diffusers, I mean. You have to admit though, it did sound a little crazy."

Callum nodded. He heard the man's words but didn't quite take them in. Something else down in the middle of the town had diverted his attention. "Malc, I think I know how to kill them. Look at that over there, man."

"I'm sorry, what?"

He pointed down at where the town's old cinema used to stand. The cleared land now had a new structure. It looked just like a giant, organic sandwich box, full of some kind of red liquid. It didn't take Callum long to realise just where all that stuff had come from, not when he saw over a dozen collectors accompanied by their armed escorts walking towards it.

The other Goliath was stood over it. A thick tube extended from under its stomach and disappeared into the crimson fluid. "That must be how they feed, how they get their energy. Now, imagine what would happen if we just happened to empty a few infusers into that gunk, Malc? Those two massive fuckers wouldn't stand a chance!"

"Man, I don't wish to piss on your parade here, but how the hell do we do that when we're stuck up on this roof? Grow wings?"

Callum ran back to Custer. He crouched beside the man. "How are you doing?"

Custer did not look great at all. His skin had blistered badly from where those tendrils had grabbed him.

"I'm not going to make it. There's something inside me. I can feel it eating my body." He groaned, turned onto his side, and coughed up a gobbet of jellied blood.

"Look, just relax, Custer. We're going to get out of this, all of us." Callum looked up at Malc. "Look over there. There's a fire exit on the other side of the roof." He pulled Custer on to his feet. "Come on, man. Let's get you back."

The man shook his head, pulled Callum's arm off him, and sat back on the roof. "I'm not going anywhere. I'm done for. The stuff in me is spreading." He grabbed the barrel of Callum's gun, pulled it down, and pressed the end against his forehead. "This is what you have to do for me now, Callum. End me, please. I'm begging you."

"I can't do that!"

"Then let me," said Custer. "I don't want to turn into one of those things"

Something banged against the other side of the door. Callum saw something pressed against the glass. He swallowed hard and tried to keep his wits about him at the sight of his daughter's distorted face. Callum crouched beside the groaning man. He placed the gun in his arms then reached into his pocket, took out the last infuser, and placed the glass cylinder into the man's hand. "Try to take some of them with you, Custer, and thank you."

Malc grabbed his arm and pulled him away just as the door flew open. Callum heard a single shotgun blast just as he reached the fire exit. He didn't turn around.

CHAPTER SEVENTEEN

There could be no doubting it. There was a foot-soldier hiding behind that blue van. Harry pulled the fleshmelta into his shoulder and allowed the scope to attach itself to his eye. As always, that sense of utter revulsion coursed through his body as it suckered itself onto his skin. Harry fought back the urge to pull it away and focused on the task at hand. He moved the weapon a couple of degrees to the left until the vehicle's window came into view.

Sure enough, there it was; a single foot-soldier, cowering on the other side of the van. He could clearly see the top of its head. His finger tightened on the trigger then he paused. Something was not quite right with this scenario. It was acting like a skittering insect. Like it was nervous of something?

He zoomed in and looked past the foot-soldier and focused on the shop window. Was there movement in there? Harry felt his companions shifting at either side. They were getting uncomfortable.

"Something about this is not right," he muttered.

Both Callum and Gavin groaned.

"It's not like we can go anywhere else," replied Callum. "We've checked all the other directions. This is the only way we can go. Look, maybe we'll be okay?" He turned around and nodded over to a fried chicken shop. Their people were hiding in the basement, ready to be told they can move. Their destination was an old butchers shop on the next street. Dosser had explained that there's an old metal door in the cellar of that abandoned building that will take them all the way across town. "I mean, they'll only be exposed for a couple of minutes, max. I reckon it's worth the risk."

Harry's reply caught in his throat when he saw the shop door opening wide. Another creature was trying to push its bulk through the gap. Oh on, they have a bio-tank with them!

"There's one!" hissed Gavin. "At last, I'm going to get myself a foot-soldier."

Harry pulled the scope off his eye and dived to the left, pushing Gavin's rifle into the wet mud. "Leave it," he whispered. "It isn't as it seems." He picked the gun off the floor, wiped off most of the mud, and handed it back to the boy. "It's a sacrificial pawn. Look at how it is moving. The foot-soldier does not want to be there. Not too surprising. Who would want to be pushed out into the open?"

"I don't get it."

"There's a bio-tank tank behind that van," he replied. "Shooting the foot-soldier would be the last thing you would ever do." He watched the creature one in between the cars, getting more confident the longer it stayed alive. "Do you have that knife, Callum?" Seconds later, Callum's blade appeared in the palm of his hand. Harry gently laid the fleshmelta on the ground.

"Callum. Believe me, it isn't worth the risk. If we don't take out that creature, then we'll all die. They can home in on large groups of people."

The man's face drained of blood. "Oh hell. So that's how they do it?"

Harry nodded. "Indeed. Stay here. I won't be long." Harry scurried past the two men. He waited until the foot-soldier had its back to him before running across the road. Only the big van separated him from being broiled alive by the bio-tank. If the foot-soldier turned around, it was bound to raise the alarm. Harry lowered himself and slithered under the van, a moment before the foot-soldier did turn.

This had to be the most insane thing he had ever done, but Harry knew that he had no other choice. The three of them were supposed to provide covering fire so the two groups could move from their current sanctuary, before they could continue with Callum's plan. Trouble was, there were too little places inside the energy curtain left which could hold such a large amount of souls.

Callum and Malc had recounted their encounter with the thing that claimed to represent one of the Goliaths. Harry believed every word, as he had heard rumour of similar encounters from his world. He also believed that the enemy knew where they were hiding, meaning they needed to disperse before they came for them.

Dosser had taken one group into the sewers while Paul intended to guide the remaining survivors into the town's school basement. They hoped to stay hidden until they either found some way to remove the energy curtain or wait until it dissipated in its own. At the time that the others were coming up with this fantastic plan, Harry was scouting the area with another two guards. If he had been there, Harry would have explained a few home truths about what the future held for them if they all insisted on staying in large groups.

He crawled towards the left wheel, aware that the bio-tank was just inches away now. He stopped. More movement from the inside of the shop caught his attention. There were others in there! Harry's guts knotted up. Oh no; he thought this beast in front of him was the only creature, apart from the other foot-soldier in this area. If he'd known about the presence of another bio-tank, Harry wouldn't have pursued this course of action. He was getting careless. Harry crawled a bit further.

The two who had taken charge, Dosser and Malc, would not listen to his arguments. He had told them over and over that the only way to survive was to split up the group into twos and threes. No more than four. There was no energy curtain back on his world, meaning the survivors were able to spread out, making it more difficult for them to be picked off. Staying in two large groups was just asking for trouble. Neither of them would listen. He tried to explain that back before he was born, during the invasion on his world, the people who lived were the ones who were quiet, who only took the minimum of food and stayed away from any old population centre.

How could those two not understand this? Even groups of four were, in his opinion, too many. The people in this world did not know how to stay quiet, and they certainly had no concept of rationing food supplies. How could they? This land had not seen true war for decades. The people were fat, bloated, slow, and noisy.

The familiars would trap and mine every single food source they could find. Every shop in this town would be a death trap. It would be difficult to keep just a couple of humans alive. Keeping two groups of thirty each would be next to impossible.

Harry got himself ready. They also were unable to listen to sound advice. Strange how they were so willing to listen to Callum's advice though. Everything hinged on the man's fantastic plan of dumping all the strong-scented fluid into a giant vat which, according to Callum, helped to feed and maintain the Goliaths. Both Dosser and Malc stated that they only needed to keep the two groups separate and protected until Callum's idea worked.

It then dawned on Harry that the two old men knew exactly what they were doing. They knew that if they failed here, they were all dead anyway. The men were just buying time until Callum succeeded; either that or just delaying the inevitable

He still needed to know what else was lurking around here. Another bio-tank would ruin everything. Harry needed to get closer to that shop window. It would only take... He froze. The bio-tank next to him was making some very weird noises. It sounded like it was trying to sniff the air. Harry silently moaned in terror when he realised that's exactly what it was doing. Just as Callum and Custer were able to smell the presence of so many familiars, it stood to reason that the same should pay to them as well. Oh no! Even now, the huge armoured creature was backing up. It must know he was hiding under the vehicle! If he didn't take it out right now, he was dead meat.

The beast roared and charged the moment he rolled out the other side. He had to shift his body sideways to avoid the heavy creature from stomping him flat. Harry slashed out with his left arm, the blade leaving a shallow score along its thick skin.

It was going to kill him if Harry didn't do something drastic! He gripped the handle left in his arm and slammed it down, spearing its large foot. He pulled the wet, slimy blade out and slammed it up, in between its legs. The creature made a strange gulping sound before falling over backwards and crashing onto the pavement.

Harry saw the shop front door starting to open. He still had no idea what was still in that shop. Not that it mattered to him if they caught him out in the open. Unbelievably, the bio-tank was now trying to get up. Considering how much he now hurt, if it did get up, Harry might as well slit his own throat.

"Not going to happen!" he growled. Harry leapt onto the bio-tank's heavily armoured chest and thrust the knife into the only soft part he could find, its eye. The creature let out one last sigh before it stopped moving. He pulled out the blade and rolled back under the van, listening to the other familiars approach the large corpse. Harry hoped that the shock of finding their heavy artillery bleeding out of its eye might encourage them to run back inside that shop.

Harry got to the other side. The foot-soldier was nowhere to be seen. It must have run off before it did get shot. That helped him to breathe a little easier. He ran across the road and scurried back around the column of cars to discover the other two had deserted him. They had even taken his fleshmelta.

"Did you kill him?"

Harry around for his lost weapon, remembering it wasn't there then threw himself into the mud. It took him a moment to realise that the voice had come from inside one of those vehicles and another moment to realise that nobody was shooting at him. He lifted his head and saw the foot-soldier looking down at him and pointing his own fleshmelta at Harry's face.

"You killed him with your knife too. That's impressive and potentially devastating to morale if the word ever got out."

The creature laughed. It sounded so human. Harry had never even conceived that the enemy's most numerous of familiars possessed intelligence equal to his own. He certainly never thought that he would hear one speak. This new information unsettled him. It just went to show how much about them he didn't know. "Are you going to kill me?"

It gave him what Harry believed to be a wink before continuing.

"This fleshmelta has been well looked after and from your look of panic, I can only assume that you're its adoptive owner?" It laughed again. "The non-standard weapon harness on your back reinforces my assumption." The foot-soldier pushed open the car door with its door and leaned closer. "You are not from this world. Imagine that, a free-mind human travelling between worlds. That too could be devastating to the troops' morale. You're supposed to be just livestock. Animals with no real feelings. Imagine our surprise when we entered this new world and discovered how much progress you dumb animals have made in just one hundred years."

Harry rolled onto his back. He sat up and turned back to face this rather talkative foot-soldier. "If you are not going to turn me into meat soup, could I please have my gun back."

To his utter shock, the creature did just that. It stood up, walked over to him, and dropped the weapon into his lap.

"My old unit, what is left of them, would not believe tales of a human soldier who had travelled from the old world and can kill one of our greatest military assets with just a knife. I am a traitor to my own kind. At least, that is the designation that I have to bear until they do kill me." The foot-soldier turned around and walked over to the car. He placed a hand-sized lump of grey material on the roof then turned around. "Good luck with your continued fight against the oppressors. Your two human friends are still alive. I didn't kill them if you were thinking that. A large patrol passed this location a couple of moments ago. They moved onto the next street." It tapped the roof of the car. "This will revive your weapon. It does take a few time units to fully recover, but the fleshmelta will be functional again."

"Wait!" Cried Harry, running towards it. "I don't understand. Why are you doing this?"

The foot-soldier gave the approximation of a shrug. "Perhaps because I am not an automaton? More likely because I can no longer follow prevailed doctrine when our so-called Gods change it when it suits them. You had better rejoin your companions, human." It jumped across the car bonnet.

Harry covered the distance between them in less than a second. He reached across the car and grabbed the foot-soldier's bony wrist. "Wait, please. Continue. I need to know. Why are you unsettled?"

It signed heavily. "Are all humans as inquisitive as you? Very well. Look, soldiers talk. It is the way. Amongst ourselves, when we're alone and away from our masters, we discuss everything from what makes you different to the beasts we used to harvest to more delicate and potentially blasphemous subjects involving our Gods." It licked its lips. "I used to hold a privileged position, you know. Privileged for my caste, that is. I was once assigned to the Right Hand of God." It leaned against the side of the vehicle. "Then our Gods decided on a change of structure and we were forced to serve some other creature." It screwed up its face. "A beast not worthy of such an esteemed position." The creature passed Harry the device. "Go now, please."

Before he could respond, it ducked down and ran across the road. Harry watched it look towards the direction of the ship where the other foot-soldiers had retreated then ran the opposite direction. He turned the device around, turned the fleshmelta upside down, and searched for the location where the lump had been removed from. 'There you are," he murmured. He pushed the lump into the hole, watched the black flesh fold over it then clipped the weapon on his back.

The other two were making their way back to his position. They must have decided to come back to him after leaving him. Had they seen him speaking to that foot-soldier? So what if they had? Thanks to that creature's sudden change of loyalty, Harry had acquired some valuable information. Harry lowered himself against the vehicle and waited for Callum and Malc to join him.

"Did you kill it?"

Harry jumped. He wasn't prepared to hear the same words come from Callum's mouth. He nodded. "Yes. It is dead. That unit had lost their heavy artillery. They no longer pose a threat. Where did you go?" He already knew the reason for their disappearance, but Harry felt they might become suspicious if he didn't ask the question.

"A load more foot-soldiers almost fell over us," said Callum. "It felt best to move until they left." He peered over the roof of the car. "So, you think it's okay to get the remaining group moved?"

"Sooner than later," replied Harry. He gave the weapon another once over. It looked to be back to normal. Harry would not know for sure until he pressed the trigger.

Callum unclipped the walkie-talkie, passed it over to Malc then walked over to Harry. "Okay, this is it. The big push, so to speak. Are you ready?"

Harry waited for Malc to give the order. He then took up position behind the car, keeping his aim on the van. The bio-tank might be gone, but those foot-soldiers were still in there. He stayed in position while their remaining people filed past him. There were no signs of any suspicious activity anywhere. He began to believe that they might have been able to move the civilians without him going to all that trouble of trying to get himself killed.

Callum tapped him on the back. "That's the easy bit." He passed out two rucksacks filled with Callum's sweet smelling glass containers to Malc and Harry. It took him a bit of manoeuvring to place the canvas bag on his back but after a minute, he managed it.

"Now it's time for the fun stuff." Callum raced along the street and took up position on the corner. He peered around the edge and jumped back as if he had been electrocuted.

Harry ran up to him and crouched beside Callum. "Are you okay?"

The other man shook his head. "You had better take a look."

Harry looked around the corner. He saw the huge organic tank which had so excited Callum. He also saw both Goliaths stood over it, several foot-soldiers, three bio-tanks and over a dozen flyers perched on the Goliaths. The flyers took off as one and flew straight towards their position. "Oh Fuck! They know we're here."

One of the bio-tanks turned to face the building they were hiding behind.

"Run!" screamed Harry. He raced across the road, fully aware that the foot-soldiers were running towards them. He felt a rush of hot air roll over his back. He didn't need to turn around to know that the building they were hiding behind no longer existed. He dived over a car bonnet, spun around, and brought up his fleshmelta, giving the other two cover while they ran towards him. Harry fired three times, two of his shots hitting foot-soldiers. He said a silent prayer that his weapon still worked.

"Look out!"

Harry threw himself down, rooted around, and blasted three diving flyers into red mush. Callum and Gavin pulled him up and dragged the man along the pavement, occasionally ducking in response to the plasma fire smashing against the sides of the vehicles.

Harry screamed as the car just behind him literally dissolved. He saw two bio-tanks rushing towards them through a car window reflection, as well as the two Goliaths. One of the bio-tanks fired again, destroying two more vehicles a couple of metres from Callum.

"What are we going to do?" he shouted. "We're running out of cars to hide behind and time."

Harry turned and fired a continuous stream of energy at the closest bio-tank, not stopping until the superheated plasma managed to eat through the creature's hardened plate armour. When it did get through, the resulting explosion took out four foot-soldiers who were running beside it.

"Do that again!" shouted Gavin.

"I can't," he replied. "The fleshmelta will now be useless for at least five minutes."

Malc pulled both Gavin and Harry into a stone alcove. "I say we make a run for it through the park and up onto the housing estate. It'll give Harry's weird gun to recharge."

"No, Malc. We can't. We only have one chance to do this. It won't take them long to realise that we've found their weakness and plug it up. If we turn back now, we'll lose that chance forever."

"Have you lost your fucking mind?" screamed Malc. "Have you seen how many of those things there are out there?" He leaned his head out of the alcove.

Both Harry and Callum grabbed an arm each and pulled him back but they were too late. A stray blast slammed into Malc's chest. The man literally dissolved in their hands.

"Oh God, Harry. We're not going to survive this, are we? How am I going to explain this to Dosser?"

"Do you want to follow Malc's suggestion, Callum? You are right. The chances of us getting anywhere close to that well are next to zero. Perhaps we can come back a bit later?"

The Goliaths had finished feeding and were now striding towards them, joining the three bio-tanks already close enough for Harry to smell their pungent chemical stench. Harry didn't think they could escape from this alcove, let alone cause enough damage to stop those gigantic monsters in their tracks.

"Bollocks. You only live once," growled Callum. "Follow me, you two, and try to keep up!" His companion ran out of the alcove, scrambled over a car bonnet, and raved straight towards the advancing bio-tanks, running straight through the middle of them. The large creatures were too slow to catch him.

Harry swallowed hard then followed Callum and Gavin. By the time he had reached the bio-tanks, they had only just started to turn their bulky bodies. Harry threw himself behind a wheelie bin.

"What a rush," said Callum. "Don't stop now, man!"

The three of them ran over to a second-hand shop. Callum started to grin. "I don't believe this!"

"Above you!" shouted Harry.

Callum saw the flyer about to dive bomb him and Gavin. Callum turned his shotgun around and blasted it into a cloud of red muck. "Thanks, man." He pushed open the shop door and pulled Harry inside. "There's another door at the end of the shop," he hissed. "It leads back into the shopping mall. I can't believe how lucky we've been. We can resupply and make sure we really turn their feeding bowl into liquid poison!"

Callum ran through the empty shopping mall. "Gavin, it feels like it's been years since we were in here. How can that be?"

Gavin shook his head. "Do we have to go back in there, man? I mean, we almost didn't make it out of there alive the last time."

164

Callum stopped dead right in front of the store entrance. "What the fuck is this?"

Harry and Gavin joined him. When Harry saw what it was, he pulled them both back. Thick sticky threads of organic resin covered the doorway. "I haven't seen this type of stuff for a long time. The Goliaths use a spider-like construction to weave this stuff. They use them to stop us from moving around in the surface, usually in the place where they keep their food stores. I don't think this is a coincidence. I think they have done this to stop you from collecting any more of your strange-smelling chemical."

"Well, this is great news!" said Callum, excitedly. "It means that they know how dangerous the stuff is. It could work, Harry!" Callum looked behind him.

"Are you okay?"

"I'm fine, Gavin. It's just that I thought I heard a noise. Harry, can you blast a way through that stuff?"

"I could," he replied, "but I'm not sure that this is such a good idea. It feels wrong."

"What choice do we have, Harry? We need more of that chemical. Come on, man, blast it!"

Harry sighed heavily and did as the man asked. The stuff stuck to the door melted away.

Callum ran through the door and straight over to a shelf. He picked up a clear, plastic box and paused. "I don't get it, the box is empty." He threw it on the floor, picked up another, and another. He groaned softly then swept all the boxes on the floor. "What the fuck is going on here?"

"I knew you wouldn't be able to keep away," chuckled a deep-throated voice from behind Harry.

He spun around only for three foot-soldiers to run out from behind a clothing rack, grab him, and pull the fleshmelta out of his hands. He stared in revulsion as another creature, one which looked similar to another foot-soldier but with twice their bulk, made its way towards them.

"It is still not too late to agree to my terms, Callum. I am a benevolent being and I am willing to forgive." It opened its arms and smiled at him. "I won't be offering you this opportunity again, my friend. You have no other choice now. You cannot get out of this situation. Choose the only possible outcome and live."

Harry jumped as the foot-soldier holding his left arm screamed out in agony then fell to the floor.

"There is always another choice," spat another voice. One more large, armour-plated monster stepped out from the shadows. Harry used the distraction to grab his weapon from one of the other foot-soldiers. He smashed the gun stock into its face, turned the fleshmelta around, and fired at the remaining creature.

It raised its own fleshmelta and pointed it at the foot-soldier hybrid. "Still playing your deal games, I see?"

"How dare you!" it roared. "You are supposed to be my Right Hand."

"Yeah well, things didn't work out. You know, with you and your other buddy giving my job to some worthless piece of excrement. You know what does annoy me about this situation? When I pull this trigger, I'm only melting an extension of your being and not the real deal. I am coming for you. I'd start running, both of you." The armour-plated monster pulled the trigger.

Harry kept the gun levelled on the new arrival while watching the liquidised remains of the hybrid run under a shelf. It lowered its own fleshmelta, looked at Gavin then at Callum before it settled its gaze on Harry.

"I'm Copperfield," it said, "and I don't think we have much time left."

CHAPTER EIGHTEEN

Callum pressed himself against the wall. He tightened his fingers around the shotgun's pistol grip and mentally dared their new pet monster to even look at him in a weird way. Copperfield lumbered past him and kneeled down next to Harry. Of all the sights that his old eyes had shown him today, seeing those two bitter enemies sharing ideas and thoughts about their current situation just had to take the biscuit.

"Gavin, how are you holding up?"

"About as well as expected, I guess." The boy looked towards the newcomer and then he peered through the gap in the line of cars. "Our new friend looks like he's made from the same stuff as that tank full of gunk. It's kinda unsettling, you know?"

That was the understatement of the century. "Look on the bright side, Gavin, at least we're not dead. There's also the added bonus of having two guys carrying those pretty phenomenal fleshmeltas."

"I guess," replied Gavin. "As long as he doesn't turn it on us."

The man from another world and his colleague, the thing from this world, both stood up. Harry looked over his shoulder. "Callum, prepare yourself, my friend. It's time to go." Harry gave him a rare smile. "I hope you can keep up."

He watched in astonishment as those two jumped over the car they were hiding behind and raced along the empty street, heading towards the huge, grotesque-looking monstrosity across the road. "Come on, Gavin. We'd better stay with them as they're the ones holding the big guns."

"Not like there's anything to shoot at," muttered Gavin.

Callum ran after the other two. He had noticed the lack of extra foot-soldiers. After what they'd done, he thought the streets would be full of them by now. He had tried to argue with himself that they were not all that bothered about him and his armed group, that they were too concerned with flushing out the last of the town's survivors. It just sounded to him like he was lying to himself, that this was yet another bloody trap.

The other two had stopped beside the huge tank. He joined them and looked up towards the tank's lip. "Is it safe to touch?"

The newcomer nodded. "The outer coating is just a hardened resin. It swallows your hand if you get too close, if that's what you're concerned about." Copperfield tapped it with the stock of his fleshmelta. "Shouldn't be too difficult to break, if the case arises."

"You suggest that we can starve them?" asked Harry. He nodded. "Yes, we can do that if Callum's plan does not work. A couple of well-placed shots will easily destroy this foul construction."

Callum could not stop looking around. "This is mental. Where the hell were they? There's no way that the creatures would leave such an important construction unguarded." He ran into the middle of the road and spun around, trying to spot signs of any movement in the windows surrounding them.

"Copperfield," said Harry. "Can you sense anything?"

He shook his head. "Yes, but not here. It feels like both Gods and all of their familiars are congregated in one location on the other side of the town." He furrowed his brow. "The images I sense are too confusing."

"You reckon that they're going for the others?"

"They could be, Gavin," said Callum. "If that's the case, then the bastards are looking in the wrong place."

"Meaning they don't attach much importance to this place," said Harry.

"More likely, they don't attach much importance to us." He grinned. "Let's prove to them just how wrong they are," replied Callum. "Come on, let's get moving before they change their minds and come back!"

"It still doesn't feel right," said Gavin. "What if he's lying?"

"I'm not lying," snapped Copperfield. "And I would advise you to keep your accusations to yourself. That is, if you wish to keep your head attached to your spindly body."

Harry held up his hand. "Enough," he muttered. "If you are to disagree, then please do it quietly. The air will carry your voice far and wide. It does not matter if the enemy is on the other side of the town or in the next street, because you can be assured that once they hear it, they will come. Remember, there is a curtain of energy around us and until that is gone, none of us are going anywhere."

"Sorry," said Gavin. "It's just…"

"Yes," interrupted Harry. "It's all a bit too much to take in." He shrugged. "I believe that goes for all of us." He nodded over at Copperfield. "This creature saved your life, Gavin. If his Gods had not changed, adapted themselves in order to conquer this world, then he would have most likely eaten you. We are here for one purpose only. I suggest we do that and see where it takes us. Agreed?"

The others nodded, including Gavin. "That let us find a route to the top as I am sure that the collectors did not fly up there." Whether Callum's insane plan worked or not, once this was over, Harry intended to end the existence of the hybrid creature. It did not matter if it had offered to help them; it had already changed side once. Harry dare not risk that happening again.

Callum had already left the group and was about to vanish around the corner. He stopped. "Guys, you have to see this. I think I've found our way up!"

Harry allowed the others to pass him and followed at a distance, watching Copperfield. As he reached the edge of the resin coated building, the others had already left his sight. He turned the corner and found exactly why Callum had sounded so excited.

The familiars had constructed an earth ramp, which progressed from the road up to the top of the tank. The ramp was wide enough for all of them to walk up, side by side. Callum was already halfway up by the time he reached the bottom. His companion had opened his rucksack and had distributed a handful of the glass containers to both Gavin and Copperfield.

So why was he still hesitant to join them? Apart from the obvious, Callum and Copperfield were now rushing to the top with Gavin just behind them. Harry swallowed down the suppressed hesitation and rushed up the slope. If this worked, he did not want to miss out on destroying a creature which was partly responsible for murdering untold billions of humans throughout thousands of worlds.

Harry ran up the first couple of metres. He slowed down and then stopped. He gazed at the floor. Small stones and gravel were vibrating across the ground! "Get down!" he screamed. "Lie on the floor!" Harry staggered backwards, urging the others to do as he said. The ground shook harder.

He moaned in terror when gallons of that crimson gunk slopped over the edges and two vast shapes rose up, out from beneath the liquid.

Both Callum and Copperfield were already on the floor. The hybrid creature had already fired off half a dozen shots but even at close range, the fleshmelta shots just bounced off the Goliath's thick armour.

Gavin had not moved. He stood rooted to the spot, frozen. Callum reached up and grabbed the youth's leg, just as three serpentine tendrils emerged from under one of the Goliaths. They all wrapped around Gavin's body and pulled the screaming boy into the belly of the beast.

"Come on!" he cried. "Get back down here." Harry dropped to one knee and fired off several salvoes while the remaining two scrambled up and ran back down the slope. His shots were just as ineffective as the shots fired from the hybrid, but they made him feel better.

The others had almost reached him when dozens of foot-soldiers slid down thick cords, dropping out of openings under the two Goliaths.

Both Harry and Copperfield managed to hit three of the enemy troops, but they just kept sliding out from under the two monsters.

"Retreat back to that bus!" Harry pulled Callum back while running backwards and firing shot after shot.

The hybrid had not moved.

"Copperfield, get back here!"

The hybrid looked over his shoulder. "Callum, throw me your rucksack."

Several foot-soldiers had almost reached the slope. Harry turned his fleshmelta on them, dissolving three before the remaining soldiers either ran back or dived off the slope and hid. Copperfield caught the rucksack. He held it in one hand while running up the slope and firing at any foot-soldier stupid enough to get in his way. Harry stayed where he was, doing his best to provide cover. He knew it couldn't last. His fleshmelta was almost out of energy.

"Oh God, I don't believe it. I think he's going to make it to the top!"

Harry heard Callum but dare not agree as his ears had just picked up the unmistakable sound of bio-tanks trudging towards them. His fleshmelta died on him. He stood up and saw the next street was full of bio-tanks coming towards him. Harry grabbed Callum. "Time to go, we'll die if we stay here."

"Wait, man! Just hang on for another couple of seconds. Copperfield has almost reached the top."

Harry saw him getting ready to throw the rucksack at the same time as several more cords suddenly snaked towards the hybrid, snatched him up, and pulled him into the beast.

"Oh God! I see what you mean. Harry, we need to get out of here!"

"It's too late for that, my friend." Harry nodded towards their only cover which was now swarming with foot-soldiers. The creatures silently stared at them with their fleshmeltas aimed at both Harry and Callum. He looked back at the bio-tanks. They had all stopped as well.

"I don't get it. Why are we not dead already?"

"Do you still have your knife, Callum?"

"You're shitting me! How is that going to stop them?"

"It's for you. After the damage we have inflicted upon them, I suspect that the two Goliaths have something special planned for us."

"We almost did it, man," said Callum. He brought the knife out. "Yeah, we showed those bastards."

Harry took hold of his friend's wrist. "Wait, perhaps we haven't completely lost. Look!"

The first Goliath, the one which had snatched Copperfield, lurched to one side. It pulled one of its legs out of the fluid and attempted to straighten itself.

A low groan rippled through the assembled foot-soldiers and bio-tanks before the Goliath emitted an ear-piercing child-like scream.

"It must be Copperfield! It's working. It's bloody working!"

Harry kept his gaze fixed on the two monsters. He heard the thump of what he believed to be explosives detonating inside that Goliath. The monster slumped forward and crashed into the side of the tank. Intense blue fire engulfed the Goliaths.

"We've really done it!"

Harry kept hold of Callum and began to walk up the slope. He heard his friend asking him to get off him, but Harry ignored that. Strange forces pulled on his body. The fire reached out and surrounded both men.

Callum started to shriek. Harry wanted to tell him to calm down, that everything was going to be okay. The Goliath was going back to Harry's world, where he and his unit would turn these evil creatures into bloody mush.

They had done it.

EPILOGUE

It took Callum a whole ten minutes to figure out that Harry had pulled him into another world. It wasn't Harry's world either. He remembered Harry telling him of the century of devastation caused by those monsters. He said that stinking mud, mixed with powdered rubble covered most of the land. The man had described hell to them.

This world looked so much like the world he had left, only perhaps with a few more airships, tanks, jeeps and soldiers.

He stood on the roof of a multi-storey carpark. Harry was beside him, clutching his fleshmelta tight. Callum had lost his shotgun somewhere along the way. From what he had seen, it didn't think it would be too difficult to pick up another weapon. "We have entered a war zone," said Cullum.

Harry nodded. "Yes, so it seems."

The Goliath, the one still standing, had brought the fighting to a complete stop. Callum had no idea who was fighting who, nor did he care. It had now reached the edge of the city. The Goliath had already lost most of its fliers to small arms fire and well as the occasional rocket fired from buildings on the outskirts. Harry had already informed Callum that it would soon replenish its stock with either flesh stored inside it or from the fresh meat it had already accumulated as it progressed through the city.

"What do we do now?"

The man turned to Callum. "What else can we do? We must finish this."

THE END?

CHECK OUT OTHER GREAT KAIJU NOVELS

MURDER WORLD I KAIJU DAWN
by Jason Cordova
& Eric S Brown

Captain Vincente Huerta and the crew of the Fancy have been hired to retrieve a valuable item from a downed research vessel at the edge of the enemy's space.
It was going to be an easy payday.
But what Captain Huerta and the men, women and alien under his command didn't know was that they were being sent to the most dangerous planet in the galaxy.
Something large, ancient and most assuredly evil resides on the planet of Gorgon IV. Something so terrifying that man could barely fathom it with his puny mind. Captain Huerta must use every trick in the book, and possibly write an entirely new one, if he wants to escape Murder World.

KAIJU ARMAGEDDON
by Eric S. Brown

The attacks began without warning. Civilian and Military vessels alike simply vanished upon the waves. Crypto-zoologist Jerry Bryson found himself swept up into the chaos as the world discovered that the legendary beasts known as Kaiju are very real. Armies of the great beasts arose from the oceans and burrowed their way free of the Earth to declare war upon mankind. Now Dr. Bryson may be the human race's last hope in stopping the Kaiju from bringing civilization to its knees.
This is not some far distant future. This is not some alien world. This is the Earth, here and now, as we know it today, faced with the greatest threat its ever known. The Kaiju Armageddon has begun.

CHECK OUT OTHER GREAT KAIJU NOVELS

KAIJU WINTER
by **Jake Bible**

The Yellowstone super volcano has begun to erupt, sending North America into chaos and the rest of the world into panic. People are dangerous and desperate to escape the oncoming mega-eruption, knowing it will plunge the continent, and the world, into a perpetual ashen winter. But no matter how ready humanity is, nothing can prepare them for what comes out of the ash: Kaiju!

RAIJU
by **K.H. Koehler**

His home destroyed by a rampaging kaiju, Kevin Takahashi and his father relocate to New York City where Kevin hopes the nightmare is over. Soon after his arrival in the Big Apple, a new kaiju emerges. Qilin is so powerful that even the U.S. Military may be unable to contain or destroy the monster. But Kevin is more than a ragged refugee from the now defunct city of San Francisco. He's also a Keeper who can summon ancient, demonic god-beasts to do battle for him, and his creature to call is Raiju, the oldest of the ancient Kami. Kevin has only a short time to save the city of New York. Because Raiju and Qilin are about to clash, and after the dust settles, there may be no home left for any of them!

CHECK OUT OTHER GREAT KAIJU NOVELS

KAIJU WINTER
by Jake Bible

The Yellowstone super volcano has begun to erupt, sending North America into chaos and the rest of the world into panic. People are dangerous and desperate to escape the oncoming mega-eruption, knowing it will plunge the continent, and the world, into a perpetual ashen winter. But no matter how ready humanity is, nothing can prepare them for what comes out of the ash: Kaiju!

RAIJU
by K.H. Koehler

His home destroyed by a rampaging kaiju, Kevin Takahashi and his father relocate to New York City where Kevin hopes the nightmare is over. Soon after his arrival in the Big Apple, a new kaiju emerges. Qilin is so powerful that even the U.S. Military may be unable to contain or destroy the monster. But Kevin is more than a ragged refugee from the now defunct city of San Francisco. He's also a Keeper who can summon ancient, demonic god-beasts to do battle for him, and his creature to call is Raiju, the oldest of the ancient Kami. Kevin has only a short time to save the city of New York. Because Raiju and Qilin are about to clash, and after the dust settles, there may be no home left for any of them!

www.ingramcontent.com/pod-product-compliance
Lightning Source LLC
Chambersburg PA
CBHW032210170626
46808CB00006B/2408